DEADLY INTENT

A SCVC Taskforce novel

MISTY EVANS

ROMANTIC SUSPENSE AND MYSTERIES BY MISTY EVANS

ACKNOWLEDGMENTS

To the men and women who strive to do the right thing even when there is no "right" answer.

Special thanks to Maria Mercedes for helping me with my Spanish, and to Adrienne Giordano for brainstorming plotlines and motorcycle gangs. To Nana for offering bail money in case I needed it, and to Linda Proud who gets kudos for the idea of Rosalie and her bingo good luck charms.

Amy Manemann, your idea to reunite Sophie and her sister was spot on, and I'm so thankful that you and Arial Michaels met me that day for froyo so I could hash out Angelique's past. Thanks, ladies!

Also to the fabulous duo, Amy Remus and JB Lynn, for keeping me on track and for understanding my brand of crazy.

DEDICATION

To Mark

You make the world a better place
and me a braver person.

A woman without her sister is like a bird without wings.
~ Luna Adriana Ardiansyah

~

We are all just walking each other home.
~ Ram Dass

~

The feeling of *I can't help you* can break your heart.
Yet it's very important to understand that even if there's
nothing else you can do,
you can love.
You can always love.

~ Dr. Barbara DeAngelis from Soul Shifts

CHAPTER ONE

Nelson Cruz thought he might throw up.

His left temple beat a violent staccato timed to AC/DC's *Hells Bells*. His eyelids scratched like sandpaper against his corneas. The left eye was swollen shut; the right didn't seem to want to obey on principal.

Swallowing past the dryness in his throat, he drew a deep breath and focused on the last thing he could remember. A humid, dark building. Body odor, cigarettes, the hiss of…

Snakes?

Someone had grabbed him. Threats had been yelled in his face. A fist had connected with his eye, another with his gut.

Interrupting the replay in his head, a floral scent brought him back to the here and now, teasing his nose and reminding him of something—someone—completely different. It smelled like…

Sophie.

Dreaming. He had to be dreaming.

Playing possum, he held still and finished his inventory. His aching head rested on something soft. *Pillow.* He was flat on his back, limbs splayed, his battered body cushioned. *Bed.*

The floral scent grew stronger. A low, seductive voice said, "You looked better last year in San Diego, *niño*. You really should have stayed there."

That voice. Smooth. Almost a purr.

Sophie.

1

His body responded like it always did at the thought of her—his cock grew hard at the thought of her luscious curves in spite of the fact that he'd just had the shit beat out of him. Memories of warm nights, too much tequila, and an ocean of stars assaulted his brain.

Commanding his good eye to open, he realized it didn't matter. Something covered his eyes. He brought a hand to his face.

Or tried to anyway. Both hands were held hostage, his wrists tied.

Metal rattled as he jerked at the restraints. *Not tied. Handcuffed.*

To the bed.

Correction: He was handcuffed to FBI Agent *Sophia Diaz's* bed.

Ah, shit. "Uncuff me, Soph."

His voice was rough. Too rough. Too many late nights drinking and smoking with the Savages Motorcycle Gang. This undercover assignment was going to kill him.

If Sophie didn't first.

The mattress dipped from her weight as she joined him on the bed. Warm fingers played over his naked bicep. "Why are you here?"

To protect your ass and bring you home.

Better to keep that a secret. At least the part about the FBI believing she was a rogue agent. Diaz had a chip on her shoulder bigger than his dick. "Uncuff me and I'll tell you."

Her fingernail dug into his muscle. Just enough to remind him she was in charge. "Tell me first, then I *might* turn you loose. Or I might shoot you."

Nothing with Sophie was ever easy. "You know what happened the last time you handcuffed me to your bed."

"Yes, you had the night of your life."

True. It had actually been two nights, but it could have been a thousand and it wouldn't have been enough. "You enjoyed it as much as I did."

"And then you left me."

After he'd found out the truth. After she'd thrown her handcuffs at his head and given a nice scar. "If you'd told me who you were up front, things might have turned out differently."

"I was undercover."

"As was I."

She lifted the corner of the blindfold covering his right eye. Her long, dark hair, beautiful skin, and big hazel-green eyes swam into focus. "Why are you in Tijuana?"

Work was as good of an excuse as ever. Except that if he mentioned his original assignment—Chica Bonita—she'd probably shoot him in the balls for good measure and *then* throw him out.

Good thing he was a skilled liar. "Just joined the Savages. I'm patrolling the border for Morales."

"You're lying." The blindfold slipped off his head. She sat back on her heels. "Rodrigo's men are the ones who did this to you."

Either his vision was screwed or the blow to his eye had messed with his head. Through the haze, it looked like Sophie was wearing nothing but her bra, some lacy black underpants, and a garter. Her breasts were pushed up and out, creating cleavage that made Nelson's dry mouth water.

Apparently, she didn't appreciate his ogling, even if it was only with one eye. She smacked him on the cheek. "Focus!"

Hard to do when she was mostly naked on the bed beside him. "God's truth, Soph. I'm undercover to investigate the gang and some of their dealings along the border. Not all of Morales's men, and certainly not Rodrigo, know me yet. Especially his personal security team. Who suck, by the way. I'm surprised he's not dead already."

"Why were you were sneaking around the grounds of the compound?"

"Can you please uncuff me so we can talk like rational human beings?"

"The only reason you're alive at this moment is because I intervened and stopped Chavez and his goons from killing you. Rodrigo Morales happens to like me and Chavez knows it. It took some begging on my part, and a threat or two, but I got him to bring you here and let me handle you."

"Chavez?"

"Rodrigo's head of security. The guy who gave you the black eye?"

"Ah. Well, he needs a lesson in protecting an asset."

"Look, I'm valuable to the Morales cartel, but I still had to lie and say you were...my lover." She gave an exaggerated shudder. "It was the only way to explain how I knew you."

"Lover, huh?" He grinned. "I'm happy to play my part."

Leaning forward, she put her luscious cleavage on full display in front of his face as she stroked his jawline with a finger. He could see the sexy little gap between her front two teeth. "You owe me your life, Nels."

Her full lips were covered in glossy, red lipstick. Her eyes danced with mischief.

Being a U.S. Immigration and Customs Enforcement agent with the Southern California Violent Crimes Taskforce had prepared him for many things in his undercover roles with gangs, drug cartels, and human traffickers. Physical violence, torture, possible death. Never had it prepared him for the force of nature contained in the five-foot-five, irresistible package known as Sophia Diaz.

Tied to her bed once more, it was fifty shades of Sophia all over again. Her beauty stunned him into silence. His cock was so tight against his zipper, it hurt.

She took his silence as stubbornness rather than speechlessness, and since she knew a thing or two about breaking his will, she straddled him.

Jesus, Joseph, and Mary. She was wearing spiky red heels.

Her curvaceous bottom nestled down on his hard cock and he moaned before he could stop himself. She planted her hands on his chest and arched her back, a blatant reminder of how she'd rode him the last time they'd spent time in bed together. "You're wasting time, *niño*. Tell me the truth or..."

She ground herself into him slowly and deliberately, licking her lips and smiling down on him.

Torture. Brutal, beautiful torture like he hadn't had since the last time they were in this exact position.

She was undercover, working on bringing down Rodrigo Morales. He was undercover, working a different angle, but on the same man and his cartel. They should be able to work together.

Regardless of the past lies and indiscretions.

In fact, working together would be better for both of them.

Except Special Agent Diaz wasn't a team player. Never had been. She was the most fiercely independent agent in the FBI. She worked alone and always got her man—the only reason the Feds allowed her to be so independent. Their concern that she'd been under too long on this mission and may have gone rogue was ridiculous. Sophie was Bureau to her lovely bones. Her track record was spotless.

With one exception.

Chica Bonita.

He couldn't tell her he was investigating the possible resurgence of the human trafficking operation that had been the only failure of her career.

So he told her the only thing he could. "Guido Ruiz."

The sex goddess morphed back into FBI agent. She stopped undulating on top of him and gave him a hard stare. "What about him?"

Nelson took one last look at all the beautiful cleavage and sighed. "He put out a hit on you at 0800 hours yesterday."

"What? Where did you hear this?"

"He hired me to do it."

That gave her pause. "*You?*"

"He doesn't know I'm with the Savages and my backstop

identity says I've done murder-for-hire quite successfully. At the bar the other night, Guido offered me a hundred-thousand to kill you—one of the reasons the FBI and the SCVC Taskforce want me to bring you home."

She looked at him wide-eyed for a second and then threw back her head and laughed. Low and husky, the sound sent ripples down his spine, not to mention what it did to his already straining lower parts.

Patting his chest, she gave another chuckle. "I'm not going anywhere with you, ICE boy. Feel free to run back to San Diego and tell the FBI, and your boss at the taskforce, to stay out of my operation. I'm not scared of Guido and I'm too close to bringing down Morales to blow this over an idle threat by a spoiled brat posing as a rival cartel leader."

Guido was no spoiled brat. He was a six-foot-three monster with a shaved head and teardrop tattoos. Six of 'em. He'd once worked for Rodrigo's father and decided to take over. A bloody battle ensued, but Ciro Morales had deep pockets and loyal employees. He won the skirmish and Guido went underground.

For a while, anyway.

Now, with Ciro dead, the monster was back and he was coming after Ciro's son. Killing off Rodrigo Morales was tough, even if his security detail wasn't the brightest, and Guido liked to make his prey suffer first. Everyone knew Rodrigo had a thing for his accountant. Guido planned to kill her off first.

"It's not an idle threat, Soph." Nelson understood Sophie's bravado. As an undercover agent, her life was always in danger, like his. Miss 99% Ball Buster wasn't about to let a criminal of any type ruin her chance at a successful bust, regardless of the fact that Guido had once been the Morales cartel's right-hand man and was the only serious menace to Rodrigo at this point. But that didn't matter. The higher-ups wanted her butt back in the U.S. "Your life is in imminent danger. It's time to pack it in."

"I can't leave. I *won't* leave. Not yet." She studied him, her eyes softening as she leaned forward, putting her face in front of his. "But maybe you can stay if you play along and pretend to be my lover and bodyguard."

Once more through the fog in his brain due to her nearness, Nelson reminded himself that Sophie never worked with a partner. Which was why he'd ended up holding shit instead of evidence the last round he'd gone with her.

Fool me once, shame on me. Fool me twice… "What do I get out of it?"

Sophie grinned and produced a key from between her breasts. "For starters, I'll release you."

That was easy.

Too easy.

Something was wrong here but he couldn't snap the pieces together when she was shoving her chest into his and her big smile encouraged him to forget his misgivings and consider her offer.

Freedom and Sophie in one package. What could he say?

"You have a deal, Agent Diaz."

CHAPTER TWO

Sophie's grandmother, Little Gran, had always told her, "Pain feeds on pain, so be happy. Pain can't feed on joy."

Somehow, Sophie was feeling both at that moment.

Joy at seeing Nelson; pain as well.

How is that possible?

Probably for the same reason she could always pick the best undercover assignments—the ones she knew she could absolutely nail—but somehow managed to pick the worst men to get involved with. The ones who used her to further their careers and broke her heart.

Case in point, the man tied to my bed.

Climbing off Nelson, she ignored his raging erection and the wetness in her panties. The last time she'd had him in such a compromising position, it had ended for her with a screaming orgasm. She'd nearly peeled paint off the walls; she'd had so much built up stress and frustration. She'd never had an orgasm like it before or since. A cleansing of her system she could use again.

From the look on Nelson's bruised face and the bulge under his zipper, she could have another any time she wanted.

Tempting. Verrry tempting.

Except for the part where her heart would get involved.

Snatching up her silk shirt, she slid it over her arms and tromped into the small, but modern kitchen. While her heart ached, and her ego cried out for revenge, she couldn't leave him there, strapped to her bed, and walk out. Well, she could, but that would be unprofessional, and she needed to stay as professional as she could with Nelson Cruz. Distance herself emotionally and mentally from his charm and absolute, God-given hotness.

Another man, her current boss, waited for her in the main house, ready to interrogate her about her interference with Chavez's response to Nelson sneaking onto the grounds. *If I hadn't had that vision…*

Like her grandmother's words of wisdom, the visions were another of the older woman's gifts. This one, however, felt like more like a curse. The visions didn't come often, thank the Holy Jesus, but when they did, it usually meant someone she cared deeply about was in trouble.

I do not care about Nelson Cruz.

Dropping cubes of ice in a dishtowel, she wrapped them up. *I don't care about anyone anymore.*

The throbbing in her temples—as usual, the vision had left her with a headache—and the wetness in her panties said differently.

In the bathroom, she grabbed a jar of wild yam cream, and caught sight of her reflection in the mirror. Her cheeks were flushed, eyes shining.

Damn. What spell had that man put her under? Even when she was furious with him, he excited her like no one else.

Provoked is more like it.

Purposely furrowing her brows and reminding herself that he'd broken her heart and she officially hated him, she stomped back to the bedroom. "I hate you," she said, to make sure they were clear.

The right corner of his lips quirked. "I hate you too."

He made a good biker gang member with his too-long dark hair spread across her pillow, scruff along his jawline, and the scar she'd given him cutting through his left eyebrow. His cold blue eyes drilled into her from above his high cheekbones, and his haughty lips smirked.

She unlocked one handcuff and handed him the ice bag. "Keep this on your eye until I get back. We'll put some cream on your bruises and then you can be on your way."

He accepted the ice bag and put it to his eye. "I thought I was going to be your lover-slash-bodyguard."

"In your dreams." *Or an alternate universe.*

Which, unfortunately, they did not live in.

She tossed the key to the cuffs on her dresser, yanked on her long skirt, and skipped the stockings she'd laid out. Although it was November, this was Mexico and it was unseasonably warm, a pressure system building in the Pacific farther south.

Or maybe the sweat running down her back was due to being in this small apartment with the dangerous and very badass Nelson Cruz, still laid out on her bed.

Either way, she needed air and lots of it. "I changed my mind."

He didn't need the Savages biker jacket with its skull and bones motif, or his recent black eye, to look menacing. "You didn't change your mind. You're screwing with me on purpose."

The damning tone of his voice stung. The challenge in his eyes said he was remembering their shared past. She'd known all along he was an undercover immigration officer. He'd thought she was an illegal and she'd done nothing to dispose him of that idea.

Until the morning after, when she'd seduced him and pumped him for information to help her with her sting. That's when she'd realized she'd gone too far.

Sometimes the harder you tried to keep people from seeing the real you, the clearer the view they got. "I work alone," she said. "You know that."

He shifted as well as he could, holding onto the cuff still securing his left wrist and using it to leverage himself up to face her. "Your life is in danger."

Just like last time. The words hung between them.

His was in danger, too, if he kept looking so damn sexy.

"Guido Ruiz is not a threat to me." It was mostly true. "I will not leave until I've wrapped up this operation."

Laundering money for the Morales Cartel was a full-time job and required a bevy of skills. Skills she had. Plus, Rodrigo liked her petite stature and substantial curves.

She'd always thought of herself as plain, a weird mix of Hispanic and white that didn't quite fit in either world, not in East L.A., not in Tijuana, both places she'd grown up.

But during agent training, she'd figured out how to handle criminals as well as enhance what she *did* have in the sexy department, working it for maximum advantage. Push-up bras and lots of spandex were main staples of her wardrobe. "I'm quite safe here inside the Morales compound."

"I snuck in." The tone of Nelson's voice had that know-it-all edge that drove her nuts. "Right past the guards and the cameras."

Taking a white lace shawl from the hook next to the door, she wrapped it around her shoulders and checked her lipstick in the nearby mirror. Rodrigo kept his study cool and he gave her goose bumps even in ninety-degree weather. "Need I remind you, you got caught?"

She opened the door, but Nelson's voice stopped her, the clang of the handcuffs echoing in the room as his anger finally got the best of him. "We had a deal, Sophia."

They had a deal, all right. One she was about to bust to smithereens, just like Nelson had done to her heart. Chica Bonita had nearly ruined her, emotionally and professionally. She wasn't making that mistake again.

She closed the door behind her, heard him raging against the single cuff still restraining him. Quickly, she ran down the stairs to the first floor and stepped out into the evening.

Her heart drummed to match the throb in her temples as she stopped on the covered patio to draw a breath. The aftereffects of the vision were going to be a bitch if her head and heart were already pounding.

The sun was sinking, thick humidity weighting the air and leaving her nearly panting. Or maybe it was the anxiety catching up with her from seeing Nelson being beaten on the floor of the pit. If she hadn't gotten there in time, he'd be dead.

A flowering bush climbed the trellis next to her, its small, pink flowers attracting bees. Low grasses and aloe encircled a birdbath in the center of the garden. From here, she could see the west wing of the main house and the tall windows of Rodrigo's office on the top floor.

Casa Morales was a mansion. Ten thousand square feet with seven bedrooms, nine baths, an in-ground swimming pool, and a staff house. The guesthouse where Sophie stayed was a miniature version on the outside, and while nice on the inside, it still lacked the luxurious furnishings of the main house.

The sinking sun reflected in the third floor windows, creating the illusion that they were the eyes of a giant. Rodrigo Morales stood there sometimes, the position giving him a birds-eye view of the entire compound.

Of her.

A sickly tightness threatened to shut off her windpipe. She closed her eyes, slowly drew air in through her nose and held it for a count of three. Then she exhaled all at once, like Little Gran had taught her, to clear her thoughts and her lungs.

A few more controlled breaths and her heartbeat slowed. The tightness in her throat eased. Even her temples stopped pulsing so hard. When she opened her eyes, a peacock had wandered into the garden. It ignored her, preening near the birdbath.

She'd been summoned half an hour ago. Rodrigo wanted an answer as to why Nelson was here. She could play it one of two ways. Go in easy and try to smooth things over, or go in bitch-on-wheels and put her cartel boss on the defensive from the get-go.

Like many men, Rodrigo liked his women hot-blooded and fiery. No problem there. Sophie tended toward both. The women in her family had always been passionate and emotional, sometimes too much.

Bitch-on-wheels it is. If she went in full of indignation and hit him with guns blazing, she might escape his probing into her past about her relationship with Nelson. She'd give the same excuse as she had given to James Chavez. Nelson was her lover—a misguided *ex*-lover looking for her. He'd be on his way as soon as she doctored the poor man back to health. Her game plan was clear:

Cut Morales off at the pass.

Rail against Chavez and his men to keep the focus on the injustice of beating up Nelson.

Reassure all that Nelson is harmless.

Harmless. No one would believe that, but maybe if she assured Rodrigo that Nelson was leaving and nothing like this would ever happen again, this would blow over quickly and she could get back to work.

The end was in sight. She couldn't let Nels or anyone else blow this mission after she'd suffered through all these months of hell.

Following in his father's footsteps, Rodrigo didn't like anyone to rock the boat. She'd played the part of the loyal and extremely valuable money launderer for him all this time, but one little slip could endanger everything.

Hiking the shawl higher on her shoulders, she had just started toward the main house when she heard the apartment door above her bang open.

Nelson stood there, looking down at her with a sneer on his lips, cuffs hanging off his wrists, the one eye still swollen to beat the band. The ice bag dangled from one hand.

Unbelievable. "How the hell did you manage to get free?"

"Are you kidding?" he said. "Child's play."

To him, it probably was. She needed to get zip ties. No keys, just hard plastic.

He could probably chew through those.

Or break them with his powerful muscles.

The image, combined with her frustration, almost made her swear out loud. "I need to talk to Rodrigo. Please stay here until I get back."

He jogged down the steps and came to stand in front of her, totally invading her space. "You're not going any where without me."

His gaze was hard, unrelenting. Bullheaded didn't begin to describe his stubbornness.

She lowered her voice. "If you blow my op, I will string you up and pour hot grease over your balls."

"Kinky."

"I'm not kidding, Nels."

His flinch reminded her how he hated that nickname. "It's Nico Raines for this op," he said.

"And what op is that exactly? You weren't very specific earlier."

"Sorry, sweetheart. That you don't need to know."

He didn't trust her. That road ran both ways. She drew farther back under the patio awning and out of sight of the west wing, lowering her voice. "Running with the Savages along the border means you're going after some part of the Morales cartel. One of the smaller businesses, I assume. But I'm going after the *entire organization*. I'm not just going to shut down the cocaine or meth distribution. I'm bringing the Morales Mexican-American Cartel to its knees."

He grabbed her elbow and got in her face. "Not if you're dead."

Pulling her arm free, she shoved at his chest to make him back up. Stubborn was one thing, but she'd never seen him so adamant except that day two years ago at Chica Bonita.

Too bad he hadn't felt quite so protective of her after he discovered she was a Fed and not some wayward nineteen-year-old. "I need forty-eight hours. Tops."

"For what?"

"Sorry, sweetheart," she mimicked. "That you don't need to know."

"Sophie, they pulled me off my op to bring you in. The brass is worried about you. Hell, *I'm* worried about you. You're in deep, I get that, but you're also in more danger than you've ever been in before."

"I'm not leaving."

A muscle in his unshaven jaw jumped. "Then I'm staying."

There was so much he didn't know. So many secrets she was keeping. "I don't need your protection."

She started to walk away. He grabbed her and hauled her back against the cool stone wall. "You *do* need my help. Shut up and take it."

"Stop manhandling me."

"Manhandling? You handcuffed me to your bed!"

His face was close to hers. Those full, seductive lips a breath away. *Don't do it, Sophie. Sexual attraction is not love.*

She glared at him and tossed her hair over her shoulder. "Like being handcuffed to my bed is the worst thing that's ever happened to you."

"My assignment is to bring you back to San Diego. If you won't let me stay and help you, then I'll throw you over my shoulder and carry you out of here caveman-style."

"You'd like that, wouldn't you?" She met his eyes, her brain scrambling for a more solid argument. He was as hot-blooded as she was, their brief relationship intense and physical. "Try it. You'll never get me out of here. Rodrigo keeps a very close eye on me."

"I bet he does."

His tone suggested she'd crossed a line with her criminal boss. She didn't appreciate the insinuation. "I can handle Morales and my job. In fact, I can do *your* job, whatever operation you're working on, and take down the cartel at the same time."

"That so?" he said in an aggravatingly thoughtful tone.

She lifted her chin. "Yes."

His glare turned more serious. He hesitated before giving a big sigh. "Chica Bonita."

The air stuck in her lungs. "What?"

He glanced over his shoulder, double-checking they were hidden and still alone. "After the Southern California Violent Crimes taskforce took down the Londano cartel, it left an open field for human traffickers. Morales may have stepped up to the plate. The taskforce believes he plans to rejuvenate his father's operation and that he has the Savages picking up girls. Human trafficking, sex slaves, he could be putting his toes in all of it."

The evening air burned in her lungs. Her younger sister's face flashed in front of her.

Don't go there. Not now. There was something going on with Chica Bonita but not what he thought. "That's not possible. I see the books, all of them. He's started dealing with a European investor for his exotic snake collection, but that's all he's got going besides the drug running. He's kept the details of that to himself, which is the last piece to wrapping up my operation. There's something going on with transporting those snakes and I need the ledger he keeps to figure it out. He's not resurrecting Chica Bonita or his father's sex slave business. I would have seen the exchange of money."

"He's not dealing in money. We believe he's bartering girls. The only thing we're not sure of is what he's getting in exchange."

A frosty chill swept down her spine. Sex slaves. Bile rose in her throat. Had Angelique been one of the CB girls?

Steeling her emotions, she knew she had to get Nelson off the Chica Bonita train. If he discovered her secret, it would ruin her career—and her career was all she had. "I would know if there was any type of exchange."

Nelson placed a hand on the wall behind her, the metal cuff knocking into the old brick. He dropped his head. "I didn't want to tell you this, but..."

"But what?"

"The Savages aren't just patrolling the border for Morales. They're transporting shipments across it. Girls with backpacks coming up from the south. The girls have to be funneled through a central checkpoint somewhere around here. We believe Morales is using the Chica Bonita camp. They're coming through Tijuana and into San Diego. That's why the SCVC Taskforce is on it."

"Those girls aren't sex slaves. They're mules for the drugs."

"And possibly more. There's a strong history of human trafficking with this cartel and I'm undercover trying to find out if Chica Bonita is back in business."

Sophie felt like throwing up. Human trafficking was getting worse despite the new laws and concentrated efforts of the United States government to shut it down.

Angel, I'm so sorry. "I should have burned that camp to the ground when I had the chance."

"We both should have. Wouldn't have stopped anything."

Might have saved my sister.

But now, Sophie knew it wasn't being used for human trafficking. Smuggling, maybe. A different side of the same coin, but she couldn't let Nelson find out what was really happening there. "If Rodrigo is selling girls like his father did, and I take down the cartel—which I'm about to do—it will shut down Chica Bonita. Like I said, I can do your job *and* mine if you let me. I only need a couple more days."

Nelson lowered his face so they were nose-to-nose. His other hand went to the wall next to her head, effectively trapping her. "When Guido figures out I didn't kill you, he'll send someone else. You won't last twenty-four hours without me watching your back."

Infuriating. She touched his swollen eye in mock concern. "Stop worrying your pretty little head. Guido won't touch me."

His eyes flared and he started to say something, clamped his lips together, and then out of nowhere, he lowered his face the final few centimeters and kissed her.

No warning, no warm-up. Just *bam*. His lips touched hers, hard, then soft, then hard again. As if he needed her. Wanted her.

No.

She wanted to push him away, even raised her hands to his shoulders to do so. Instead, she found herself cupping those hard, muscled shoulders and tugging him closer. Parting her lips, and…

The peacock squawked, a man cleared his throat.

All of the lust drained right through her toes. Fear shocked her back to reality.

She broke away from Nelson's lips and forced her eyes to open. Sure enough, the man of her nightmares was standing at the entrance to the patio staring at her with one dark, bushy brow raised in question.

"Rodrigo," she said, trying to shove Nelson aside. The ICE agent-turned-biker was a brick wall, refusing to move other than to glance over his shoulder. "I was just coming to see you."

Rodrigo was a tad short and thin. He was barely older than her—twenty-eight—but his hairline was receding from its widow's peak. He compensated by growing the rest long. The black strands were perfectly straight and hung around his pointed chin. His cold eyes and narrow nose completed the look.

The perfect vampire in some teen movie, Sophie thought.

"I became concerned," the cartel leader said, speaking in perfect English thanks to his European schooling.

He wasn't looking at her. He was looking at Nelson.

Nelson stilled pinned her between his arms. She smiled at Rodrigo over one bulging bicep and pinched Nelson in his side.

"Ouch!"

At least he moved, jumping back enough she could duck around him. "My friend was moments away from leaving," she told her boss. "We were saying goodbye."

Nelson snorted. "More like a long-overdue hello."

Rodrigo's glare went from Nelson to Sophie and back. "I don't believe we've officially met."

"Nico Raines." Nelson stepped forward offering Morales his hand. The cuff danged from his wrist. "I'm one of the Savages."

Rodrigo ignored his outstretched hand. "One of my Savages?"

"I've been with the Savages now for nearly three months."

"And you're a special friend to Miss Ramirez, or did I misunderstand?"

Sophie elbowed Nelson. Maria-Sophia Ramirez was her undercover identity.

The ICE agent didn't need the nudge. Seamlessly, he nodded and produced the key Sophie had left on the kitchen table, uncuffing his wrist as he answered. "Miss Ramirez and I go way back."

Rodrigo's cold gaze bored into her. "Is that so?"

Sophie swallowed. During her interview nine months ago, he'd asked her if she had any close relatives or a boyfriend. She'd answered no—it was the truth.

"A very brief affair a long time ago was all it was." *It could've been so much more.* "Nico has been overly protective ever since. He heard about Guido putting a hit out on me and thought he would come to my rescue."

She gave her cartel boss her brightest smile. "I was telling him to go back to the Savages and not worry about me. We already knew about Guido's childishness and I'm perfectly safe here." *In my prison.*

That prison was a godsend, however. Since Rodrigo insisted she live inside his compound, she had access to things. Not just the luxurious accommodations, but things that helped her case. Gossiping house staff, the comings and goings of other nefarious criminals, access to Rodrigo's study when he was out. Not that he kept a lot of evidence casually lying around, but she had become an expert at picking the lock on the door and had documented everything, knowing that innocent-looking papers or photographs could contain some bit of evidence that would tie her case shut and lock it up tight.

"Your security could use a reboot," Nelson said. He pocketed the cuffs. "If I'd been Guido's assassin—which he did try to hire me, by the way—I could have killed her with ease. And if I could get on the grounds without much trouble, that means you're not safe either."

Rodrigo crossed his arms, his suit's silk sleeves making a shushing sound. He tapped a slender finger against his lips as he considered Nelson's words, all the while studying him from top to bottom.

Sweat trickled down Sophia's spine. If there was one thing she knew about Rodrigo Morales, he didn't like looking foolish.

"Come with me," he said, turning on the heel of his expensive leather dress shoes. "We'll discuss this in my office."

"But...but," Sophia rushed after him. "There's nothing to discuss. Nico's being ridiculous. Your compound is completely safe."

Rodrigo stopped and glared at her. "I wish to talk to Señor Raines alone."

With that, he stalked away.

As she stood speechless, Nelson walked past her, grinning, and tossed her the ice bag as he followed.

CHAPTER THREE

"Tell me again how you met Maria-Sophia," Morales said. He poured whiskey from a crystal decanter into two squat glasses.

His study was office-like with a large desk, leather chairs, and doublewide wooden doors. A guard stood by the doors, face blank, legs wide, a black gun on display. The floor-length windows revealed the orange and peach rays of the dying sun. Bookcases lined the north wall. A three-by-five section of one bookcase held a display of colored rocks.

On the opposite wall was an aquarium of sorts. A blanket covered most of the glass, but Nelson could see it didn't contain water or fish. Maybe the guy had a lizard or something.

Morales handed him a glass and the leather chair complained with a soft squeak as Nelson sank into it with the whiskey.

Backstories were tricky lies and he had no idea what Sophia had used for hers. "Maria-Sophia and I were moving in some of the same circles a few years ago." Best to stick to the facts and keep his answer general. "She has a thing for bikers." Truth. "She got on my radar."

Morales sat behind the desk, removing a box of cigars from a drawer and choosing one to his liking. "Bikers, huh?"

He did not offer Nelson one, but that was to be expected. Nelson tapped his Savages' leather vest. "It's the bad boy thing."

"My little Maria-Sophia pursued you?"

This was said as if Nelson were dog shit, and Nelson didn't particularly care for the possessive tone. "From the first time we met." Another truth. "And believe me, she's impossible to ignore when she wants your attention."

Morales gave him a half smile, as if humoring him.

So far, so good. He was piling up truths. The fewer lies he told, the better.

A cigar cutter sat on the top of the desk. Single blade. Morales grabbed it, lined up his cigar, and brought the blade to touch the wrapper, a large diamond ring on his finger twinkling in the light. Then, like a skilled surgeon, he slammed the blade home swiftly and confidently, making a slick wedge cut.

The second cut was equally impressive, and Nelson had the distinct feeling as the man stared at him over the tip of the cigar that that was exactly what Morales wanted to do to his dick.

Morales used a cigar lighter, then sat quietly enjoying his smoke and studying Nelson with empty eyes. He put his feet up on the desk, taking another puff and slowly letting the smoke escape his lips. "A brief affair, she said. *Si?*"

He really needed to change the direction of the conversation. Morales obviously had a thing for his *little Maria-Sophia* and this discussion was sure to endanger both Sophie and him. "Yes, very brief, but I care for her even though she wants nothing to do with me."

"Some encounters are quite powerful, but it seems a bit extreme that you should track her down after all this time because of idle gossip."

Idle gossip? What had Morales been smoking with his premium cigars? "She's hard to forget, and even though I tried, when I heard about the threat against her life and that she was working for you, I had to see her. As I mentioned, Guido offered me money to kill her—I have a reputation for being good at that kind of dirty work—so I'd say that's more than idle gossip."

"If you had no intention of hurting her, and you are…friends…why sneak onto my property, rather than using the front door?"

At least he'd diverted Morales from their backstory. "Rude and improper behavior and I apologize for that. Just ask Maria-Sophia. She'll tell you I'm an expert at both. I knew she would turn me away and refuse to hear me out if I showed up at the front door. I had hoped to check on her in secrecy, make sure she was safe, and leave her be. Your men caught me before I had the chance."

Morales wanted to protect himself at all costs. His assets as well. Another drag on his cigar, and Nelson saw the change from jealous male to astute businessman. "You were caught, *si*, but you still managed to evade my security cameras, bypass my fence, and elude my security patrol to gain access to the grounds. I wish to know how."

Bingo. The cat was too curious for his own good. Nelson stood and set the whiskey on the man's desk. "How about I show you."

———

The living and dining area inside the apartment was exactly ten paces each direction. Sophia had paced it over a hundred times as the sun sank in the west.

Her fingers tingled. A dull throb had set up shop in her temples. Where was Nelson?

He's going to blow my case.

What to do? Sit tight until Morales's men came for her and end up in *el nido de serpientes*—the snake pit—where Rodrigo's men did their dirty work, or go on the offensive and see if there was anything of her operation she could still salvage?

The pit held a collection of snakes. Rodrigo had a thing for them. She certainly didn't want to be "interviewed" as he liked to call it when people went in alive and came out dead, or didn't come out at all.

One of the snakes in the collection, Medusa, was a 20-foot

anaconda. Another, Goliath, was some type of rare albino python from Asia that gave Sophie nightmares. She'd barely kept Nelson from ending up snake food earlier that day.

There were few things that could break her—she'd had extensive training in resisting threat manipulation and torture; in fact, she'd scored the highest in her graduating class for being the last to break during interrogation training—but snakes might just be the thing to do it.

Goose bumps raced over her skin. What if Chavez already had Nelson there, torturing him? From the look in Rodrigo's eyes, she knew that was a real possibility. The cartel leader was as paranoid as they came and too young and inexperienced to be an effective leader of such an extensive operation. He was more modern than his predecessors, but relied on violence just as much, if not more, to assert his control. No one dared question him. No one crossed him either.

And Nelson has gone off with him to be "interviewed."

She stopped pacing and rubbed her arms. *Enough.* Even though she hadn't asked for Nelson's interference, and found his appearance more than annoying, she couldn't leave him dangling in the wind. One false move, one slip of his tongue, and everything she'd worked so hard for would go up in smoke.

Or down a snake's throat.

The last thing I need is his death on my conscious.

Snatching up her shawl, she left the apartment, nearly snagging her heel on the fringed edge in her haste to run down the stairs.

House or the pit?

Rodrigo and Nelson had been heading for the house when they'd left. Sophie took off in that direction, keeping to the stone path that glowed a pale gray in the moonlight.

Her kitten heels clicked on the stones as frogs and other nocturnal creatures called to each other. Still thinking about snakes, she kept a close eye on the palm-fringed walkway. The compound stretched over several acres, most of it filled with vegetation. Occasionally, a snake left the cover of the trees and bushes to soak up the last of the heat from the stones.

A light was on in the office window. The heavy drapes were drawn and she couldn't see any shadows moving behind them. But it was a start. Hopefully, he and Nelson were still there.

The house was a two-story, Moorish-style white stucco adobe with a copper roof, beautiful arched doorways, and immaculate gardens on both sides. It had been in the Morales family for several decades and had fallen into disrepair after Rodrigo's mother had passed from a blood cancer. When his father died two years later from a heart attack, Rodrigo had stormed in and repaired it to its original beauty. Probably for his mother's sake and to relieve his guilt that he hadn't been there when she died.

Rodrigo Morales. A family man who didn't want the family business, but was now a cut-throat businessman, even in the world of international drug cartels.

Quite a conundrum.

Sophie nodded at the guard on duty by the west entrance. "Hello, Sanny."

She knew every one of them by name, including the ones like Sanchez who went by a nickname. Most of them were loyal to the Morales family, and even those who didn't like Rodrigo respected his ability to keep them well paid.

Sanny's only response was a subtle nod in return, but like most of Morales's men, he liked her because she went out of her way to show him respect.

And maybe a little because she flirted with him just enough to appeal to his very male ego when she brought him homemade treats. No one could resist something made from Little Gran's recipes.

Inside, the house was mostly dark, a few lights here and there on in the expansive living room and coming from the kitchen down the hall. Sophie heard a soft noise; the maid and part-time nanny to Rodrigo's little sister hummed along to the radio as she cleaned up the dinner dishes.

Sophie's heels were now soundless as she climbed the carpeted stairs past a portrait of Ciro Morales and photographs of his family. Many were in black and white and sepia tones dating back to the 1800s. The original family had been cattle ranchers in South America. Their sons had migrated to Central America, starting large families of their own. Successive generations had continued the climb north, ending in Tijuana.

Upstairs, outside Rodrigo's office, there was no guard. Which meant Rodrigo wasn't there.

Too late!

Double-checking, she knocked. No answer. Rodrigo always locked his door when he was out, but she tested the knob anyway.

The door opened.

Had he fallen asleep at his desk? It happened on occasion, but the bodyguard would be there if Rodrigo were inside.

She inched the door open. "Señor Morales?"

The study was empty, a single light on the desk lit, throwing a yellow glow on the highly polished wood top. One wall was a library. The other held the snake tank.

Sophie shivered. *God, I hate snakes.* She steeled her nerves and refused to look at the tank, even though the draped cloth over the top hid the reptile from view. She crossed the floor to the windows.

Parting the curtains, she scanned the yard and gardens from Rodrigo's favorite vantage point. The shadows were plentiful and she saw no movement anywhere.

There was only one other place he would have taken Nelson.

Laying her forehead against the cool glass, she considered her options. Maybe she could still save the operation, but how would she save Nelson?

"Maria-Sophia?" A soft voice behind her made her jump. "Is that you?"

Alexa, Rodrigo's eleven-year-old sister, stood in the doorway, her service dog by her side.

"Hi Lexie."

The girl came in, stopping at the chair on the other side of the desk. "Where's Rigo?"

Feeding my arch nemesis to Medusa. "I'm not sure. I thought he was here, and the door was unlocked, but apparently, he went out." Sophie went to her and touched Lexie's shoulder, letting the blind girl know where she was standing. "I see you had spaghetti for dinner. Are you saving some for later?"

"I spilled *again*?" The girl's braids danced on her shoulders as she shook her head. "How bad is it?"

Sophie scraped a lone noodle with a touch of sauce on it off the collar of Lexie's blouse and dropped it in the wastebasket under Rodrigo's desk. "I've seen worse, but we should get that stain in some cold water or it won't wash out."

"Why doesn't Kristine tell me when I have food on my shirt?"

Sophie needed to find Nelson, but staying with Lexie held more appeal than heading to the snake pit. "She knows you don't want anyone to call attention to your blindness. It's her way of respecting that."

Which was a lie. Kristine only cared about her paycheck and fooling around with Xavier, Rodrigo's favorite guard.

"And she doesn't think me walking around with food on my shirt calls attention to the fact I can't see it?" the indignant girl asked.

"Believe it or not, it is not uncommon for eleven-year-olds to spill their food, regardless of their eyesight. You're not the first, and certainly not the only one of us to walk around with spaghetti sauce on her collar."

Lexie set her lips and squeezed her brows together, considering Sophie's words. "Is that true?"

Having been blind since the age of five, Lexie had worked hard to overcome her disability. She was astute for eleven, and definitely mature under the circumstances, but she didn't always know what "normal" constituted for kids her age. While she'd been around other children at the school for the blind, she had little experience with non-blind children. "We all spill, grown-ups included. My nemesis is salsa. No matter how careful I am, I end up with it on my shirt or in my lap. Little Gran used to make me wear red all the time to hide the stains."

Lexie giggled. "Will you help me wash the stain out? I don't want Rigo to be mad."

She didn't have time for this, yet she hated leaving the girl in a lurch. "I'm on an errand. Why don't you change for bed, and after my errand, I'll come back and take care of your shirt."

"Is it an errand for Rigo?"

"Yes," she lied.

Lexie stroked her dog's ear. "Will it take long?"

Sophie looked out the window again. *Not if Nelson and I both end up dead.* "I'm not sure. Why?"

"Will you read more of that book to me when you come back? The one about the woman who had the farm in Africa?"

Lexie loved books and Rodrigo had a whole section of books for her in braille, but the girl preferred stories well above her age range and about daring women who traveled and explored the world. Sophia had already read Anne Morrow Lindbergh's complete works to the girl, even though Rodrigo frowned on the adult nature of some of the stories.

Movement on the grounds caught Sophie's eye. She moved to the window again, spotting two figures walking toward the house. A small glowing ring cut through the shadows, growing brighter for a second and illuminating Rodrigo's face.

He took the cigar away, returning his face to shadows. The small light had not captured the other man's features. Was it Chavez? Had they already disposed of Nelson?

The second man broke off from Rodrigo and headed toward Sophie's apartment. Yep, Chavez was going after her now. He didn't know she was in the main house.

God, Nelson. She made the sign of the cross, grateful Lexie couldn't see her. *I'm so sorry.*

Should she run or she should she stay and see if there was any way to save the operation? Maybe Nelson wasn't dead yet. She could sneak into the pit and save him.

First, she had to deal with Lexie. "If I return before you're asleep," Sophie told her, hustling her back through the study door, "we'll read, okay?"

"Okay." The girl stopped. "I want to know what happens to the woman now that her coffee bean crop is ruined."

If only life were as simple as reading to a child before bed. Sophie tugged on one of Lexie's braids, hoping to make good on her promise. "Your brother's coming. If you don't want him to see that shirt, you better head to your room."

Downstairs, the door rattled as Rodrigo entered the west wing. The girl and dog started walking. "See you later, alligator," Lexie stage whispered.

"After a while, crocodile," Sophie whispered back.

And then she waited for her fate, and that of Operation Gangs Without Borders, as Rodrigo Morales climbed the stairs.

CHAPTER FOUR

"Maria-Sophia?" Rodrigo's gaze took her in and then the open door behind her. "Is there a problem?"

There's a problem all right. Or was there?

Rodrigo's demeanor seemed relaxed, at ease.

"I'm sorry to barge in." Sophie moved so he could enter the study. "I wanted to talk to you about Nico and the door was unlocked."

"Nico, yes." He brushed past her. "Unusual man."

Nelson was arrogant, determined to undermine her, and sexy as hell, but she'd never considered him *unusual*. "I wanted to apologize again for his rude manners. He's really not a bad guy, just…unpredictable."

Rodrigo sat in his chair, leaned back, and motioned for her to enter.

She did, but didn't sit. Better to stay on her feet in case this went downhill.

"I like him and the fact he didn't ask me to top Guido's price on your head. He seems to truly care for you." Rodrigo's cigar was nearly gone. He stubbed out the end. "He knows security like the back of his hand."

Wait. Was Rodrigo *complimenting* Nelson?

Sophie gripped the back of the chair she stood behind. Had the ICE agent kept their covers intact?

I will kiss him if he did.

Kiss him *back*, actually. She hadn't even had time to analyze what he'd done to her earlier. She'd tucked that memory, the feel of his lips, into a safe place to think about later. *Much later.*

"He told me about his tour in Iraq for the Americans," Rodrigo was saying. "You know, I toured the Middle East during my schooling. Never have I seen such security extremes. Dubai...now that was my favorite place. It is one of the top three trading hubs in the world for diamonds and other gemstones."

Rodrigo had loved traveling. Loved going to university and getting his gemologist degree. He talked about both on a regular basis. What could he have been if not dragged back to Tijuana and his family's criminal enterprise? Perhaps he would have lived in Dubai and made an honest living as an international master gemologist.

He seemed to be waiting for a response. She knew Nelson had been a ranger in the U.S. Army, but he'd never spoken of his tours of duty to her. Of course, during their brief time together, there hadn't been a lot of talking. "War-torn countries tend to take defense and personal security quite seriously. I'm sure he learned quite a bit in Iraq."

Rodrigo's face was still lit up with the memories of his past. "That is why he's going to be staying with us."

She had to take a moment to process his words. "He's *what?*"

"I've made him a deal."

Relief that Nelson was still in one piece flooded her body, yet a cold slice of apprehension at Rodrigo's words caused her to grip the back of the chair tighter. "What kind of deal, if I may ask?"

Rodrigo smiled, cold, calculating. The cartel leader in him rising past the memories of his unencumbered college years. "Nico Raines is my new head of security."

A beat of silence passed, her nails digging into the chair back. "What about Chavez?"

His face hardened. He didn't appreciate being questioned,

and failure by anyone on his team was not allowed. "Chavez's security failed. He was shown the door, as they say."

Chavez was out. Nelson was in.

She almost burst out laughing, her apprehension sky-rocketing once more.

The irony.

Instead, she held herself still, not moving as anger heated her blood and a dozen arguments ran through her head. *Never argue with Rodrigo.* The first lesson she'd learned. He was prone to snap decisions, had loyalty to no one but himself. Everyone at the compound, everyone who worked for him, was disposable.

"That's...wonderful," she said, plastering on a fake smile.

"He will be staying in the guest house in the empty apartment next to yours. He said you wouldn't mind."

The smile threatened to turn into a grimace. *I'm going to kill him.* "Is that what he said?"

One of Rodrigo's brows rose. "Is there a problem?"

Only a six-one, one-hundred and ninety pound undercover agent screwing up my operation. "I just assumed he would stay in the staff house. Like Señor Chavez did."

"Yes, well, I am beefing up security based on Señor Raines's recommendations. Chavez's quarters will be soon be assigned to a new security member based on Nico's recommendation."

"I see."

"Tomorrow, we will head to town at noon for rounds like usual. Raines will accompany us. He needs new clothes, and I want him to keep a close eye on you."

Their weekly "rounds" constituted picking up money drops in a six-mile radius of downtown, a section they called Old Tijuana that had existed when the town was nothing more than a few strip clubs and gambling dens. The area was a ghetto with plenty of seedy businesses with a healthy drug trade. Sophie picked up the drug money and protection fees and ran the cash through legit small businesses to clean it. "Of course."

"Rigo!" Lexie appeared, dressed now in her pajamas, and

made her way to her brother's side, dropping her service dog's handle as Rodrigo lifted her for a hug.

When he set her down, she tugged on his hand. "Maria-Sophia is going to read to me, and then you can tuck me in."

"You are too old for me to tuck in, *chica.*"

Her brows scrunched in that telltale sign. "Is that true, Maria-Sophia?"

"You're never too old to be tucked in by someone you love." Sophie wished she'd tucked her sister into bed more, especially since their mother was often MIA. "But I'm sure your brother still has work to do, so how about we read and I'll tuck you in?"

"I will do it." Rodrigo stood and smiled down at his sister even though she couldn't see him. "I've been too caught up with work. Alexa and I should spend time together."

"I could skip school tomorrow," the girl volunteered.

Lexie had left her boarding school in Mexico City only a month ago to come home and live with Rodrigo. She was privately tutored by nuns at the local convent and hated it.

Sophie didn't blame her.

"No skipping school." He winked at Sophie over Lexie's head, once more a normal human being and not the cold-hearted cartel leader. "We all have jobs tomorrow and yours is learning Latin and History."

"I hate school!" she said in Spanish, and then again in English as if to emphasis her point.

"Lexie," Sophie said, "your brother and I will be in town. We'll pick you up after school and go for ice cream. How does that sound?"

The girl had a weakness for orange sherbet. She tugged on Rodrigo's hand again. "Can we?"

Rodrigo gave Sophie a look. "You're spoiling my sister."

Be grateful you still have one. "She deserves it."

He threw up his free hand in exasperation. "I'm losing this battle, aren't I?"

Lexie's little-girl laugh was contagious and Sophie laughed

33

with her. Her service dog, Harry, named after Lexie's favorite fictional sorcerer, barked.

Such a normal family conversation. If only I could keep them together.

But she wasn't part of this family and the family owned a cartel that hurt people every day.

Still, guilt ate at Sophie that she was about to take Rodrigo away from Lexie. "You should know you'd never win against two strong females."

"That's right!" Lexie dragged him out the study door, Harry by her side. "See you tomorrow, Maria-Sophia."

Sophia followed and gave Rodrigo a smile as he shut and locked the door behind them. He gave her a small bow. "Until tomorrow, Maria-Sophia. Sleep well."

There was a message in his eyes. The same one he gave her every night—she was always welcome in his bed if she found hers lonely.

She wondered, not for the first time, if he had a snake in his bedroom.

Tonight, the invitation seemed to hold more weight, letting her know he preferred she sleep with him rather than Nico. Time to put the idea that Nico was coming anywhere near her to rest. "If it's alright with you, I'll grab extra bedding on my way out for Nico since the vacant apartment has none."

A pleased smile passed over his lips. "Of course."

Lexie tugged him away. Watching the two of them laugh and talk as they walked to Lexie's princess-inspired room, guilt consumed Sophie again. Lexie had no idea what her brother did. The biggest reason—maybe the *only* reason—Rodrigo had come home from Europe and taken up the family reins was to take care of Lexie. He'd studied to be a master gemologist. Had left the family biz behind and planned to start over in another part of the world.

When he went to jail, the little girl would end up in foster care if Sophie couldn't track down any relatives. Foster care here would be a death sentence. Rodrigo's enemies would hunt her down.

Every operation took its toll, but this one was one for the books. How had she let herself fall for Rodrigo's little sister, knowing she would bring the girl's world crashing down on her when this was over?

Disgusted with herself, she headed down the stairs and out the door. Collateral damage from her job would have to wait. She had a bone to pick with the new head of security.

Where is she?

The apartment was empty, only the hint of Sophie's perfume lingering in the air. She liked to walk at night, he remembered. Maybe she'd gone for a stroll to work off steam after he'd kissed her. Boy, the look in her eyes when he'd done that. *Pure fire.*

She was always steamed about something.

He sort of liked it.

His stomach growled. The swelling in his eye had gone down and he could crack it open now. He found the kitchen, washed his hands, and rolled his shoulders. What a day.

Rodrigo had shown him the grounds and the security set up. The tour wasn't complete without another stop at the snake pit. The caretaker, an exotic animal vet, was feeding Morales's pets. Rats. Yeesh. Nelson hated rats almost as much as snakes.

But during the tour, Nelson had shown Morales how he'd gotten into the compound without detection. He'd made several suggestions to increase security and make the existing security more efficient. Sanny, one of the guards, had a cousin in the Savages. A call was made; Nelson's backstory confirmed. He'd dug himself in deep with the motorcycle gang and his hard work had paid off.

Not exactly in the way he'd intended, but if it meant keeping

Sophie safe and all of his limbs attached to his body, so be it.

Sophie's fridge was filled with fresh fruit, cheese, cold rotisserie chicken, and three different flavors of hot salsa. He found chips in a cabinet and, whistling to himself, went to work building a plate of chicken nachos.

The door opened and slammed shut again in the other room as he was pulling them out of the microwave. Warm, gooey cheese covered the pile, and he opened a salsa jar and poured some on top. "I'm in here," he called.

Her heels clicked furiously on the tiled floor and he saw her enter from the corner of his slitted eye. Her face was a storm of worry and anger. The energy radiating off of her reminded him of a tropical storm building down south.

He held up the plate. She had a soft spot for spicy food. "Dinner?"

She dropped a set of bed sheets on the table, then took the shawl from her shoulders and tossed it on the back of a kitchen chair. Her face was set. She grabbed the plate from his hands, slid it onto the counter, and pointed a finger at him. "I should…"

Here it comes. His ass was about to take a beating.

"I should…" she said loudly again. Then, without warning, Sophie Diaz threw her arms around him.

She went up on her toes and hugged him hard enough to force the breath from his lungs. Her breasts pressed against his sore ribs, her chin barely clearing his shoulder.

She was warm and soft in all the right places, and this was completely not what he'd expected.

Which was normal for Sophie. She was always turning left when he thought she'd go right.

But fuck. Who was he to look a gift horse in the mouth?

He ran his fingers down her back and let his hand linger just above her sexy ass. His other hand went to the back of her neck and he slipped it under her braid and massaged her neck. Man, what he wouldn't do to cup those heart-shaped ass cheeks and bend her backward over the table…

He closed his eyes and let the hair at the edge of her ear tickle his nose. *God, I've missed you.*

As if she read his thoughts, she jerked back, breaking his hold. Before he could take his next breath, *whack!* She slapped him across the face.

"What the…?" He touched his stinging cheek. "What was that for?"

"First, for kissing me."

Okay, he'd expected payback for that. "I heard someone coming when we were on the patio and I needed to shut you up. You said you'd told them I was your lover, so I figured I'd better play the part. Good thing I did since it was Morales."

"*Former* lover, and don't ever shut me up like that again. Got it?"

He grinned. "You didn't seem to mind."

Heat-seeking missiles generated less intensity than the rage coming from her eyes. "Secondly, you nearly blew my op."

He spread his palms wide. "I have everything under control. Morales hired me as his new head of security. I can watch your back and help you with the investigation."

"So I heard. You can't seriously think you can stay here as the head of security."

"Chavez screwed up. I pointed out a bunch of spots Morales needed to beef up on and I looked over his security protocols. Big holes."

"Morales would never hire someone he hasn't vetted."

Nelson shrugged. "I'm vetted. After our walk around the grounds and a thumbs-up from the Savages, Morales offered me the job." He smiled. "What I can say?"

She eyed him suspiciously. "You planned this, didn't you?"

"What? Of course not. Chavez screwed up and I had an opportunity to step into his shoes. Which is perfect. Now I have a reason to stay and help you."

"I don't need help!" She caught herself, took a deep breath, and seemed to rein in her emotions.

Sort of. Her hands balled into fists at her sides. "I thought you were snake food. You gave me heart palpations."

"Snake food?"

"Yes, you idiot. I thought you'd blown the operation and Rodrigo had realized you were lying. You know what he does with liars? He takes them to the pit. The snake pit, that red building at the back of the property. He keeps snakes there. Gigantic ones that he feeds liars to."

"I know. I had the grand tour." He shuddered. "Jesus, Joseph, and Mary, I hate snakes."

She made the sign of the cross. "I thought you were dead."

She cares for me. The truth was like a sucker punch to his stomach, yet it made his heart do weird things inside his chest. "I figured you'd dance on my grave when I died."

Snatching up her shawl, she glared at him again, but the missiles were fizzling. "Don't for one minute think that I'm okay with you being here. You're staying in the apartment next door, by the way." She tapped the folded bed sheets. "For your bed. Over there."

With a swirl of her skirt, she tilted up her chin and left him standing there. He heard the bathroom door slam shut.

Grinning, he grabbed his plate of nachos and went to make himself at home on her couch.

CHAPTER FIVE

San Diego
2200 hours

Cooper Harris crouched in the dark beside the basement window of a gift shop in a not-so-nice alley on the rough side of San Diego.

"What do you see?" the head of the SCVC Taskforce whispered sotto voce to his partner, Thomas Mann.

Shuffling, along with a sound of metal scraping on metal, rose from inside where Thomas was looking around. "A bunch of shit," the DEA agent answered softly. "Shelving, perfume, knickknacks, office supplies, a couple of crates. Wait... What is this?" A pause and the squeaking of dry hinges. His cell phone's flashlight illuminated a crate. "Oh, yeah, come to papa."

Cooper's body went on high-alert. "What is it?"

"Ronni's going to love this. She was right. The crates are full of bath salts." He emphasized *bath salts.* "Purple Wave, Ocean Snow, Tranquility."

In the world of designer drugs, stimulants were sold as bath salts under a variety of names. Ronni Punto, Cooper's undercover FBI agent working Project Bliss, had nailed another one. She'd told him about this gift shop and her suspicions at their morning taskforce meeting.

Bliss was an op to crack down on manufacturers, wholesalers, and retailers of synthetic designer drugs. They were after a dealer in San Diego, but the operation spanned at least twenty states. They suspected the manufacturer was in Mexico. Everything from tobacco shops to convenience stores was selling the stuff over the counter. A seven-year-old kid had recently died from eating his mother's bath salts, a white, powdery substance more widely known as ecstasy.

A block or two away, he heard the chirp of a police siren. This alley was quiet, but the ones surrounding it saw a good number of homeless squatters, drunks, and street dealers. "Come on out," he told Thomas. "I'll call Dupé and get a warrant."

Cooper heard the snap of Thomas's cell phone camera, saw a flash of light. "Coming."

A minute later, they were headed back to Cooper's SUV. He was dialing his boss, deputy director Victor Dupé, when his phone beeped with an incoming call.

Make It Rain was the ID.

Cooper climbed into his vehicle. "It's Cruz." He answered the cell. "Tell me you have Agent Diaz and are headed back to San Diego."

"I have Diaz, but…"

The agent's hesitation made his hackles rise. "No. No buts. Project Bliss is about to explode on us. We've taken down three shops this week and we're closing in on the supplier. I need you here."

"I haven't completed my mission with Chica Bonita."

"Chica Bonita has to wait. Bring Diaz back and help us nail this supplier."

"No can do."

Cooper refrained from banging the phone into the steering wheel, but his stress must have been obvious on his face. Thomas grabbed it from his hand and put Nelson on speaker. "What's up, man?"

"Diaz is safe. I've got her back. But I've found myself in a little situation that could lead to something bigger than Chica Bonita. I'm going to follow it."

Thomas shot Cooper a questioning look. Down the street, blue and red strobe lights illuminated the surrounding buildings. A crowd was gathering at the corner.

The distraction was helpful after their little B&E, but it was time to go. Cooper put the SUV in gear. "Agent Diaz is not safe until she's back in the States, Cruz. There's no breathing room on this. The Feds want her back, like yesterday."

"She refuses to come back until she finishes her op. She's not gone rogue, man. She's still on the job like a dog on a bone. If I'm going to protect her, the only thing I can do is play bodyguard, and it just so happens, I have the perfect cover."

"As an assassin outlaw gang member?" Thomas asked.

"Rodrigo Morales made me his head of security today."

The Southern California Violent Crimes Taskforce was a conglomerate of agents from the FBI, ICE, and DEA. Each and every one of them had incredible undercover skills, a ton of training and experience in undercover ops, and a penchant for taking risks.

Didn't mean they couldn't give Cooper a giant headache when one went off the deep end. "Head of security. For Rodrigo Morales. Are you fucking kidding me?"

"God's truth. All I need is forty-eight hours, maybe less. Agent Diaz will have this op wrapped up and we'll be in the sweet U.S. of A. by Saturday."

Cooper shook his head and drove east, away from the commotion down the street. "What aren't you understanding? Her op is *done*. The FBI has enough on Morales, according to Dupé, The Attorney General will be sending warrants down the pipeline in twenty-four hours, maybe less. Bring her in. If she causes an international incident, your ass is in deep shit. The president can't afford that right now, not with his approval numbers in the toilet after the Chicago debacle."

Cooper's former NSA agent, Bianca Marx, and her SEAL husband, Cal, had been at the heart of that, revealing that the prez's VP had turned traitor. While many of the president's constituents believed he was innocent of any of the VP's wrongdoing, the majority of people blamed him for allowing a traitor into the White House. "He's got to get his new immigrant policy worked out with Mexico and through Congress ASAP. Even a whiff that we have a rogue agent ruffling feathers in Tijuana with the Morales cartel, and President Norman can kiss his negotiations with Mexico goodbye."

Nelson's voice suggested he didn't care. "Diaz claims there's another ledger she needs to find, one Morales keeps hidden. She's going after that. I'll keep it all quiet—her, the operation, everything. There won't be any blow-back on the president."

Thomas chuckled. "How the hell did you pull off landing the head of security, Cruz?"

"I'll tell you over a beer when I get back." His voice faded in and out. "You still owe me one for backing you on Operation Truth."

"You got it, Make-It-Rain Raines." Thomas was texting Ronni with his other hand, probably to tell her they'd found the bath salts. "You need backup?"

"Not yet. Gotta see how deep the shit is first. Hopefully, Diaz can find that ledger in the next day or two."

"You have twenty-four hours." Cooper let go of a deep sigh. He hated giving Cruz rope on this, but pushing his agent into a corner wouldn't help any of them, least of all Agent Diaz. "If things get ugly, Mann and I can be there in thirty-five minutes, less if necessary."

He was low on manpower with Ronni undercover and Bianca gone, but if Nelson needed help, Cooper and Thomas would ride to his rescue. "Don't take chances. Morales is no one to mess with. You say the word, we're there."

"Sorry I can't help with Bliss."

You and me both. He hit the main drag, heading for the SCVC Taskforce headquarters. "I'll call in replacements. Watch your six, and whatever you do, do not let Agent Diaz get hurt."

"Roger that, boss. Will Dupé fire me over this?"

"I'll do what I can to cover for your insolent ass."

"Thanks, Coop. Beg, borrow, and steal to get me a full twenty-four hours before the Feds come for Morales."

The line went dead and Thomas handed him his phone. "Replacements, huh? Who you got in mind?"

"Mitch Holton is back from his offshore assignment and Sara Rios is also interested." Both had worked with the taskforce before. "What do you think?"

"Holton is good with tech stuff and knows his way around weapons. Sara's former stint with the CIA can't hurt and she's a damn good fugitive recovery agent. She knew her stuff when we took down Emilio Londano. Either would be a strong addition to the team. Which one are you leaning toward?"

Cooper hit a speed dial for Dupé. He needed a warrant for the gift shop, and he needed to inform the director that Nelson was not bringing back Agent Diaz yet. "Both. After Dupé puts my ass through the ringer over Cruz going off the reservation with the Diaz op, you may be the only man left standing."

"Dupé's going to give you hell, but your hands are tied. It's Nelson who's going to get fired."

True, but then Dupé liked his taskforce agents to push the limits. That's how they accomplished all they did.

As usual, Dupé answered on the first ring. Cooper took a deep breath, glad for the physical distance between him and his boss. "I have good news and bad news," he said. "Which do you want first, sir?"

CHAPTER SIX

Tijuana
Morales compound

Her bed was in pieces. Nelson, with only one free hand, had managed to dismantle it to free himself earlier and it still lay in a state of disarray.

The aftereffects of the vision had finally caught up with her. Her headache had spread from her temples to the back of her head. Her legs were weak. Her eyes would barely focus, and all she wanted to do was lie down with a cold rag on her forehead and sleep.

But there was her bed, the mattress askew, the headboard detached from the frame and cockeyed on the floor. In the other room, Nelson was whistling softly. She had just enough strength to pick up the headboard and curse him, leaning it against the wall, but she didn't exactly relish the idea of it falling on her during the night.

With the way her body was shutting down, maybe she wouldn't notice.

She slumped to the floor, ignoring the sound of Nelson entering the room.

"I'll fix that." He moved past her, shuffling the frame around and bolting it back to the headboard. He'd removed his biker vest and boots. "All I had to do was release this pin,"—he tapped a metal brace on the frame's wooden spindle—"and voila, freedom."

In thirty seconds flat, he had the bed put back together.

Sophie didn't speak, using the nightstand to steady herself as she rose. Her head felt like a hundred-pound weight, her eyesight blurring. Her hand bumped the jar of wild yam cream, sending it to the floor.

Disregarding the sheets that were still askew, she climbed into bed. The pillow gave way under her head and she sighed, closing her eyes. "Leave."

"The room or Mexico?"

"Both."

"Are you okay?"

"Headache," she mumbled. "Go away."

She thought she'd gotten her wish when Nelson walked out without another word.

Until she heard water running and the clank of glass coming from her bathroom.

What the hell was he doing?

She felt his engulfing presence return. A soft, cool cloth landed on her forehead as if he were a fairy godmother fulfilling her wish. She blinked open her eyes as the mattress dipped from his weight. He set down a bottle of lavender essential oil and a second one of peppermint on the nightstand. "What are you doing?"

"My mom used to get migraines." He scooted next to her, his hands going under her neck to lift her head as he removed the pillow. "She was a holistic practitioner. I know a few things that might help."

Before Sophie could protest, or tell him she'd already used the oils on her temples—a Little Gran staple—he lifted her upper body and climbed onto the bed. He sat with his back against the headboard and lowered her head into his lap.

Oh, no. He could *not* be in her bed. Not like this.

"Close your eyes," he instructed.

She wiggled, trying to get away from him, but she was as weak as a baby. With every protest, her head sent a spike of agony to the base of her skull. "Oh, God."

The scent of lavender drifted to her nose. Little Gran had been a holistic practitioner of sorts herself, using natural herbs and oils all her life. She'd never gone to the doctor, and had treated her family, including Sophie, with her concoctions.

Nelson's fingertips, gentle and coaxing, rubbed her temples, then tapped softly along her hairline. "Shh," he said. "Relax."

Relax? He was the reason for her vision, the reason she was now in pain. He'd wormed his way into her op and now into her bed. Her body might have betrayed her at the moment, but as soon as she felt better...

He moved the wet cloth off of her forehead and placed it on her throat. Pressing a thumb into the area between her eyebrows, he rubbed up and over the arches of her brows, stroking, stroking, stroking...

Sophie lost her train of thought. Her temples weren't pounding anymore, and as Nelson worked the lines out of her brow, her whole body felt softer, lighter.

Those diligent fingertips moved to the back of her neck. His oiled thumbs pressed into the tight muscles there, working calmly and firmly from the back of her head down into the sensitive top of each shoulder, then returning to her neck with smooth strokes.

Sophie felt a twinge as the tendons in each shoulder began to loosen under his ministrations. His thumbs continued their path from her shoulders, up the back of her neck, massaging the base of her skull. Up and down, and...*ahh*...her tense neck muscles unwound in one satisfying release.

Gently, he moved to her jaw, kneading the tightness there away. He tapped her cheekbones, stroked the indentations of her cheeks. She lost track of time, a strange electrical pulse running from her head to her toes, thrumming through her entire body.

He rubbed the edges of her ears between his thumbs and forefingers, massaged her scalp through her hair. The next thing she knew, he raised her right arm over her head. "Just let it fall back," he said in a low, husky voice, guiding her hand to his neck. "Put your hand here."

Her fingers skimmed the hair at the base of his neck, her right side exposed now to his hands. As his hand steadied hers, he ran his other down the underside of her arm, tapping and stroking over her ribs, then switching to a gentle rubbing through her shirt as he ran his hand back up her side.

It tickled and it didn't. His big hand brushed the side of her bra. Her nipples tightened in response.

She forgot all about her head, opening her eyes to stare up at his face. His eyes were focused on what he was doing and she could watch him without his return gaze making her uncomfortable. He caressed the back of her shoulder, his hand diligent and confident, then ran it down her side again.

The focus on his face brought back memories of the previous time he'd taken such care with her body. Her lower belly tensed. Warmth bloomed between her legs.

He was irreverent and flippant on the outside; intense and powerful on the inside.

He switched sides, bringing her right arm down and raising her left as he started the sweet torture all over again. She sighed deeply and his gaze met hers for a second.

"Better?" he asked.

That low, sexy voice, his very presence, would be her undoing. "Your mother knew her stuff."

The right side of his mouth quirked. "Most people thought she was loco, but I think she just walked to the beat of a different drummer."

Bet she didn't have visions. Sophie watched Nelson's hand moving up and down her arm, her side. Other parts of her body fired up, begging for his touch. "Don't we all?"

"Mmm," was his only response.

He moved both of her hands to the back of his neck, doing double duty on her arms and sides. For some reason, she felt exposed, even though she was still fully clothed and he hadn't so much as leered at her.

After a minute, he brought her hands back down.

Taking her right hand in his, he massaged it from wrist to fingertips. His thumb pushed into her palm, then he gently pinched the end of her index finger. His own index finger and thumb slid to the soft tissue where her thumb joined her hand. "Pressure points," he told her. "These points are linked to the head and neck."

They seemed to be linked to other places as well. Sophie covertly squeezed her thighs together, wishing he would end the torment and praying he never did.

Sweat beaded on her top lip. She longed to strip off her clothes and let him work over the rest of her.

Stop it, Sophie. No getting involved. Not again.

Never. Again.

Pulling her hand away, she sat up, using the cloth to wipe at her face. All the coolness had evaporated and it had instead soaked up the heat of her skin. "Thank you. I feel much better."

His hand lingered on her arm. He sat forward, putting his face next to her ear. "How about some peppermint oil on your neck? It will cool you down."

Nothing but a cold shower would cool her down at this point. She swung her legs over the edge of the bed and stood. Her thighs trembled, but she knew it was from sexual frustration, not the headache. "I'm good."

Outside the window, night had totally enveloped the compound. Clouds covered the sliver of moon, leaving the grounds deep in shadows.

Nelson stood as well, taking the washcloth and moving her braid to dab at her neck where a trickle of sweat coursed over her skin. He was too close again. "Why don't you turn on the air conditioning?"

"It's old and loud. I can't hear if someone's outside or coming up the steps." She pointed up. "I use the ceiling fan and open the windows."

"You've got me now to protect you. Turn on the air and get some sleep."

Tempting, but she couldn't let her guard down. Not even if she wanted to. Being on constant alert, always vigil, was a way of life.

He tossed the washcloth onto the dresser and headed for the living room. "Sleep well, Soph."

When she didn't hear the front door of her apartment open or close, she peeked around the corner. Nelson had the stack of linens she'd brought and was making up the couch.

"You can't sleep here."

He didn't look up. "My job is to protect you. I sleep here."

By the tone of his voice, there was no arguing. She closed the bedroom door and sank down onto the edge of the bed, hands shaking.

Forty-eight hours. She had forty-eight hours to figure how to save Lexie and stay away from Nelson and his magic hands.

For the second day in a row, Nelson woke up in Sophie's bed. This time, he could open both eyes and he wasn't handcuffed to the frame. Moving, however, wasn't recommended since she had him by the hair, his head pulled back, neck exposed.

Two of her fingers jabbed him in the Adam's apple as she loomed over him. "What the hell are you doing in my bed?"

He looked down his nose at her face. Overnight, the outside temp had dropped and cooled the room, but her body oozed heat as she leaned over him. She had wicked bedhead, her tangled brown locks showing highlights of burnt orange and golden yellow in the morning sun coming through the window.

A wary spark lit her eyes even though her lids were still

heavy with sleep. Better than the night before when the headache had caused her pretty peepers to be glossy and unfocused.

Hard to speak with her fingers pressuring his throat, though. "Couch...was...too small."

Removing her fingers, she gave his hair a tug. "Bullshit."

"I'm six-one. That couch is made for midgets. I kept getting a kink in my neck and cramps in my legs. I needed a real bed."

"So you invited yourself into mine?" Now that he could halfway move his head, he saw her pajama top had a deep V. "You have a bed next door!"

Releasing his hair, she started to swing herself off the bed. He caught her by the wrist. The sunlight bathed her face as the last of the sleep left her eyes.

Something sizzled between them. His morning boner grew fatter. "You have a king size bed, Sophie. It practically swallows you up. The one next door is a single."

He saw her throat contract as she swallowed. "I don't share and you don't belong here."

Like he didn't already know that. "I kept to my side. Never touched you."

Her gaze fell to his hand, still locked around her delicate wrist. "You're touching me now."

All he wanted to do was drag her back into the pillows. "You didn't seem to mind my touch last night when you were in pain."

"I was nearly comatose. You could have been a Martian and I wouldn't have fought you off."

"Do you have migraines often?"

She tried to pull her wrist away. "Only when you're around."

He held on for a second, enjoying the way her breasts jiggled under the top as she fought the restraint. "Seems to me you slept pretty damn well after I made you feel better. You didn't even wake up, except to cuddle me, when I slipped into your bed."

"How did you get in? I locked the door."

He tapped his chest. "Expert lock picker."

She stopped struggling, giving him a look that could have singed his hair. "You watched me sleep, didn't you? Stalker."

He rolled his eyes. "Get over yourself. I have to keep an eye on you to make sure Guido doesn't get you. Won't be long before he knows I turned on him and I'm now working for Morales. Hell, he probably already knows." He rubbed the inside of her wrist with his thumb. "When I tried to nap on that fucking couch, I nearly ended up in traction, so I came in here and decided the best way to keep you safe *and* get my beauty rest was to bunk down next to you. I'm on bodyguard duty, remember?"

Her gaze raked the length of him, caught on his flagrant erection. "How could I forget?" She gave another jerk and he released her. "I did not cuddle up to you last night. You're living in fantasy land."

He'd been in fantasy land all right. A visit to fifty shades of Sophia once again. Hearing the shower run for a good, long time after he'd set up camp on the couch, he'd had to fight the urge to join her and see if he could make her scream his name like she had back in the day. Imagining her naked under the water, all those curves and gorgeous skin wet and willing was too strong a temptation no matter how much she annoyed him every time she opened her mouth.

She was breathing hard after trying to get away, and looking like she wanted to hit him. "Get. Out. Of. My. Bed."

Maybe not so willing, but…

Restraint was his middle name these days. Had been since she'd screwed him over the first time they both tried to shut down Chica Bonita. So last night, he'd washed off in the kitchen sink and ignored his hard cock. Later, when he'd crawled into her bed, exhausted—he hadn't slept in three days—and she'd sidled up next to him, it had been a test of every last, fucking nerve he had not to take her right there.

But he was telling the truth. While she may have touched him, he'd never laid a hand on her, lying there like a statue.

Yeah, he'd known better. Known being that close to her sleeping body and not able to strip her naked and make her moan was the worst form of torment.

He did it anyway.

Hello, my name is Nelson and I'm addicted to Sophie Diaz.

Women. Always his downfall. The one vice he'd never given up.

Until Sophie.

He touched the scar over his eye. In his post-Sophie world, the only woman he'd wanted was her. The one who'd screwed him over, literally and professionally, and left him with a souvenir so he'd never forget her.

This morning, with her only inches from him again, her curvy body, sexy hair, and clean skin giving him another round of sledgehammer cock, he was finding it hard not to act out every one of the fantasies she was accusing him of.

But the look on her face bode evil for him if he so much as smirked. So instead of goading her more, he took his fantasies, and his treacherous addiction, and headed for her bathroom.

When he emerged after a quick shower, he smelled like Sophie's gardenia shampoo. He had no clean clothes, so he skipped the underwear and ruined T-shirt and pulled on his dirty jeans.

She was in the kitchen, dressed in a hot pink number that dipped in the back, exposing her graceful shoulders. He remembered tracing his tongue down her spine, sucking at the indents above her heart-shaped ass.

Mind blank except for damning memories of their all-too-brief set of nights together, he stood motionless for a long minute, watching her now sip from a coffee cup and move something that smelled of eggs, peppers, and onions around in a skillet with a spatula. A jar of hot sauce sat next to a stack of tortillas. For a moment, it reminded him of his mom, cooking breakfast for him and his brother.

Without looking at him, Sophie said, "There are clothes on the couch for you."

His brain struggled to shift gears. "Huh?"

She set down the cup and spatula and started spreading a pale pink, creamy concoction on a tortilla. "Rodrigo had the maid bring a set of clothes for your trip into town today. He wants to walk you through how the team handles our trips into Tijuana. If Guido knows you've jumped ship, and he's found someone else to take a shot at killing me, it will be in town."

"Oh, uh, okay." Clothes from the cartel leader? That was weird, but Nelson guessed Morales didn't want his head of security looking like a biker. "What are you making?"

"Breakfast."

Answered his question without actually answering it. "Smells delicious."

She scooped some of the mixture from the skillet and laid it in the middle of the tortilla, then rolled. Once finished, she lifted the burrito, turning to face him. The tortilla stopped midway to her mouth as her eyes landed on his naked chest. Her gaze surfed across his pecs, dropped to his ribs, and lingered on his bruises. Whirling back around, she set the breakfast burrito down and hastily worked filling another. "Coffee?"

"I'll get it." He crossed the small kitchen and took a cup from the open shelves, his elbow brushing her shoulder.

She shifted sideways, giving him more space, although there really wasn't any. After he poured a cup that was the color of mud, he leaned a hip against the counter and pointed at the bowl of pink stuff. "What's that?"

"Secret ingredient." She shooed him out of the way and spread some on the next tortilla, repeating the process and handing it to him. At least six more lined a platter.

"You made me breakfast?"

"You're too skinny." She busied herself cleaning up and

53

eating her own burrito. "Plus, I owe you for last night. For relieving my headache."

He was not skinny. Sophie never allowed herself to be in anyone's debt, and that was the real reason she'd made him breakfast.

He bit into the burrito and savored the simple ingredients that made a glorious and satisfying meal all wrapped in a small package.

Small package filled with spunk. The thought made him take a second look at the chef.

She avoided glancing at his chest. At him.

He sipped his coffee. "I hardly think rubbing your temples and massaging your neck for a few minutes is worth anything more than a thank you, but if that's all it takes to get you to cook for me—"

She slapped him with a dishtowel. "Get out of the kitchen."

He took his coffee and burrito and went to get dressed. A pair of black jeans and a deep blue button-down were folded and tied together in a neat bundle with string.

He was buttoning up the shirt when Sophie appeared in the living room. Her eyes were serious. "Can we talk?"

"Sure." He shoved his ragged biker jeans and leather vest aside from where he'd tossed them on the couch. After a shower and a filling breakfast, he was ready to get down to business and discuss the op. "What's our plan for getting that ledger?"

"It's not *our* plan." She sat on the edge of the couch, looking up at him. "It's mine, and although I understand the fact that you need to complete your mission to bring me back to the States safely, I do *not* need a bodyguard. I know what I'm doing, and… I'm sorry, but I can't involve you in this, Nelson."

Such a Sophie thing, trying to give him the boot. She was the same old Fed she'd been two years ago. Operation Gangs Without Borders was her op and she didn't want him honing in on it.

He'd gotten too close to her with Chica Bonita and that had

ended badly. She'd never worked with another agent again. Now, here they were, and she was trying to give him the shaft.

"I'm not going to take credit for anything you accomplish here, Soph. All I'm here for is to watch your back and help any way I can."

"That's just it. You can't help. In fact, I'm still worried about the way you usurped Chavez and got hired on the spot by Morales. He doesn't do that, Nels, not ever." She reached out and touched his hand. Softly, fleetingly, her eyes wide and pleading. "You could be in some serious danger here."

Oh, she was good. Playing him with the eyes and the touch and the troubled voice.

He didn't take her hand, instead stepping back. "You find that ledger, I'll handle Morales. This isn't my first cartel rodeo. I can take care of myself." *And you.*

She stood, brows furrowed, and moved in close. "Nels, I'm worried about you." She reached out and skimmed her fingers over his ribs, down his side. "Did you use the yam cream on your bruises?"

The woman who claimed she hated him was pretending to care? *Like I'd fall for that.*

If only her eyes didn't look so damn sincere.

In his mind, he saw the vet feeding the snakes, heard the hiss of the snakes in the pit. "It's not the first time I've been beaten up."

At some point when he had been lying stock still next to her during the night, he'd thought over his experience at the compound so far and wondered how Sophie had known he had been getting his ass handed to him by Morales's men. "How did you know I was here, yesterday, by the way? What brought you to the snake pit?"

Her hand fell to her side. She backed up, hesitating for a second before her eyes lost their concern and went hard. He'd seen through her bluff and she was pissed. "I heard you crying like a baby. I wanted to know who was about to be killed."

He hadn't made a noise. "The ledger's hidden somewhere in there, isn't it? That's why you were there."

For half a second, she looked surprised. "Good thing I was, or like I told you yesterday, you would have been snake food."

"Where do you think it's at? Under a cage or buried in the pit itself?"

"I don't know."

"But you have a guess."

"Sunday is the anniversary of Rodrigo's father's death. He's taking his little sister down the coast this weekend. Ciro is buried behind their vacation home. I've been through every square inch of the house and most of the out buildings. Everywhere but that damned snake pit. I plan to thoroughly check everything again, that's why I need forty-eight hours. I hope the ledger isn't hidden in the pit, but if it is, I'll find it."

"You don't have forty-eight hours. You have twenty-four."

"But that's not enough. I already told you"—

"The Feds took your information on Morales to the Attorney General yesterday. Morales's arrest warrant is in the works as we speak. I bought you twenty-four hours, but that's all you get."

Her mouth dropped open. "No. I need more."

"What you need,"—he leaned in, putting his face in front of her—"is me. Fucking snake pit or not, I'll find that goddamned ledger, all right?"

"Oh, Nelson." Her voice shook and she looked like he'd hit her with one of those damn snakes from the pit. She sunk down onto the couch again. "What have I done?"

CHAPTER SEVEN

"Sophie?" Nelson sat beside her on the couch. One of his hands went to her knee, the other to her back. "What's going on?"

Those hands were warm, the one on her bare back calloused but gentle. The one on her knee gave a slight squeeze as he shifted an inch closer. "You can tell me," he said, his voice comforting.

But she couldn't tell him. She'd screwed up and let herself get attached to a criminal's little sister. Displacement. She shook her head. *Classic Psych 101, Sophia. The very thing the Bureau teaches you not to do.*

What was I thinking? Lexie was not a replacement for Angelique, and it had been wrong of Sophie to let herself get emotionally close to the girl. The old guilt was too hard to get around. She hadn't protected her younger sister and fooled herself into believing she could protect Lexie to make up for it.

And then there were the others. The girls she was helping get across the border in the most illegal of ways...

Lifting her head and standing, she shook off Nelson's concern, and his hands. Emotionally vulnerable was the last thing she'd ever let him see her as. She had to act cool and in control, keep her reputation intact. *I still have twenty-four hours.* "It's nothing. I've just been undercover with this assignment for so long, I can't believe it's almost over."

The weight of his gaze rested on the back of her shoulders as she paced away from him. His silence suggested he didn't believe her, so she wrung her hands a little as she faced him. "You said it yesterday... I'm in deep. For months, I've been thinking this operation was never going to end, and now you're telling me it'll all be over in a day."

Again, total silence. He shifted back on the couch, one arm coming to rest across the back. She glanced out the window and gazed at the garden below. The morning air was still cool even as the sun climbed higher in the sky. The peacock pecked at the ground and preened. A couple of other nondescript birds bathed in the birdbath, flipping water out on him.

Nelson's intense stare didn't let up, his silence sucking at her energy. She'd known he was in bed with her during the night and she hadn't kicked him out. For the first time in months, she'd slept soundly and didn't startle at every noise.

No way was she letting him know that.

But she'd gone and put her foot in her mouth. *Distract him.* Change the subject, kiss him, do *something*!

Distracting Nelson wouldn't buy her more time, however, and in the end, time was the only thing that could save Lexie and the other girls.

There were so many lost girls...

Swallowing hard, she walked back over to the ICE agent and forced herself to kneel in front of him. It took all her willpower, but she batted her big eyes and added a pleading tone to her voice.

For the girls.

Giving him a dose of his own medicine, she placed her hands on his knees as she looked up at him. "Nels, is there any way you can buy me more time? Please. You know I wouldn't ask if it wasn't important."

His dark eyes studied her, his arm still resting on the back of the couch like he didn't have a care in the world. His body totally insouciant. "What's in the ledger, Sophie?"

She had to tell him the truth. It was the only way he'd help her.

First, he'd tell her she was a fool and shake his head at her ridiculous pie-in-the-sky hope after all these years.

Maybe I am *a fool.* She took a deep breath and considered her options. He wasn't leaving, and if she only had twenty-four hours to find a home for Lexie and a way to secure her personal human smuggling operation, she really had no choice.

Sitting back on her heels, she dropped her hands and put them in her lap. "I believe it holds a link to finding Angelique."

CHAPTER EIGHT

Downtown Tijuana
Two hours later

The bingo hall was hopping with a motley assortment of senior citizens, the jobless who'd scrounged up a few dollars to gamble away, and tourists with plenty of disposable income. The building had once been a church and pictures of saints still hung on the walls, watching the gamblers with solemn, stoic faces.

The sinners didn't seem bothered, and as Nelson scanned the room for exits and potential troublemakers, he saw a husband and wife team take turns holding up their winnings next to a painting of St. Paul so the other could take a picture for those back home.

"B12." The caller read from the chip she'd pulled from the basket. In unison, a bevy of those with B12 marked their cards with stamps.

After Sophie had laid the Angelique bomb on him, Nelson had endured a tug-of-war with his conscience. While Sophie had always assumed responsibility for her sister's disappearance, Nelson knew he'd played a hand in it. A part of him strongly believed it was the only reason Sophie had become a Fed in the first place—to track Angelique's movements from the time she'd run away from home. The trail had gone cold by the time Sophie had earned her badge, but she'd managed to find it again. That cold trail had led her to Chica Bonita.

And him.

Now she'd confessed that there was more than one ledger she was after—not only one with the European money-making operation, but also one that held a complete timeline and history of all the girls shipped into and out of Chica Bonita during the past seven years.

He wanted to kick her square in the ass for not being upfront with him in the first place, but he'd known what he was getting into when he agreed to follow Director Dupé's orders and bring Sophie home.

Home. He'd promised his sister he'd be home in time for Thanksgiving. She and his niece, Carly, were counting on him. He'd promised he'd be there to carve the turkey.

If he gave in and bought Sophie another day or two, he'd still have a day or so to spare.

Why are you even considering it? Angelique, if she was still alive, had been gone for years. The last whiff of her had been on the failed CB op two years ago. Even if the mysterious ledger held the information of where she'd been shipped to, it didn't mean she was still there.

But what could he say? He was a sucker for family. Sophie was alone. Angelique was her last living relative—if she was still alive. He still had his father and several siblings with their extended families.

Heading for the upstairs back room where Sophie was working, Nelson absentmindedly kept an eye on everyone he passed. After the previous night's crash course in Morales's security setup and a discussion that morning with his team, Nelson had hit the ground running. The first thing he'd done was switch up today's schedule. Morales came to town with Sophie in tow once or twice a week to exchange money and lean on the businesses in a multi-block section of Old Tijuana that resembled the hood, to produce protection fees. The routine never changed and Nelson was sure that Guido Ruiz knew it as well as the rest of the hood.

Instead of hitting the dry cleaners first and ending at the

strip clubs, Nelson sent a small team ahead to scout the other locations while he did a sweep of the bingo hall. No one had tripped his warning system, but he'd posted several lookouts and was on his way to position himself next to the woman who drove him crazy.

A flight up the stairs showed she wasn't in the office. A heartbeat of panic shot through Nelson's chest. Taking the stairs back down, he hustled through the kitchen, down a hall, and into a back storage room, spotting her at a back door, handing a pyramid of wrapped burritos to a young boy dressed in ragtag cutoffs and a plaid shirt two sizes too big for him.

Burritos? Where had those come from? She hadn't been carrying them in her money bag.

Her voice was too low for Nelson to hear as she spoke urgently to the kid. The boy nodded, his tongue slipping out to lick his lips as he juggled the stack of burritos.

Sophie lifted the edge of her skirt, and suddenly, her transportation method became clear. From pockets sewn under the long skirt, she withdrew a roll of money and a handful of colorful bracelets made from thread like his niece, Carly, liked to make. Friendship bracelets, she called them. Nelson had a stack she had made for him—the school therapist said it helped calm her. A better outlet for her autistic mind might have been a new school.

But his sister didn't have money for that.

Nelson hugged the shadows, not wanting to alert Sophie to his presence. She slipped the roll of money into one of the boy's pockets, the bracelets into another. After a second nod from him, he slipped off, Sophie watching him with a sad expression on her face.

In the background, Nelson heard the bingo caller over the speaker and a cheer erupted. *Bingo*, someone yelled.

At the noise, Sophie turned, saw Nelson watching her. Quickly, she fluffed her skirt and headed for the stairs to the office.

He caught her before she could pass. "What were you doing with that kid?"

"Nothing."

She tried to go around him; he blocked her path. Crossing his arms over his chest, he stood there, looking down on her. "Sophie...?"

Her chin rose. "Wipe that threatening look off your face and stop trying to intimidate me. The boy and his mother are homeless, like so many around here. I brought them some food."

He didn't change his expression, nor did he stop lording his bigger body over her petite one. "How many other strays have you taken in since you've been here?"

She balled her fist and slugged his arm.

"Hey!" He uncrossed his arms, but refused to rub his stinging bicep. Instead he set his hands on his hips and glared down harder on her.

"Don't call them that. They can't help it that they're poor."

"You have a job to do, sweetheart. I suggest you stop flirting with danger and get to it."

She lifted one pretty eyebrow. "Flirting with danger? Are you referring to yourself or the *strays*?"

The tough FBI agent who wouldn't let anyone inside her head or her heart felt deeply about many things besides work. Saying that to her, even *suggesting* it, would earn him another slug, this one in the gut. Stepping out of her way, he motioned for her to climb the steps. "After you."

She took the first few stairs, realized he was following her, and turned on him. "Where do you think you're going?"

"I'm your bodyguard. If you're going upstairs, so am I."

"I work alone."

"So you keep reminding me."

She put her hands on her curvy hips hidden under the skirt. "Morales gave me explicit instructions not to let you near the money."

"I don't care about the money. I care…" *About you.* "You're not leaving my sight."

Her lips turned down in an exaggerated frown. "Aw, poor Nico." She reached over and patted his cheek. "Rodrigo Morales doesn't trust you after all."

Shifting her weight, she leaned her right hip against the stair railing. "Did you really think after knowing you for less than twenty-four hours, he would let you in on the cash side of the entire operation? It took me three months before he trusted me enough to leave me alone with the cash, and another five before he trusted me completely with his books, and I studied at the feet of his father's beloved accountant. Rodrigo may trust you enough with security to give you a test run, but that's as far as it goes."

With that, she whirled and jogged up the steps. Biting off a curse, he let his gaze follow her exposed shoulder blades and lovely back.

Then he followed her. "Stay away from the two-way mirrors."

Her hand was on the doorknob. She looked over her shoulder. "Why?"

"According to my sources, everyone knows that's where you sit, watching the hall while you work. One of Guido's men could walk in and machine gun those windows. You may believe you're bulletproof, Sophie, but even you can't survive that."

"You've already changed our normal schedule and screwed up my pickup timeline," she huffed. "This stop is normally my second to the last one for the day. Today it's my first. If Guido was going to send someone to shoot me down, they won't be here for another three hours."

The gambling hall's flow of money from tourists made it the perfect laundering establishment for good, hard cash. From what he'd gathered from Morales and the other men, Sophie preferred it to be the final stop on cash days because she picked up the marked money from the other drops and brought it here to exchange it for the constant flow of clean bills. When the staff paid out winnings or gave change for food and drinks to tourists, the tourists unknowingly took marked bills home with them.

"Even without a bounty on your back, you know better than to keep the same routine. You make yourself an easy target. Morales too."

She didn't move, but something changed in her eyes. The muscles in the back of her hand, still on the doorknob, flexed ever so slightly. "I know what I'm doing."

Disappearing inside, she closed the door behind her. He heard a lock click into place.

She was hiding something; he could feel it in his bones.

The hallway was poorly lit, the worn, brown carpet smelled like grease and body odor. He checked the handgun Morales had given him, an HK45 pistol with the registration number filed off. Ten rounds in the magazine, another in the chamber.

There were five more drops to make after this. If Guido was smart, he would have lookouts at every stop along the way. A plant inside the bingo hall could have already tipped him off that Sophie was here.

Which is why Morales isn't here.

Fucker wasn't all that bright, but he was smart enough not to put his ass on the line.

Nelson had done his scan of the players in the hall and none had set off his internal warning system. He'd established a three-layered security circle with Morales's men, and he knew their loyalties were probably as strong as he could hope for. Not to him or Sophie but to their boss. They were in position around the bingo hall—one inside with him, three outside the building, one on the roof and another in the lead SUV for a speedy getaway if needed. His radio occasionally buzzed with their background chatter as they checked in with each other.

All he could do now was pray Sophie was fast at her job. The sooner they got out of Old Tijuana and back to the compound, the sooner he'd be able to breathe.

Leaning back against the door, he listened to the sounds below in the hall and wondered how to buy Sophie the extra time she'd begged him for. He tapped the handgun against his leg and whistled softly under his breath.

CHAPTER NINE

That damn sexy whistling would drive her to do something stupid. Like kiss Nelson just to shut him up.

Sophie stood in front of the two-way, like Nelson didn't want her to, and watched a woman enter the hall from the east side.

At least we aren't too early to catch Rosalie. It might be the last time she'd see the woman who reminded her so much of her mother.

Sophie crossed herself.

And hoped the boy she'd given the burritos to remembered to give her the one marked with a red X.

As Nelson whistled a seductive tune outside the door, Rosalie slowly made her way across the bingo floor to her lucky chair. A tourist was sitting in it, some young, bleached blond who'd spent too many hours baking in a tanning booth before coming to Tijuana to gamble her rich father's money away. A set of gold bangles fell back and forth on her arm as she stamped her card and laughed with her group of equally rich, young female friends.

Rosalie stopped and frowned for a second when she saw her. Then she hefted her bag a little higher on her shoulder and made her way to the table, an air of righteous indignation trailing behind her.

Oh, boy. Not good. Habitual gamblers were superstitious. Lucky clothes, lucky jewelry, lucky chairs.

As Rosalie passed their tables, a few regulars spoke to her.

She spoke back, her gaze never leaving the young woman invading her chair.

Rosalie was a legend in the area for her sixth sense when it came to gambling. Some of the regulars who feared her, ducked their heads as she passed by, others crossed themselves behind her back.

The bleached blonde and her friends stopped laughing once Rosalie reached their table. The older woman's size alone could be intimidating, and her self-confidence even more so. The regulars never ventured near her table during bingo. Bingo was her job these days, her very life.

But the tourists seemed mildly confused by the smile on Rosalie's face as she towered over them. Words were exchanged and Rosalie motioned for them to leave. A couple of disdainful looks passed between the girls. Finally, Rosalie simply grabbed the back of her chair, lifted it, and sent Miss Bangles tumbling to the ground.

A minor bit of outrage ensued, Rosalie ignoring it as she sent the cards already on the table scattering like the women. She plopped down in the now-vacant chair, making Sophie smile, and began her ritual of setting out her lucky charms.

Three trolls with orange hair emerged from her bag first, then a lace doily upon which she reverently sat a Madonna statue. Next came a picture of a young girl that Sophie knew was Rosalie's dead daughter. Lastly, she draped a rosary bead necklace over the Madonna and around one corner of the picture frame.

By the time Rosalie brought out her own specially selected set of sixteen bingo cards, Miss Bangles and her friends had gone to find the manager. The same manager who let Rosalie break the house rules with her cards and sometimes with her antics. Sophie knew the tourists would get comped a drink and shown to a new table in the VIP section normally reserved for parties of ten or more.

Watching the woman, memories of Sophie's early childhood

materialized. Her mother's lucky trolls had sported green and pink hair and had been holding hands. A miniature bluebird of happiness had to be positioned just so at their feet. A candle engraved with Sophie's father's initials and a bundle of sage came next. Rounding out the setup was a diet Coke and a chocolate bar.

Sophie wasn't allowed to touch any of Juanita's lucky charms, even when she was dying of thirst or her stomach growled loud enough to illicit questioning looks from those around them.

Juanita had always worn her charm bracelet and a set of blue bird earrings. She haunted the bingo halls, making enough money each month to keep her girls in clothes and shoes and the cable hooked up to the TV. On days when Juanita was in a foul mood, she'd sometimes forget to take Sophie with her. So Sophie stayed home alone and watched cartoons.

Juanita had been an illegal immigrant, squatting in an abandoned hotel in East L.A., and Sophie hadn't attended school until first grade. But she'd received enough training in the way of letters and numbers, thanks to bingo and Nick Jr., that she'd fared just fine. She'd also learned enough social skills in the bingo halls, begging other players for sips of their drinks and bites of their food, that she managed to convince her first grade teacher, Miss Krandle, not to tell the principal when she caught Sophie setting up her own bingo den on the playground with chalk drawn cards and pea gravel to mark the letter-number combos she called from memory.

By fifth grade, however, the gig was up. Juanita, now pregnant with Angelique, was kicked out of the country. Sophie, who'd been born in America and was a U.S. citizen, left the country of her birth and went with her, back to Mexico and a grandmother she'd never met.

The whistling outside died away and Sophie shook herself out of her reverie. Rosalie was firmly entrenched in the game, and Sophie knew it was time to get back to work.

She just hoped in her heart of hearts that Rosalie never met the ending that her mother had. If she got the burrito marked with an X, with its hidden immigration papers wrapped inside instead of food, she had a fighting chance.

Nelson secured Sophie in the black Range Rover and checked that the rest of the security team was packed and ready to go. As the afternoon sun reflected off the stucco buildings and storefront windows, a storm system built over the ocean to the southwest. While the last few days had been dry, the November rains were never far away.

He had a couple of new suits from the local men's shop in the back, thanks to Rodrigo Morales who insisted he wear suits while working for him. Nelson checked in with his lead security team, already half a mile ahead of them, to make sure the path to Casa Morales was clear. The team confirmed what Nelson wanted to hear, but the twitch in his shoulders insisted something was wrong. If Guido had put a target on Sophie's back, why hadn't anyone taken a shot at her today?

He'd instructed the different teams to chat up store owners, people on the street, even contact their snitches and offer a reward for anyone with information that might be pertinent. Not one response, not even a hint of what Guido might be up to.

Climbing into the front passenger seat, he tapped the dash. "Let's go," he said to the driver.

Leaning forward from the backseat, Sophie disconnected a call on her cellphone. "Change of plans. Señor Morales is involved in an important meeting. We are to pick Lexie up from school."

The Range Rover pulled away from the curb, merging into traffic. Nelson half turned in his seat. "Who's Lexie?"

Sophie gave him a look usually reserved for ignorant men,

slanting a look at the driver, then back to Nelson. "Señor Morales's sister. She lives with him."

His intel was obviously not up to date, and Rodrigo hadn't mentioned the girl at all. "Alexa? I thought she went to boarding school in Mexico City."

"After her parents were killed and Señor Morales returned home from Europe, he brought Lexie here a month ago. She receives her schooling from a private tutor, Sister Leslie, at the Holy Francis nunnery."

The driver took a turn that lead them away from the Morales compound to the west. "I take it Sister Leslie lives in the opposite direction I had planned to take home."

Sophie simply shrugged and sat back.

This wouldn't do. Guido could be lying in wait, anticipating exactly this sort of thing. "Pull over," he said to the driver.

"What are you doing?" Sophie leaned forward again. "We have to pick up Lexie at three-thirty. We'll barely make it in time."

"We're not going without my team scouting the area first."

"You're kidding, right?"

"Do you have the number for the good Sister? Better call her and tell her we'll be a little late."

"We can't be late. Lexie has a fear of no one being there for her."

Grabbing his radio, Nelson buzzed his lead team. "And Guido could be waiting for us. Taking out Lexie, as well as you, would definitely cripple Morales and his operation. Lexie should have a full-time bodyguard herself."

Her righteous anger deflated. "You think he'd come after Lexie?" She raised a hand to stop his confirmation. "Of course he would. I should have thought of that."

As Nelson rerouted the teams, Sophie called Sister Leslie. A minute later, they were on their way and the nun knew to keep the girl sequestered and safe until they arrived.

Security confirmed the convent was locked up and no one

was hanging around outside. After doing his own scan and finding nothing, Nelson insisted on walking Sophie to the door and escorting her inside.

The girl was sitting in a small room with a cot and a large golden retriever next to her. She looked up when the door opened.

Skinny and pale, Alexa Morales was a miniature of her brother, except her eyes were hidden behind dark glasses too big for her face. She wore pigtails, her widow's peak on display, and her too-big clothes hung on her like her glasses—as if she wanted to disappear behind her coverings.

When she heard Sophie's voice, she charged off the edge of the bed and flew toward her. Sophie lined herself up and bent down to accept the hug. The girl's arms wrapped around Sophie's neck, a stack of colorful friendship bracelets encircling her left wrist.

A dog came to stand at Alexa's side. Sophie patted his head and spoke soothingly to Lexie. The girl was clearly anxious, but within seconds, Sophie had her relaxed. "Your brother is very sorry he couldn't be here, *chica*. Next time, okay?"

Lexie released Sophie and stepped back, tilting her face up. "Is someone here with you?"

Sophie stood, guiding Lexie's hand out. "This is my fr—I mean, your brother's new head of security, Nico."

"Nice to meet you, Nico," Lexie said.

Nelson took her small hand in his and shook it. "A pleasure, *señorita*."

Lexie giggled. "Can we go for ice cream now?"

Nelson met Sophie's eye and shook his head. They needed to return to Casa Morales where he could control the situation.

"You can have one, too, Nico. My brother will pay," Lexie added. "He owes me for not showing up."

Sophie patted the child's shoulder. "Today may not be the best day."

Lexie frowned an exaggerated frown. "Pleeeease."

Sophie sent a pleading look in Nelson's direction. He shook his head again.

"I suppose," Sophie said, ignoring him. "But only if you promise to follow Nico's directions explicitly."

Lexie's expression morphed instantly into delight. "Is it a game, Nico? Like Simon Says?"

Sophie's lips moved, miming Lexie's plea. *Pleease.*

Rolling his eyes at Sophie, Nelson bent down so he was on Lexie's level. "Simon Says is for babies. We're going to play the adult version. You think you can handle that?"

Lexie's head bobbed up and down. She tapped her glasses. "I may be blind, but believe me, I can handle a lot."

He hoped that was true. The kid had no idea what she was about to be handed once her brother went to prison in America. "Fair enough." He took her hand and barked instructions to his security team waiting outside. Once everyone was set, he led her and Sophie out the door.

Ten minutes later, they stopped at an out-of-the-way ice cream shop. The wind had picked up and fat drops of rain landed on the Range Rover's windshield. Lexie had insisted on going to her favorite place, but Nelson had told her no. Staying away from any further usual haunts was a must.

He also insisted they get the ice cream to go. He radioed one of the men in the SUV bringing up the rear and gave the man Lexie's order.

"What about Maria-Sophia?" the girl asked. "She likes two scoops of café au lait."

Sophie grinned at him over Lexie's head. "One scoop will do."

God help him. "And a scoop of café au lait," he said into the radio.

"Sugar cone, please" Sophie added.

"On a sugar cone, Miguel."

Once they had the ice cream and resumed their drive, Nelson kept an eye on the road ahead. At least the ice cream had shut the two females in the back up.

The peace and quiet didn't last long. Soon he heard Lexie say, "Tell me another story about your sister, Maria-Sophia."

There was a pregnant pause. Sophie had told Lexie about Angelique? Nelson dared a glance at her over his shoulder.

Her gaze was fixed on the scenery flying by outside, the ice cream cone in her hands forgotten. "She was beautiful, like you, and almost as smart, Lexie. She had the most amazing voice. You would have sworn the gates of heaven parted and the angels were singing to you when you heard her."

Lexie, not seeing the sadness of Sophie's face, must have still heard it in her tone. The little girl placed a hand on Sophie's arm. "Why did she leave you?"

The pain on Sophie's face was too much for Nelson. He faced front again, focusing on the road ahead of them.

"Our mother died. Angelique was very sad and very angry." Nelson heard Sophie's soft sigh. "She took drugs and"—

"Drugs are bad," Lexie said.

"Yes. Drugs are bad. You must promise never to take any."

"I promise."

Nelson shook his head at the window. Leave it to Sophie to tell a drug cartel leader's little sister to stay away from drugs.

"It wasn't enough," Sophie continued. "She had so much pain, even the drugs wouldn't dull it."

"So she ran away?"

Sophie's voice came out stronger. "She was trying to escape the pain."

"Do you think she did?"

Another pause. Then, "No, I think she found more trouble, and with trouble comes more pain."

"I wish she would come back. I bet she'd like my bracelets."

"She would love them." Sophie's voice took on a forced brevity. "Have you made any more for me?"

"I'm going to work on new ones tonight," Lexie said. "Rodrigo said he would pick up thread for me today after his meetings."

Nelson frowned. Were these the same bracelets Sophie had shoved in that boy's pockets at the bingo hall?

He heard shifting on the leather seat and glanced back. Sophie was putting a rolled up stack of bills into Lexie's free hand. "Payment for the last set. Keep 'em coming. My friend with the shop says they're selling better than her gold bangles."

The kid's face lit up. "Really?"

Sophie licked her ice cream, not meeting Nelson's eyes. "You're very talented."

"You always lay out which colors I should put together. You should get some of the profit."

"Oh, no. You're the artist. I could never weave them in such interesting patterns."

Nelson faced forward again. What was Special Agent Diaz doing with a little girl's homemade bracelets? Giving her an ego boost or something else?

"You should ask my brother for help finding Angelique," Lexie said.

Nelson's insides froze. No way. Surely Sophie hadn't told Lexie her sister's real name.

"There's nothing he can do, I'm afraid," Sophie said. "But I appreciate you trying to help. If I learn anything new and think Rodrigo might be able to find her, I'll certainly ask him."

CHAPTER TEN

Nelson completed his report to Morales and was leaving his office when Lexie caught him in the hall.

"Who's there?" she asked.

"Nico Raines."

She stroked the top of her dog's head, her too-big glasses turned toward his face. "Thank you for ice cream today, Nico."

"You're welcome."

"Are you on your way to see Maria-Sophia?"

He was, but decided this was an opportunity to find out more about the bracelets. Besides, last he'd checked, Sophie was still holed up with Morales's books. "I'm on my way to check the grounds. Would you and your dog like to go with me?"

"Do you know Latin?"

"Only enough to get by as an altar boy."

"Your church didn't do the Mass in English?"

"They did both Latin and English up until I was a teenager."

"So you could help me with my Latin homework?"

"Only if you want Sister Leslie to fail you."

Lexie grinned. "I really hate Latin."

"It's the root language for Spanish, French, and Italian, and many English words derive from those languages. It's like the grandfather of the big three. I'd say it deserves some respect."

She pondered this a moment, her tiny brow scrunching. "I can see that."

And then she giggled, her hand coming up to cover her mouth. "Get it? I can *see* that?"

The kid was cute. No wonder Sophie had fallen for her.

Nelson bent down in front of her. "So you're a joker as well as a bracelet maker, huh?"

Her dog wagged his tail, his mouth opening so he could pant. Lexie giggled again. "Do you want to see my room? I have lots of cool stuff."

"Sure." He could check her security while he was there. "What kind of cool stuff?"

She talked nonstop as she led him down the hallway and to her room on the opposite end of the house. "I'm a big fan of Frozen. Harry likes it too."

Lucky for Nelson, he knew about the movie since his niece loved it too. "Who's Harry?"

She stopped and gave him an exasperated look. "My dog? Duh."

She wasn't lying. Her bedroom looked like a giant Barbie had vomited in it. Pink walls, pink bedspread, pink rug. Sparkly pillows and throws. A large dollhouse dominated one corner. Dozens of stuffed animals covered her bed and an oversized upholstered chair. The four-poster bed was white with pink tulle hanging from the posts. A white desk with a computer and braille keyboard rounded out the furnishings.

Carly would have loved it. Being socially awkward and intensely shy, Nelson's niece spent many hours in her room, singing Disney songs over and over again and stroking a favorite stuffed bear.

"Where's Señor Chavez? Is he sick?" Lexie released her dog's harness and felt her way along the edge of the desk. "Is that why you're taking his place?"

Nelson stopped in the doorway. How to explain? "Sort of."

Lexie plopped on the bed and patted it for Harry to come lay beside her. A pile of brightly colored threads lay in the center.

"So tell me about the bracelets. How long does it take you to make one?"

"I usually make two a night unless I run out of thread." She ran her fingers through the pile of colors. "I could make you one. What's your favorite color?"

Um…he'd never really thought about it. "Black?"

Her brow knit again. "That's boring. I don't have black. How about purple?"

Purple. Yeesh. "Got any blue?"

"Three shades! I could use all three if you like."

"Need me to lay them out for you?"

"I know the dark blue one." She pulled a ball of the blue from the pile. "It feels different than the others. It's Maria-Sophia's favorite. She gave me a whole bunch of it. I use it in all of the bracelets."

There was something odd about that but Nelson couldn't put his finger on it.

Or maybe he could. "Can I feel it?"

Lexie held out the ball of thread and he ran his fingers over the smooth strands. "See?" she said. "It's super smooth."

He touched some of the other colors and found she was right. They were all soft, but the dark blue thread seemed to be coated with a waxy substance.

"Did you find the other blues?" Lexie asked.

He handed her two other balls of lighter blue. "Here you go. Need anything else?"

Lexie tipped her head toward her desk. "Are you sure you can't help me with my Latin spelling words?"

Nelson sauntered to the desk, found a page of braille that he assumed was the Latin. "Only if you can teach me braille."

"Maria-Sophia knows it. She can teach you." Lexie started pulling threads. "She knows everything, except…"

"Except what?"

Lexie's fingers stopped. She reached for the dog and patted Harry's head, her face turned away from Nelson. "I like her a lot."

"I'm pretty sure she knows that."

"I want her to stay here. Forever." She cautiously turned her face toward Nelson. "I want her to marry Rigo."

Ah, shit. How was he supposed to respond to that?

Luckily, he didn't have to. Lexie went back to her threads. "It's a secret, though. You won't tell her, right?"

Nelson was glad she couldn't see his face. "Mum's the word." He tousled her hair and headed for the door. "Goodnight, kid."

"Goodnight, Nico."

When he glanced back, Lexie was hugging the dog as Harry's mournful gaze locked with Nelson's over the girl's shoulder.

———

It was shortly before midnight by the time Sophie finished balancing all the ledgers and made the corresponding wire transfers to the offshore accounts. She'd avoided Nelson all evening—he was thankfully tied up with Morales—and she hoped now, as she made her way to her apartment, that he would already be fast asleep in his.

A storm had moved through and left the trees dripping with heavy rain. Morales would want a full report in the morning about the day's profits and she had left a copy of the ledger on his desk before she'd left.

She hadn't gone far when a broad shadow emerged from behind a palm tree and made her catch her breath. "Finally calling it a day?" the man said. "Or were you avoiding me?"

Of course, Nelson would be waiting for her. "You startled me."

He fell into step beside her. "When were you going to tell me about the kid?"

Pulse already jumping, she picked up her step. The garden outside the guesthouse was in sight, a night-blooming cactus showing off under the tender moon. "Tell you what?"

"The real reason you've been stalling this operation."

He knew.

Or thought he did. The truth was, what he believed wasn't half of it.

"Can we not discuss this out here?" she half-whispered, hustling for the safety of her apartment.

He would follow her. She had no doubt about that. And being inside her tiny apartment talking about Lexie wouldn't slow her pounding pulse, but at least she could escape into the bathroom or bedroom and lock him out if necessary.

Passing the cactus with its white flower, she hated Nelson all over again for intruding into her op, her world. She'd had everything under control until he'd arrived.

Under the portico, the stairs were dark. Nelson's hand brushed her elbow as if to steady her in case her footing slipped on the stairs. His touch unnerved her and she nearly sent herself tumbling anyway.

Before she could protest, he put an arm around her waist, guiding her up the stairs and into the apartment in silence.

Once inside, he locked the door and turned on her, putting a finger to his lips. As she watched, he went around the living room, examining the tables and lamps and running his fingers along the edges of all the furniture.

Bugs. He was checking for listening devices.

She'd found a couple when she first came to work for Morales and had left them alone. After a few months, they'd disappeared. She still routinely checked, but had never found one since, confirming that Morales did indeed trust her to a certain degree.

But now, Nelson was here. A newcomer. Someone who'd been vetted to a certain degree but had yet to prove his undying loyalty.

While Nels moved into the kitchen, Sophie took up his search, checking the bedroom.

They met back in the living room, both having come up empty.

Nelson shrugged. "Someone new inside my territory? It's the first thing I would have done."

"Me, too," Sophie agreed, hoping that maybe he was going to drop the previous discussion. "I'm bushed. I'll see you in the morning."

She got two steps away when he said, "You're compromising the mission because you have a soft spot for Alexa. That's why you keep refusing to wrap up the op, isn't it? You think you can save the girl."

Damn. Facing him, she kept her face stoic. "I never get emotionally involved. You know that."

His eyes were dark with emotion. Bitterness? "You did once."

Once. She would never live it down, not if he insisted on constantly reminding her. "And I blew it. Is that what you want to hear? I screwed up. With you, with Chica Bonita, with finding my sister. Because I got *emotionally involved*." She drew a deep breath, lowered her voice. "I haven't done it since, and that includes this operation."

"You deny you care for the girl and that she's not the reason you're dragging out the arrest of her brother?"

"She's innocent in all of this, and who wouldn't have a soft spot in their heart for that child? All that proves is that I'm human. It doesn't mean I'm not doing my job."

"What's the deal with the bracelets?"

Oh, shit. He'd caught on to that too?

She looked down at her copper bangles and a vintage Coro bracelet that had belonged to Little Gran. Inexpensive costume jewelry that was priceless to her. She'd removed the friendship bracelet Lexie had given her and hidden it in her pocket, hoping not to call further attention to it once she'd seen Nelson eyeing it in the car on their way back to the compound that afternoon. "What's wrong with my bracelets?"

"Why are you buying a bunch of friendship bracelets from Lexie and lying to her about the shop that's selling them?"

"She's good with her hands and it gives her purpose. I wanted to instill some confidence in the child. Between the boarding school and the convent, she can't do anything but tie her shoes and dress herself. She's learning obsolete and useless things like Latin and they make her pray for an hour a day. She's not a nun, and just because she's blind doesn't mean she can't do normal things. I taught her to cook and bake and make things, like the bracelets. She's a natural."

"She loves you, Sophie. She wants you to marry her brother and the three of you to live happily ever after."

"What?"

"That's what she told me a few minutes ago when I went to talk to her. She sees you as her surrogate mother, a big sister, whatever."

"That's ridiculous. I've never given her a reason to believe I have feelings for her brother."

"She's a kid, living in a fantasy world."

This had to end. "You're living in a fantasy world, too. Yes, I may have taken the girl under my wing while I was here, but in no way is it affecting my judgment about wrapping up this operation."

He didn't say anything for a moment. His usual silent treatment tactic, hoping if he kept those dark eyes locked on her, she'd suddenly confess all her sins.

She stared back with the same intensity, as stubborn as he was.

"What's the boy do with the bracelets you give him? Sell them?"

Oh, no, something much more damning. To her, anyway. "I told you. He and his mother are penniless." It wasn't a lie. "Anything they can do to raise money is welcome."

"I can't imagine he makes much money from selling friendship bracelets."

Their street value was nominal, but their value on a young, homeless, runaway's arm was priceless. "I imagine not." Time to go on the offensive. "Did you buy me any extra time before the warrants are issued?"

"Not necessary. After today's commotion, I convinced Morales to leave for his beach house early. He and Lexie are taking off tomorrow at noon with a security detail of my picking. Once they're gone, you and I will comb the snake pit for that ledger."

"Tomorrow?" That was too soon. She needed to finalize her replacement to take over helping the girls reach sanctuary across the U.S. border. She also had yet to find a good home for Lexie. "Doesn't he want his head of security to go with him?"

"He seemed more concerned about you. Apparently, his meeting this afternoon had to do with an important deal going down on Sunday. He wants to make sure you're healthy and alive to handle the exchange of money. He insisted I stay here and continue my bodyguard duties."

"The meeting Sunday is to buy another exotic snake for his collection."

"Whatever." Nelson shrugged. "It works for us. He leaves early, with no plans to return until Sunday. By then, we'll have found the ledger and he'll be under arrest."

If she complained or begged him once again to buy her more time, it would only confirm his suspicions that she had indeed put the operation in danger because of her emotional involvement. For tonight, she had to go along with the plan. By morning, she'd figure out how to sabotage his efforts and buy herself the necessary time she needed.

"Okay, then." She headed for the bathroom. "I don't suppose locking my bedroom door will keep you out of my bed tonight, will it?"

No response except silence. Sophie sighed. She'd have to rig up a new lock system if she was going to keep Houdini away from her.

————————

Nelson had two text messages from Cooper Harris. Once he heard the shower kick on in the bathroom, he pulled out his phone and called his boss.

It was nearly one in the morning, and Cooper answered on the third ring with the voice of a hibernating bear unhappy to have his sleep interrupted. "'Bout time, Cruz." Nelson heard bed springs groan as Cooper shifted to a sitting position. "Hold on a sec."

In the background, he heard Cooper shuffling from his bedroom to another room, probably so he wouldn't wake Celina. "What's going on with Diaz?" he finally said.

Nelson's gaze automatically eyed the bathroom door, behind which she was no doubt already naked and under the shower spray. "Agent Diaz is safe. We'll have things wrapped up by this time tomorrow night if things go according to plan."

"There's been a change in orders. The Bureau's been told to stand down on serving the warrants. Word came today that the CIA is after a European player named Kronos who's making contact with Morales in the next few days for an exchange. Diamonds for missiles. Heard anything about that?"

Nelson walked to the window, staring out at the dark grounds. Rain had once again started and the palms tree in the courtyard blew back and forth in the wind. "There's a meeting scheduled for Sunday. Agent Diaz says Morales is buying a new snake for his collection. Nothing's been said about diamonds or missiles."

"Hmm." Cooper didn't sound happy. "The missiles are a prototype of surface-to-air that can operate 24/7 in all weather conditions and simultaneously destroy up to four aerial targets. Made by a Syrian company with ties to Isis. China and Russia have already placed heavy orders for them. Venezuela and Iran want a few too."

"What does Morales want with SAMs?"

"He already has 'em. That's what Kronos is trading the diamonds for. He has buyers in Iran and Venz."

"Shit. How did Morales score them?" And why hadn't Sophie caught wind of this?

The sound of a fridge opening and ice clanking in a glass came through the line. "His father was close friends with certain members of the Mexican Army back in the day. One of those men is a founder of the Syrian company. The Agency believes Morales has a tidy stockpile hidden near his compound."

"So the CIA's going to swoop in and steal our operation?"

"Bureau offered a deal so they get Morales and the CIA gets Kronos and the weapons."

Nelson heard the shower shut off. "Morales doesn't deal in diamonds. He deals in drugs."

"But unmarked stones are small, easy to transport. He studied gemology, right? K9 sniffers can't normally detect the stones, nor are they trained to do so. And diamonds will buy anything."

Snakes, diamonds, SAMs. Crazy motherfucker. "So the FBI isn't coming until Sunday?"

"Correct. Justice Department wants this one bad, on orders from the Prez. Capturing those weapons and taking out a major cartel leader will boost his approval rating by twenty points, easy. CIA wants Kronos. In the end, everyone gets what they want."

But will Sophie? "If I pull Sophie out before Sunday, the deal could go sideways."

"The deal *will* go sideways. You and Agent Diaz are to stay put and maintain your covers until further notice, clear?"

The bathroom door creaked open. "Clear."

"Stay in touch."

"Yes, sir."

Nelson disconnected, a dozen more questions racing through his mind. No time to ask them, however, with Sophie bearing down on him. She was toweling her hair dry. "Who was that?"

"Security team by the gate." Nelson stood, pocketed the phone, and headed for the door. There was one building on the grounds besides the pit. He'd check it for missiles and mentally sort through this change in plans. Darkness and the rain would provide the cover he needed to do a little digging unnoticed by the night guards. "I need to check the backup generator in case we lose power during the storm. Don't wait up," he said.

———————

What is he up to?

Sophie stared at the closed door, exhausted, and ready for sleep.

But instead of going to bed, she sighed deeply, tossed the towel on a chair, and threw on a fresh set of clothes.

Wherever Nelson Cruz was going, she was about to follow.

CHAPTER ELEVEN

Slipping her compact handgun into a specially modified sling attached to her right leg, Sophie fluffed her skirt—soon to be soaked—and drew on a rain slicker. She closed the door of her apartment quietly behind her and stood still for a moment on the landing, letting her eyes adjust to the darkness.

She took the stairs down and paused at the patio, listening and sniffing the air for a hint of Nelson's clean, tangy soap smell.

All she heard was the rain and wind. The only smells were wet mud and humid night air.

Sticking to the shadows was easy once her eyes adjusted, a fingernail moon peeking through the clouds. Reading Nelson's mind, on the other hand, was impossible. Was he really headed to the generator shed or was that an excuse for something else?

The building was a shack compared to the house, but it held an assortment of tools and ground maintenance equipment. Sophie opened the door, flinching as it squeaked and she faced almost utter darkness.

With only a single window and the cloudy sky, the light filtering through was minimal. Her fingers skimmed the wall next to her and stopped on the light switch. If Nelson were here checking on the generator, why hadn't he turned it on?

Because he didn't want to be seen.

Which meant it wasn't the generator he cared about.

A slick coolness licked down her spine. She told herself it

was because of the rain, not the ominous feeling in her stomach.

I should go back and get some sleep. Leave him to whatever foolishness he's up to.

But as usual, curiosity got the best of her. What had that phone call been about to send him out into the rainy night?

Flipping on the overhead light might attract unwanted attention from the main house or the guards on duty. How would she explain being inside the generator building? Leaving the light switch alone, she pulled a penlight from her pocket and turned it on, keeping the beam pointed at the dirty floor. Her ears picked up the sound of the rain, but nothing else, and she swept the skinny ray of light past the generator in the center of the floor and around the perimeter.

Landscaping equipment was parked along the south end. Gardening tools hung on the walls. Gas cans, a work bench, various boxes, and several shelves rounded out the inventory.

Again, Sophie wondered why Nelson cared about this shed. Or was he really headed somewhere else? She stepped farther in, walking slowly around the generator that was nearly as tall as she was. A wheelbarrow with a machete and shovel blocked her way to the tool bench. Dirt covered the end of the shovel as if someone had been digging. An almost black substance also lined the machete's blade.

Sophie leaned closer, eyeing the shovel, and trying to remember if she'd seen the gardener lately. Unless he'd come today while she was in town, it had been at least a week.

She shined her light on the machete and her stomach dropped. The dark substance was nearly as black as wet dirt.

Blood.

She felt a presence behind her right before a hand went around her mouth and she was jerked backwards, slamming her into a rock-hard body. The flashlight flew out of her hand, ricocheting off a wheelbarrow handle. It hit the floor and went into a spin, the beam throwing a flickering kaleidoscope of light around the room.

"What are you doing here?" a low and dangerous voice said in her ear.

A deluge of relief swamped her as Nelson took his hand from her mouth so she could answer. "Looking for you, asshole." She stomped on the top of this foot for scaring her.

"Ow!" He jumped back. "Dammit woman, stop hurting me."

She whirled to face him. The flashlight stopped spinning, the beam reflecting off the metal of the generator and throwing a weird shadow up under Nelson's face. "You're lucky I didn't elbow you in your bruised ribs or kick you in the knee and cripple you."

She bent down and picked up the penlight. "You're not checking out the generator. What *are* you doing?"

"It's nothing."

"Nothing, huh?"

He sighed. "Looking for weapons."

In the shed? "Rodrigo's gun safe is inside the house. Why would he store anything out here?"

"Not guns. SAMs. A special prototype the U.S. wants to keep out of the wrong hands."

"Surface-to-air missiles? He doesn't deal in weapons. He deals in drugs."

"Possibly a leftover from his father."

Rain slid down the single window. Gusts of wind blew enough through the open door to form random puddles. "First of all, how did you get this information, and secondly, why would he store SAMs here at the compound?"

Nelson ignored her first question. "Where else would he store them? He mentioned a warehouse outside of town. He said it was for drug repackaging, but could he be storing SAMs there too?"

"Doubtful, but I guess it's possible."

"You've never been there?"

"I only handle the money. I have no reason to visit the drug storehouse."

Thunder rumbled overhead. A flash of lightning followed a moment later, throwing a strobe of light through the tiny window. In the brief flash, Sophie saw the tight set of Nelson's jaw.

"What aren't you telling me?" she asked. "Why are finding these missiles suddenly so important?"

"The European operation you mentioned. Is that legit? The ledger we're after contains information about it?"

"Yes, it's legit. Why?"

Since they were standing close in order to hear each other over the storm, she saw him nod. "The deal going down on Sunday is most likely a trade of the missiles for diamonds."

"No, it's not. He's getting a new snake."

"Not according to my source."

"What source?"

"My boss. What I can't figure out is why he wants you there on Sunday for the exchange."

"He told me to prepare thirty-five thousand dollars for Sunday. That's why he wants me there, but it doesn't matter. We'll be out of here by then."

He didn't reply and she had a moment of stolen hope. "Did you manage to get me more than twenty-four hours?"

He blew air through his lips and ran a hand through his hair. "We're to stay put until the deal goes down on Sunday."

The one-eighty gave her a moment of whiplash. "On whose orders? I thought the Bureau was ready to swoop in with warrants?"

"According to Cooper, my boss, word came down that the man Morales is meeting with on Sunday is an international criminal named Kronos. The Agency's been after him for years. They believe this is their chance to snag him and get their hands on the SAMs."

Quick as the flash of lightening a moment ago, anger raced through her blood. "The CIA? You've got to be kidding me." Why hadn't Agent Blue, her partner in crime, warned her?

"They can't just waltz in here after all the work I've done and snatch Morales out from under me!"

Of course, they could. It would be just like that bastard Blue to steal her thunder.

"They want Kronos," Nelson said, "not Morales."

Blue wanted Morales. He'd made that clear as a bell since the moment he'd revealed himself to Sophie and tried to blackmail her. "Oh, please. The Agency will take credit for both. You know that."

She turned and kicked the generator. "Dammit all to hell!"

Without warning, Nelson grabbed her, his hand once again covering her mouth as he wheeled her around behind the generator, her backside to his front. "Shh," he whispered. His lips brushed her ear. "We have company."

He released her mouth but one arm stayed wrapped around her waist. Carefully he lowered them both into a crouch.

Heart hammering, Sophie listened intently. She heard nothing except the rain on the roof, maybe because the drum in her chest was drowning out everything else.

But then a sweep of a flashlight flooded the shed, spilling light on the walls, the tool bench, the lawn mower. The generator blocked it from falling on them.

A man's voice called out in Spanish, "Who's there?"

A night guard had seen the open door when he'd canvassed the grounds. Had to be. Why hadn't she shut it?

Nelson's hand on her stomach was warm through her clothes. His face was close to the back of her head, his breath sliding down her neck, calming her. They could explain this if they had to, right? He could say he'd been checking on the generator and she could claim she'd followed him, concerned when he hadn't returned.

Close enough to the truth.

Footsteps entered the shed. She and Nelson held perfectly still. He stopped breathing—his warm breath replaced with cool, damp air—and Sophie followed suit.

Another sweep of the flashlight, the guard pausing for a long, tense moment, as though he sensed their presence. Then the footsteps retreated.

Sophie heard the door to the shed close and she let out the breath she was holding.

And then she heard the clank of metal.

The guard had locked the door.

She started to rise, but Nelson held her in place a moment longer. "Wait," he breathed against her hair.

She did, heart still hammering. She heard the guard say something. The words were too muffled to understand, but then she heard the squawk of a handheld radio. He was checking in with the security team, hopefully giving the all clear.

A rainy silence fell, and she could almost sense the moment he walked away.

Nelson, arm still around her waist, helped her to a standing position. "We should get back to the apartment," he murmured.

She turned to face him, found herself bumping into his chest. She stepped back, ran into the generator, and bounced sideways into the wheelbarrow.

Nelson grabbed her arm, keeping her from falling.

She tugged her arm from his grip. "He just locked us in."

In the dark shadows, Nelson's grin looked extra menacing. He brushed wet hair from her neck. "I would think you've known me long enough to know there is no lock I can't pick."

"Good, because I have no intention of spending the night in this gross shed with you while the CIA is waiting in the wings to ruin my operation."

His finger moved to her cheek, caressing it. "Don't worry, Soph. I've got it under control. I promise, you'll get your man if you work with me on this and follow my orders. We'll find these ledgers and bring down Morales, and let the CIA bag their guy. Your reputation at the Bureau as a ballbuster will remain intact."

For a heartbeat, maybe two, she let herself believe him. Let herself believe in the Nelson Cruz myth—that he never gave up and no matter the circumstances, he always came out on top.

It was easy to let his reassurances cajole her into believing that nine months of undercover work wasn't about to be handed over to the CIA on a golden platter and her part in this sting reduced to nothing but a footnote on a report.

The two of them would find the ledgers and one of them would lead her to her sister. And to add to the dream, her sister was alive and well somewhere, just waiting for Sophie to find her.

Maybe if she didn't move, didn't breathe, just stared into Nelson's eyes a little longer, she might even believe he'd help her find a way to save Lexie. That he wouldn't hate her for helping young women get across the border illegally to start a new life in America.

Pipedreams, Sophie. Lots of wishful thinking.

But they were her pipedreams.

Well, hell, as long as she was dreaming, why not wish for a happily-ever-after for herself and Nelson?

Leaning in, she licked her lips, wrapped her arms around his neck, and did just that.

CHAPTER TWELVE

Nelson was ready for her. But then, again, he was probably used to women throwing themselves at him. As Sophie pressed her lips to his, she heard another grumble of thunder.

Only it wasn't thunder. The low growl was coming from Nelson.

Like the man himself, his response to her kiss was insouciant, smooth, and demanding. He parted her lips with expertise, backing her up against the old generator, and teasing her tongue with his.

He smelled of heat and rain and male sweat. The scruff on his jaw scratched her skin as he dropped kisses on her cheeks, her eyelids, her temples. He dipped his head and trailed his tongue up the side of her neck and behind her earlobe. "Partners?" he murmured in her ear.

Her head felt light, like a boat bobbing in water without an anchor. Her body, under his touch, felt unmoored too, as if she could close her eyes and float away on the pleasure. "If I say no?"

"You can't beat the system alone." He brushed a thumb over her lower lip, raised his eyes to meet hers. "The CIA will grab Kronos and snag Morales too. They'll take credit for bringing down the cartel along with nailing their European smuggler. Sweeping a single FBI agent under the rug will be a piece of cake."

She couldn't let them do that, but... "And how do you think

you—an immigration officer—can keep that from happening?"

His hands skimmed a trail from her ribs to the top of her thighs and back up. His thumbs brushed against her breasts under the fabric of her jacket and shirt. "I have the entire SCVC Taskforce to back me up. My boss can cut a deal with the Agency. No Kronos if we don't get Morales."

"And if they won't deal? Are you willing to blow the CIA's chance at arresting Kronos?"

"For you, yes."

His response surprised her. "Tell me the truth."

"I am telling you the truth. You've already got Morales. If they want us to draw things out until Sunday, they'll have to agree to the deal."

If she didn't have her arms around his neck already, she would have thrown them there now.

Too bad old habits and past conditioning were so damn hard to break. "Being anyone's partner isn't my cup of tea."

His lips went to her chin, trailed up her jaw. His hands softly cupped her breasts. "We both have a job to do."

Screw the job. Like his earlier response, the thought caught her by surprise. He was doing it to her again. She couldn't think straight with his teeth nibbling her earlobe and his hands teasing the sides of her breasts.

"Stop," she said, but it was weak. Too weak. The rain slanting down on the window drowned her out.

"You're stuck with me, Sophie. Might as well put me to good use."

Oh, she had uses for him. More than she could count. She slid her hands down to his chest, meaning to push him away. Instead she kneaded his hard pecs and sighed into his mouth. "Do I have a choice?"

His grin was dirty, nasty as could be. "Do you really want one?"

No, she didn't. Not at this moment. "This isn't only about arresting Rodrigo. I need to find out what happened to my sister."

95

"I know," he said, and he kissed her long and deep and passionately. He was breathing hard when he broke away. "Agree to work with me and I'll do everything in my power to help you find her."

"We're already working together. Sort of."

"You're holding out on me. If we're going to do this—if you want my help making sure the CIA doesn't steal your op—I want full cooperation and honesty."

Because she'd screwed him over last time. "There are some things you don't need to know."

Like the fact I'm infatuated with you.

"You're wrong," he said, kneeing her legs apart and pressing his hard length into her body. "I want—*need*—to know everything about you."

His mouth came down on hers, his hands cupping her breasts. Everything inside her gave a cry of joy.

She kissed him back, knowing that sadness would follow, just like it always did.

The rain eased, the worst of the storm moving north, as Nelson kept himself and Sophie tucked in the shadows of the house. Making their way back to her apartment without being seen wasn't easy, but then he never liked easy.

He'd had her skirt up around her waist, his fingers finding her hidden gun but moving on to more interesting territory. He'd liked reliving what it felt like to caress the warm, slick folds between her legs when she'd finally shoved him away.

"I can't," she'd said, her breath coming in short gasps. "Not here."

He'd always prided himself on his self-control. Tonight, with his cock straining for release, it had been difficult to find. He was still gritting his teeth at the constrictive tightness in his jeans as he walked softly through the night.

"Did you see Chavez leave the compound when you took over his job?" Sophie murmured as she tiptoed behind him.

As per normal, she couldn't focus on anything other than the op. "I escorted him out myself. Why?"

"The machete in the shed. Did you notice the blood on the blade?"

The wind gusted, blowing a sheet of water off a nearby palm and smacking him in the face. He tugged her closer behind him, making sure they stuck to the shadows and stayed out of the camera angles. "Yeah, so?"

"That's what they use to cut up body parts to feed to the snakes and the piranhas. I just wondered if Chavez was the latest victim."

"Piranhas, too?"

"There's an underground tank of them. They literally swim under the floor of the pit. Each interrogation room has a grate they can open to send the blood, flesh and any leftover body parts into the piranha tank. The goons wash down the walls and the floors with a high pressured hose and it all runs into that tank."

Nothing surprised him anymore, but it still made him wonder about humankind. "Easy cleanup, I suppose."

Sophie fell silent. How many people had disappeared into that place and never come out? Guilt at not saving them, whether they deserved saving or not, had to be eating at her.

"Nels?"

God, he hated that nickname. "Yeah?"

"What if she's dead?"

"Who?"

"Angelique."

A platitude was on his tongue quick as lightning. Sophie wanted hope, but she wouldn't buy empty assurances any more than he would. "What if she's not?"

It was the best he could give her. The hope that Angelique

was alive somewhere. The probability was remote, but a possibility did exist. "If she's alive, we'll find her," he added.

"What if we do and she wants nothing to do with me?"

"Come on, Sophie. She's your little sister and she's been through hell. She'll be amazed that you came for her and forever grateful that you found her."

"I screwed up, left her with Mama. Angel longed to go to America, to become a citizen. I should have tried harder to get her there."

He didn't know the full story about Sophie's past. He doubted anyone but Sophie did.

A sound ahead of them made him freeze. He raised his fist, signaling for her to be quiet. She stopped, her body pressing into his backside. Her hands rested on his waist.

A guard appeared, MK-4 in his hands, scanning the area as he made his rounds. Sophie's fingers on him tightened. He held motionless, willing her to do the same.

The guard moved on without breaking stride.

Once he was clearly out of earshot, Nelson took Sophie's hand once more and guided her around the end of the house. "They need night-vision goggles," he said under his breath.

"Good idea. Then they can see us when we're sneaking around and shoot us on sight."

Better than being chopped to bits and fed to the snakes and piranhas.

When they at last reached the garden surrounding the apartment, Nelson double-checked the area to make sure no one had seen them, no one was following them. Only a highly-trained SEAL should have been able to, but he didn't put it past the guards to accidentally stumble upon them.

Sophie climbed the stairs, lost in thought and not waiting for him. He stayed silent, listening to the croak of frogs and the buzz and hum of nocturnal insects. A light on the upper floor of the main house came on and Nelson watched from the shadows as a figure moved to the window.

Tall, dark hair. Morales. He was backlit, but it didn't take Nelson long to notice two things.

Morales had something draped around his neck. Something that moved and slithered.

Snake.

The second thing Nelson noticed was that Rodrigo Morales was looking right at Sophie's apartment.

CHAPTER THIRTEEN

A thin, high-pitched whining invaded Sophie's dreams, shooting adrenaline straight to her heart. She woke with a start, sat up in bed, and had a moment of vertigo. The dark room seemed to whirl dizzily around her and she stuck out both hands to anchor herself.

Her hands sank into the jumbled, messed up sheets. Instinctively, she felt her way to the left, searching for Nelson. He wasn't there.

For some reason, her heart skipped a beat. Where was he? Had he finally gotten the hint that he wasn't welcome in her bed?

Another skip.

Sophie rubbed the spot over her heart. *Don't be stupid, Sophia.*

The whining continued, rising and falling, a new sound joining it—pouring, gushing rain.

Blinking away the dizziness—God, she was tired—she tossed her legs over the edge of the bed and stood.

The vertigo immediately lessened and she took a deep breath, wiggling her toes on the bare floor. The air was cool and thick with the scent of the rain. What she wouldn't give to crawl back under the covers—preferably with Nelson, if she were honest—and go back to sleep.

But sleep didn't seem to be in the cards for her, a soft banging now accompanying the wailing noise. She tiptoed out to the living room.

A dark shadow stood resolutely next to the window overlooking the grounds. The window wasn't open, but it also wasn't locked, the wind slipping into the crack and causing the eerie noises. It clapped shut as the wind disappeared.

Nelson had constructed a bed on the floor with couch cushions and pillows. He was dressed only in his boxers. A soft glow emanated from his cell phone on the coffee table, showing her the time was slightly after 4 a.m. The screen was a mass of Doppler greens, yellows, and reds shifting in halting movements from left to right. The glow illuminated Nelson's left side.

The female inside Sophie took a few seconds to admire the length of him, all smooth skin and muscle working in synergy to create a beautiful, untamed creature.

She noticed a scar on his left thigh, another on his lower back. She hadn't seen either during their one night together two years ago.

"Nels?"

He didn't move, didn't even glance back at her. "Go back to sleep."

"Is someone out there?"

"Not in this storm."

The rainy season in Mexico combined with an approaching tropical storm. Sophie had liked the rainy season during her younger years here. The worst of the summer's heat was over, the hurricane season nearly done. It was a time to hole up inside with her books and her imagination and dream of the life she wanted to live one day back in America.

She'd made it back, but things hadn't quite turned out the way she'd planned. So she'd learned to plan better, down to the last detail. Contingencies had to be accounted for. Various outcomes anticipated. She couldn't control every factor in her job or in life, but she could strategize and devise a response to most, no matter the situation.

So far, her formula had worked.

Except for Chica Bonita.

Except for Nelson.

He still hadn't moved, his gaze locked on the courtyard below. What was he seeing? Not the storm, she'd bet, and not even the grounds. He was lost in his own world, or maybe he was worried about their upcoming job. Sophia, herself, had spent many nights looking out that same window, planning her exit strategy in case her operation became jeopardized. No way she was ending up in the pit.

A gust of wind lifted the edge of the window again, the force creating another howl of resistance from the framework. Sophie shivered and moved closer to Nelson. She knew the answer but asked anyway, hoping to gain his attention. "Why didn't Guido come after me today?"

Without preamble, he answered, as if he'd already given the subject some thought. "Either he hasn't found out about me taking over Chavez's spot, or he has, and figures I'm undercover, waiting until I can get close enough to kill you."

"Surely Chavez ran right to him and told him you usurped his position."

"Or the blood you saw on the machete in the shed was actually his."

Another shiver ran up her spine. "You said you escorted Chavez off the grounds yourself."

"Doesn't mean he didn't end up piranha food."

Sophie's stomach did a flip. She'd never liked Chavez, but no one deserved that type of death. "Why not go after Lexie? She's the only family Rodrigo has left. If Guido really wanted to hurt his arch enemy, wouldn't Lexie be the ultimate way of doing that?"

Again, Nelson has a ready answer. "Morales and I discussed exactly that. I don't think Guido knows Lexie's here. Few people do. Hurting or killing her wouldn't cripple the business the way taking you out would. Morales could get another bookkeeper, but it would take months to trust her and train her with everything.

"Striking at Lexie would start a true war between the two cartels," he continued. "Guido doesn't have that kind of manpower. He'd rather keep taking potshots at Morales, guerilla-warfare style, while he looks for vulnerabilities and builds up his own troops. That's one of the reasons Morales insists I stay here with you when he and Lexie go to their beach house."

"You think Guido will come here and try to get me when Morales leaves?"

"Both of us, if he thinks I turned traitor."

Guido wouldn't show up. Not even if he'd figured out who Nelson really was. Still, it was good to keep Nelson talking. "So while we search for the ledger, we also have to watch out for Guido."

"Guido and,"—Nelson grabbed the window handle and pulled it in, locking it tight and shutting out the wind—"this storm system."

Reaching out, Sophie took his hand, winding her fingers through his. "It's just the remnants of the tropical storm out in the South Pacific. A little rain, a little wind. I've been through them before. The worst will be over in a day or two."

"They revised the forecast," he said. "The tropical storm has been upgraded to a Cat 3 hurricane."

"Oh, no."

He finally turned his face toward her and she saw the concern etched in the creases of his eyes. He squeezed her hand in his and his gaze dropped to her lips as if he longed to kiss her again.

"Sophie, the storm is headed right for us."

CHAPTER FOURTEEN

Cooper dialed Cruz's number, copies of the Morales warrants lying on the table in front of him, courtesy of Sarah Rios. The FBI fugitive recovery agent stood in the corner, talking to one of her bosses on her phone about the chance that the Bureau, and hence the taskforce, would be moving in on Morales soon, regardless of what the CIA wanted.

Three rings, hang up, one more ring and done. Three and one was their code.

Within thirty seconds, his caller ID lit up with Nelson's call sign. "Yo, boss." Nelson said when Cooper answered. "What's up?"

"You sound like hell." Cooper sipped coffee from his mug. His gut was already rebelling from his recent diet of coffee, coffee, and more coffee. "Agent Diaz making things difficult for you?"

"We're laying low. Waiting for our opportunity to find the ledgers and look for the missiles. Don't want Morales to suspect anything before the deal goes down on Sunday."

Maybe the connection was bad. Cruz sounded off, his voice tight, even more controlled than usual. "You sure you're okay?"

"Never better."

Right. "Storm's moving in." He hated ending an op before

they had what they needed, but being in a foreign country during a hurricane jeopardized Cruz and Diaz's lives in ways Cooper couldn't justify. "We may have to move up the timeline and have you pull out early anyway."

Rios ended her call and strolled over to the table, listening to Cooper's phone call.

"If we leave," Cruz said, "it will ruin the chance to catch Kronos."

"Cruz, if the hurricane hits land anywhere near you, the meeting will be postponed. Dupé and I both want you out and on this side of the border if that thing is going to get anywhere near Tijuana."

There was a pause. "I've got no desire to ride out a hurricane, Coop, but they're saying it won't do much here. We should be okay."

Cooper pinched the bridge of his nose. Rios signaled him and shook her head. The CIA was not ready to call it quits on the op. "Not an option. Dupé says you have twelve hours, that's it. He wants you and Diaz on a bus back to the States by nightfall. You feel me?"

A heavy sigh. "I'm getting tired of being jerked around by everyone not actually working this op. First you won't give me the time I ask for, then you tell me to stay put. Now you're ready to pull the plug again before I've got what we need. It'd be nice if you had some faith in me."

The line went dead.

"He's not pulling out, is he?" Thomas said from across the table where he was doing paperwork with Mitch Holton, showing him the ropes on Project Bliss.

"Hell, no," Cooper said, pinching his nose again. "Bullheaded son-of-a-bitch."

Ronni, on Cooper's left, lifted her gaze from her phone where she was mapping out their next "bath salt" supplier. She was still wearing her pharmacy coat from her undercover job. "He'll be okay, won't he?"

Not if Hurricane Olympia got hold of his shorts. But the damn storm would have to beat Cooper to the punch.

Thomas waved off Ronni's concern. "He's in more danger from Agent Diaz than Mother Nature."

He and Holton shared a chuckle. Cooper didn't think it was funny. His phone buzzed with a call. Dupé. "Yes, sir," he answered.

The man sounded tired…and in a hurry. "Chica Bonita. Did Cruz get any info for us?"

"We pulled him off before he had a chance."

"I've got an informant who claims girls are coming through there again. With papers. They look official, but aren't. They're forged. I want to know who is providing them and how." Dupé went on to give him the few details he had. "Jump on this ASAP, but don't pull Cruz off Diaz, got it?"

Which only left…him to find the forger. Great. Nothing like heading into a hurricane and a cartel business. "You got it, sir."

Standing, he disconnected and grabbed the copies of the warrants. "Rios? You're with me."

"Where are you going?" Thomas said, sitting back in his chair.

"To get my agent and look into a new complication with Chica Bonita." Cooper went for his jacket and started texting Celina, his live-in girlfriend, to let her know he wouldn't be home for dinner. "And, no, you're not going. You, Holton, and Punto stay on Bliss."

They all started talking at the same time. He ignored their arguments, heading out the door, Rios on his heels.

In the parking lot, he jumped into his SUV, checked that he had all of his ID's and paperwork, and fired up the Explorer. Rios climbed into the passenger seat.

"This is a delicate situation," she said, her voice soft but steady. "We don't want to blow their covers or scare Morales away."

"Cruz doesn't seem to comprehend the risk he's taking by

staying down there. Meantime, I can't pull him off Diaz to find the source for some legit looking paperwork some illegals are crossing the border with."

"I think he does understand the risks. Maybe you should give him a little while to think it through and call him back. Maybe he and Diaz can investigate this paperwork trail."

Cooper eyed Rios. "Are you insinuating I'm not handling this situation correctly?"

Her smile was as soft as her voice. "No, sir. I've read up on Agent Cruz, however, and I do believe he's quite capable of determining his risk accurately and deciding when it's time to clear out. I also know if illegals are getting official-looking paperwork, an immigration officer with as many commendations in his folder like Agent Cruz will have a nose for finding the source."

Cooper put the SUV in drive, but kept his foot on the brake. "He's a bullheaded SOB and I can't afford to lose him. I'm going to Tijuana, Agent Rios, in case he needs my help or I have to drag his ass back to the States so he doesn't end up dead. And while I'm at it, I'll track down the source of the forged paperwork. I'd like you to back me up, but if you don't like the assignment, you're free to return to your regular day job."

She raised her hands in an act of surrender. "I wasn't questioning the assignment, sir. I'm happy to accompany you and be on hand to arrest Morales if the opportunity presents itself."

Better. He liked an agent who spoke her mind, but knew when to shut up and get the job done.

"Good." Cooper took his foot off the brake. It was his turn to soften a little. "Glad you're on board. Dupé appreciates your joining the taskforce again to help us out, and so do I. I never got the chance to properly thank you for helping save Celina's life last year. You ever need anything, holler, okay?"

Rios's smile widened. "I'll do that, sir."

Tijuana

The apartment was empty except for her.

Sophie showered and dressed, then checked the weather forecast. The tropical storm had indeed been upgraded to a hurricane, but a low-level one that would probably peter out the minute it hit land.

Although they were going to get a bevy more of rain and wind, landfall was expected within twelve hours and far to the south in the desert area of southern Baja.

As it stood, when she looked out her window, everything appeared normal. The rain had stopped, the sun was out. A jumble of dark clouds could be seen on the horizon, but for now, things were peaceful. Even the peacock in the garden was doing his normal strut around the birdbath, not a care in the world.

Where is Nelson?

Breakfast was an egg and toast with grape jam. As she sat at the small kitchen table, the morning news droning in the background, she fiddled with the bracelet on her wrist. The apartment seemed too big, too empty this morning without Nelson's lugging presence.

Her bed had felt too big last night as well.

Shutting down that thought, she stuck her plate and glass into the sink. Thanks to the impending storm and Nelson's quick thinking, today was the day Rodrigo and Lexie were leaving for the beach house to pay their respects to their dead father and mother. Her morning would be spent sorting the cash she'd picked up yesterday. She'd hold out the thirty-five thousand as instructed, and distribute the rest to various banks and Morales's private investment house later.

Once Morales was gone, she and Nelson would sneak into the pit and have a look around.

Where is Nelson?

Probably doing security stuff to make sure the security team kept the cartel leader safe until she and Nelson arrested him.

Oh the irony.

We're almost done. And I still don't know what to do with Lexie or the other girls.

Yolanda had been helping her with the girls, but it was a lot to ask for her to take over completely, considering she had so much else on her plate, including taking care of her son.

She's my only hope. Once the arrests were made, Sophia would have to get back to Tijuana and find Yolanda some help.

In the meantime, she had work to do.

The main house was bustling with excitement. Suitcases were packed and sitting by the front door. Lexie came down the stairs, Harry by her side, with a book bag slung over her shoulder.

"Good morning, *Señorita*," Sophie said to the girl.

"Maria-Sophia! We're leaving early for the beach. Can you come with us?"

"You're still going? Even with the storm?"

"Rodrigo says the storm is nothing." Lexie made her way to the pile of suitcases and set down her bag. "And we're Moraleses. We're not scared of storms. A little storm isn't going to stop us from honoring Mama's and Papa's memories."

Outside, in the distance, Sophia heard the sound of gunshots. She reached for the girl. "What is that?"

"Nico took Rodrigo to the south end for gun shooting practice!"

Nelson was teaching Rodrigo how to shoot a gun?

"I wanted to go to," Lexie said. "They both told me no."

"And they were right to do so, young lady."

Lexie had not had breakfast yet, so Sophia hustled her into the kitchen and left her with the maid and a bowl of cereal. She wanted to see what Nelson was up to, but decided to ignore him and get down to her business. Morales would want a full report on the week's profits and losses.

The interior of the small office she used on the first floor snugged under the grand staircase and was sparse but accommodating. Computers, printers, and a host of files waited for her. The room was windowless and had a special insulation in the walls to block outside intrusions, be they eavesdroppers or wireless hackers.

Three black cash bags sat on the floor waiting for her. The system was twofold: cash and investments. Yesterday, she logged the cash from all of the local merchants, and replaced everything in their registers and safes with drug money. The clean cash would now go into the banks, once she had finished sorting it. As a precaution, the money would be mixed together before she sorted it back out to deposit. Tomorrow, she would get online and transfer various amounts to offshore accounts.

Sophia closed and locked the office door behind her and reached for the first black bag.

CHAPTER FIFTEEN

Nelson finished prepping the team of security agents escorting Morales to his beach house shortly before noon. He'd shown Morales how to handle a handgun, because although the cartel leader had lived in a world of violence and was constantly surrounded by men with weapons, he'd never received training himself.

Nelson cared little if Morales lived through an attack from Guido, but no head of security worth his salt would let the man he was in charge of leave the security of his home without some kind of defense training.

Which made Nelson wonder all over again at the incompetence of James Chavez.

When Nelson entered the house and went to do a final check-in with Morales, he found Sophie in the man's study with him.

"I beg you to reconsider going to the beach house this weekend with the storm and everything," she was saying as Nelson entered the room.

He pulled up short, wondering what she was talking about. They needed Morales out of the house, out of town, if they were going to search for the ledgers and the missiles.

"Your security team is ready, sir," Nelson said. "I've handpicked a group of Savages to ride with you and a second group is already at the beach property, securing the area."

Morales closed his laptop and stuck a file in his bottom

drawer before locking the desk. "Very good." He snapped a finger at the guard hovering by the door. "Load up Felix."

The guard went to the tank containing Morales's pet snake and covered it. A second later he carried it out the door. Nelson gave the tank a wide berth.

Sophie still sat in the chair across from the desk. "Think of Lexie. If the hurricane does hit land, she could be in danger."

Now Sophia's pleas made sense, but a part of him was shocked. She was more worried about the safety of the girl then she was about finding a link to her sister?

Morales came around the end of his desk and stopped in front of her. He leaned his butt on the edge of the desk, the look on his face one that bothered Nelson. "You worry too much, Maria-Sophia. Lexie and I will be fine. We have survived much in our lifetimes, including several tropical storms."

"Yes, but—"

He reached out and touched her cheek, the intimacy of the gesture making Nelson tense. "If it looks like we are in danger, I promise to bring her back. But it is important that she remember and honor our parents, and she has been looking forward to this trip for months."

Sophie stood and gave a small nod. "I will see you on Sunday, then, if not before."

She started to turn away when Morales grabbed her wrist. It was gentle but still restricting. "You are welcome to come with us."

Nelson saw the way her body stiffened, but she didn't pull away. "I have the banking to do today and I must get the money ready for Sunday."

Morales didn't like being rebuffed. His face hardened.

But Sophie knew how to save her backside. She laid a whopper of a smile on the man and touched his arm. "Perhaps next year? I do love the sea. It's especially beautiful this time of year." She chuckled. "Unless there's a hurricane, of course."

Her charm was infectious. Nelson wondered if any man could resist.

A half-smile broke the line of Morales's lips. "I would like that, *si*."

Nelson had reduced the security staff by half, sending most of the guards with Rodrigo and Lexie. The maid had gone with them, Rodrigo locking up the house.

Normally, she would be on her way into town to deposit money. Today, Rodrigo had told her to wait until he returned. She didn't know if he was actually worried about her or still feared deep down inside that she'd steal his money and run.

Her apartment was empty, and once more she felt a pang of loneliness. How pathetic that Nelson had only been there two days and he'd already wormed himself into her life to the point she missed him when he wasn't around.

For a brief moment, she wondered if he'd gone to the pit without her. They had mapped out a plan during the previous night when they couldn't sleep, and Sophie knew without a doubt that Nelson wasn't one to suddenly change the plan without due cause. He was a quick thinker and talented at going with the flow, but he didn't wing things when it came to tactical operations. He always had a plan and stuck to it if possible. He wouldn't go to the snake pit until nightfall.

While she'd been in her office, she'd done some digging and found contact info for an old friend in child services back in the States. Not exactly a friend, per se, but a woman who had tried to help her mother gain citizenship and get a job when they were living in L.A. If anyone could help her with the Lexie situation, Wanda Kohl could. Sophie had emailed her and crossed her fingers when she hit the Send button.

Once done with that, Sophie had erased all traces of her Internet searches and the email off the computer.

Now inside her apartment, she changed into black knit pants, a black cotton shirt, and braided her hair so it was easy to hide under the hood of her jacket she would be wearing later. She was getting a drink from the refrigerator when Nelson arrived.

He was tense, his eyes darting around. When she started to speak, he held his finger to his lips and silenced her. "How was your day? Did you get your work done for Señor Morales?"

As she answered, he began checking once more under furniture and tables looking for bugs. She joined him. "All of yesterday's pickups are accounted for and will be deposited when Rodrigo returns. Tomorrow I will get the cash ready for Sunday's exchange."

"Very good. What are you cooking me for dinner tonight?"

She raised an eyebrow at him but played along. "Enchilada casserole, my grandmother's favorite dish to make. Since it's not raining, I thought we could sit on the patio and enjoy it."

He winked at her and moved into the kitchen. "Smells delicious."

The kitchen was clean of bugs. He moved off to the bathroom. "I'm going to clean up."

Sophie went into her bedroom and searched there while he pretended to take a shower. Again, she found nothing. What had made Nelson suspicious that Rodrigo had bugged her apartment?

Maybe nothing had tipped him off. Nelson was always suspicious and constantly on his toes.

Just like her.

Starving, she busied herself in the kitchen making a simple casserole. When Nelson emerged from the bathroom, he was dressed in black like she was. "I'll take the plates down to the patio," he said.

Obviously, he still wanted to take precautions and not speak inside about what they were up to. A few minutes later, they were seated downstairs on a pair of white wicker chairs with a small table between them.

Nelson began inhaling his portion of the barely warm meal. Sophie pointed upstairs. "You want to explain that to me?"

"Just a feeling," Nelson said around a mouthful of food. "You keep telling me that Morales doesn't trust me and I can't quite figure him out. Your paranoia must be rubbing off on me."

Nelson didn't operate on feelings. At least not from what she'd seen. "Why were you teaching him how to shoot today? Isn't that sort of counterproductive when we go to arrest him?"

"Why were you trying to get him to stay here instead of going to the beach house?"

"I was worried about Lexie. Tropical storms are highly unpredictable."

He gave her a palms up gesture. "I was worried about her too. Guido Ruiz is unpredictable."

Sophie tipped her wine glass at him. "Touché."

"Morales already knew how to shoot, by the way. Not well, but it's obvious he's had a few lessons. I was simply evaluating how much of a threat he might be if we are still here to arrest him on Sunday, and against my better judgment, I was trying to make sure he could, indeed, defend himself and Lexie if Guido's men ambushed them."

Guido. There was a conundrum. "When Guido finds out you double-crossed him, he'll be out for blood."

Nelson shoved another forkful of food into his mouth and chewed. "I'm keeping an eye out for him. Right now, I'm more worried about surviving the snake pit. Why would Morales hide ledgers anyway? How did you find out about them?"

The sun was sinking, fingers of pale peach and pink striping the sky. Sophie set down her glass and pushed her plate away. "The woman who held this job before me, Rosalie, worked for Ciro for nine years. Quite possibly, she and Ciro had a little thing on the side. Either way, he trusted her with everything.

According to her, he was fastidious about his business and wrote down every transaction, every contact, every exchange. They're like diaries of his life. By the time he passed, he had gone exclusively into the drug trade, mostly with synthetic versions created at the labs in and around Tijuana. Bigger profit, lower risk. Rosalie and Ciro had a falling out and she left right before he died. She didn't know where Rodrigo might have put them." She rubbed her forehead.

"But they're not in any of the safes inside the mansion."

Nelson stopped chewing. "How do you know?"

"I broke into them and looked."

"You cracked the safes?"

"Don't look so surprised. You're not the only one around here who can pick a lock."

"Safe cracking is different than picking a lock."

She grinned. "I have a varied work skill set."

"When you and I worked on Chica Bonita the last time, there were girls from Western Europe and Russia being funneled through CB into points south. If Rodrigo is resurrecting the human trafficking side of the cartel, he might be planning to reverse the process and ship American and Mexican girls to Europe."

"As drug mules or sex slaves?"

"Both probably," he said. "That's why he needs Kronos."

"His focus is on drugs so most likely he wants to get a foothold in Europe with those first." Sophie wanted to change the subject. "It won't matter once we take him down. But I've got to get my hands on those ledgers. I can find out if my sister's name is in any of them and where she was sent."

"Are you sure they're in the snake pit?"

"If you were Rodrigo and you were hiding the history of your family's cartel, where would you put them?"

"Sure as hell not surrounded by snakes."

"That's why you can't figure him out. He's not your typical cartel leader and you're not able to think like him. After all of these months, I am. I've seen the way he operates. The snake building is exactly where he would hide his father's criminal history and anything else that he wants to protect."

"Like a pair of missiles no one is supposed to know about?"

"Seems possible."

Shadows crept along the edges of the garden. The peacock waddled away from the birdbath, tucking himself near an aloe plant. A toad hopped across the concrete, hesitating for a moment to look at Sophie and Nelson, before venturing off into the bushes.

Nelson wiped his hands on a napkin and sat back in his chair. "The night guard will make his rounds in fifteen minutes. We'll have a half hour window before he comes through again, but we'll have to take a circuitous route like we did last night around the shed to avoid detection by the cameras."

A flash of lightening in the distance brightened the sky for a split second. Pressure was building in her head along with the barometric pressure.

Nelson eyed her from across the table. "Once we grab the ledgers, do you have an exit strategy?"

"Get the hell out of the snake pit?"

"You know what I mean."

The unlit house across the way grew fuzzy as the night crept closer and the clouds grew thicker. "If the missiles are there, we know the CIA's supposition is legitimate and then we have a judgment call to make. We stay and keep things status quo until the meeting with the European, or we blow out of here and at least get our man. Either way, the Morales cartel and the missiles will be out of commission, right? So, in the end, it's up to you and me to make that call."

A low rumble echoed over the compound. Nelson continued to study her. "You ready for this?"

Sophie took a sip of wine. At the thought of what she was about to do, the wine tasted like acid. She swallowed and took a deep breath.

She needed a moment. One small heartbeat in time to consider the fact she was about to enter a death pit.

And that she was about to find out what had happened to her sister.

No point stewing. She'd been waiting for this moment for two years. Longer if she were honest.

Setting down the glass, she met Nelson's steady gaze. "As ready as I'll ever be."

CHAPTER SIXTEEN

The pit was cold.

Nelson remembered that from his previous visits, one conscious, the other, not so much.

Floor to ceiling glass ran the length of the main room, framing the two largest snake enclosures. *Put them together*, Nelson thought, *and they're nearly the size of my apartment back home.*

Trees grew inside the giant terrariums, vines winding their way up the trunks and along the branches as if mimicking the snakes that lived there. Sophie followed on his heels, the beam of his flashlight bouncing off the glass and catching a beady eye or shiny scale here and there.

"Missiles are big compared to ledgers," Nelson said, "but these cages could hide them, don't you think?"

"Inside?" Sophie's voice faltered slightly. She stopped in front of the python enclosure. "You think he hid the missiles, and possibly the ledgers, *inside* with the snakes?"

Nelson stopped and went back to her. His arm brushed against hers has he shined the light along the bottom of the cage. "Isn't that what you were thinking?"

He felt her shiver. "Actually," she said, "I was hoping they were stored in a safe like any other valuable."

Possibly, but the missiles were too big to put in a safe.

Something that resembled a white log moved on the enclosure's floor. Sophie took a sudden step back, knocking into his elbow. The flashlight beam jerked right and landed on the giant snake's head.

The python was a rare albino with a couple of very pale yellow spots on its back. One beady red eye stared straight at them.

"Gah," Sophie said, shaking her head and letting loose a jittery laugh. She tapped on the glass and pointed at the snake. "You, my friend, would make a beautiful handbag and matching shoes."

"Taunting a snake we may have to get cozy with, is probably not a great idea."

"God, I hope there's a safe."

A safe would be nice, tidy, and far less dangerous.

Nelson hadn't been looking for missiles when Morales had given him the official tour, but he also hadn't noticed anything resembling a safe. "Alright. Let's sweep the building and see what we find."

What they found was a wall of smaller snakes in glass terrariums, and a supply room filled with cleaning products and various equipment to handle and move the snakes. Sophie uncovered what looked like a spare tank and found it contained rats.

"Eww." She made gagging noises. "Nothing like a diet of rats and body parts."

Dropping the cover back over the glass terrarium, she avoided the rest.

Leaning against the wall in one corner was a large, black terrarium base. Next to it was a tall cabinet with a lock. Sophie motioned Nelson over and it took him about five seconds to pick the lock.

Inside, the shelves looked like a serial killer's wet dream. A pile of plastic sheeting, a chainsaw, a short handled axe, and a tray of what looked like surgical tools.

"I overheard Chavez once," Sophie said. "He was talking about his top five favorite torture sessions. His number one favorite involved cutting off a man's fingers and toes one by one and feeding them to one of the snakes in order to get the man to talk. The man was either extremely resilient or extremely stupid and refused, even after they had taken off all of his digits, his ears, and one of his hands at the wrist. He was bleeding out and still wouldn't talk. Then Chavez got smart and threatened to cut off his penis. The guy spilled everything he knew and then some."

Nelson gave a mental shudder. "You don't mess with a man's dick."

"He still ended up food for Goliath." She closed the doors and relocked the cabinet. "God only knows how many men have fed that python. Where's the interrogation room?"

Nelson led her out of the supply room and around the corner. There were no windows inside this room, so he flipped on the lights.

Dingy beige walls, a chair, chains and ropes for tying men up. Old blood stains hopscotched across the concrete floor. Along the back wall there was a dip in the floor, a trough that led to a grate. Nelson assumed that underneath that grate was where the fishies lived.

The wall to their right was the backside of the anaconda's enclosure. It was entirely sealed off but for a sliding door in the glass about head high where rats and body parts could be dropped inside.

Seeing the light, and perhaps anticipating a late-night snack, the anaconda appeared, slithering up out of some vines to watch them. Sophie stood for a moment, eyeing the green twenty-foot snake and his enclosure. She took out her own penlight and headed for the door. "I want to do another sweep of the front."

Nelson followed, this time peeling off to the left and checking for any hidden doors or storage possibilities he might have missed while she went right. After a half hour of searching every nook and cranny, and tapping on every wall and floor, he'd found nothing. No safes, no hidden compartments, no false doors.

Back in the main area, he found Sophie crouched in front of the python's enclosure, running her hands along the black, plastic base. "The cages can't sit directly on the floor. I examined that base in the supply room and it has a heater and some type of ventilation fan. Got me to thinking. Maybe that one wasn't functioning properly or..."

She ran her hands along the side of the plastic, stopping when her fingers found what she was looking for. Nelson heard a distinctive *click*. "Maybe Rodrigo or his snake caretaker had a different one designed for under this cage in order to make room for a safe."

Another click. She gave a tug and the end of the black plastic casing popped off. "If Rodrigo needed to make a quick getaway and wanted those ledgers, he wouldn't want to fend off a giant snake to do so. What if he hid them *under* the enclosure?"

The terrarium bases were long and deep enough to fit a dozen men inside. Definitely big enough to hide SAMs as well. Why hadn't he thought of that?

Jogging to the other end, Nelson set his flashlight to shine on the base and ran his hands along the edges until he found one clip, then another. Popping them off, he helped Sophie ease the long cover away from the wall.

Sophie shined her light along the inside and they both sat for a moment studying what they'd found.

Three fans and a base heater lined the underside of the enclosure as suspected, but Sophie's beam swept over and then came back to stop on something else. Something as black as the dark underbelly of the terrarium.

"What is that?" she said.

Not missiles. "A suitcase?"

Above them, the python made its way to the glass. As lightning split the sky outside, a ray of light tripped across the enclosure. The snake stared down at Sophie, his long tongue slithering out and smacking into the glass.

Sophie flipped him off.

"It has drawers." She inched her knees closer to the cavernous space under Goliath and reached toward the black, soft-sided suitcase. She removed it, brushed some dirt off the top and found a zipper on one end. Unzipping it, she slipped off the fabric to reveal what looked like a toolbox with a set of five drawers. A clasp with a lock hung on the front of the drawers.

She snapped her fingers at him. "Do your thing."

He slid in next to her, and she ran her hands along the narrow fronts of the drawers as he worked his magic on the lock.

"I know what this is."

The lock sprang free and he flipped the clasp up and out of the way. "What?"

"Not ledgers or weapons," she said, grabbing one of the drawer's handles and opening it. "But something that makes a lot more sense."

As her penlight beam swept over the contents, Nelson had no idea what she was talking about.

———

Sophie stared at the tray of odd-sized rocks, disappointment flooding her system. This was not at all what she was looking for.

Nelson leaned forward. "He's keeping a bunch of rocks in a locked case under the snake's cage? Shouldn't the rocks go inside the cage?"

They did indeed look like the exact rocks inside Goliath's cage.

But these rocks were far more valuable.

"They're uncut gemstones." She ran her fingers over the rough stones. "They don't look like much in this state, but once they are cut and polished, they could be worth hundreds of thousands of dollars. Much like the ones Rodrigo has displayed in his study."

Nelson whistled low. "Why is he hiding them here?"

Good question. She pulled out another tray, found the same thing and closed it again. "As a backup in case the house was raided or burned down? Most anyone who found them would be like you and think they were just rocks."

A tug and Nelson dragged the black carrier out from under the terrarium. He hefted it with one hand and set it down. "Easy to carry off in an emergency."

Something had fallen over when Nelson pulled out the carrier. A sweep of the interior with her penlight and Sophie saw a backpack lying on the dirty concrete. "Or he could dump them in that backpack and take off. He trained to be a gemologist in Amsterdam. He could cut and sell those stones anywhere, anytime, and fund a new life for him and Lexie."

"And leave his precious snakes behind?"

"A six hundred pound python is hard to carry when you're on the run."

Across the way, the anaconda was now watching them too, wound around a tree limb, his upper half hanging down and swinging slightly. "Touché."

Before she knew it, Nelson was belly crawling under the cage. "What are you doing?"

His flashlight bounced off the sides as he went deeper. "Looking for missiles."

The built-in cage had to be at least seven feet deep. Sophie watched as Nelson's legs and feet slowly disappeared into the dark cavern. Above him, Goliath continued to stare at her and stick out his tongue.

Ignoring the snake—she would have nightmares for years after this—she focused on following Nelson's flashlight beam. "You really think they could get missiles into that space?"

The upper half of his body was hidden behind the fans. "They could have buried them."

"You don't see anything else unusual in there, do you?"

"Just a massive cobweb and a couple of spiders that I'm pretty sure are both venomous."

Spiders! Another of her favorites. Along with cartel leaders, Mexico was full of them. "Please come out. I can't afford for you to get bit by a venomous spider and ruin my entire op."

As Nelson inched his way back toward her, Sophie opened the bottom drawer of the carrier. Her pulse leapt in her throat. "Nels? I found something."

A deep thud sounded from the enclosure, making her jump. The stupid snake was banging its head against the glass.

"Stop it," she yelled, completely sick of the thing. Sticking out her tongue at him, she barely kept herself from slapping the glass. "I'm not your goddamn next meal, you freak."

Nelson emerged, brushing dirt from his shoulders and chest. "What is it?"

Sophie shined her penlight on the last open drawer. A set of three worn, leather-bound journals were tightly tucked into it. The ledgers.

Angelique.

Pulse leaping again, this time with joy, she threw her arms around Nelson's neck. "We found them. We found *her.*"

CHAPTER SEVENTEEN

Nelson didn't want to dash Sophie's hopes, but they hadn't actually found anyone yet. He hugged her back, then hated himself for saying what had to be said. "You're sure those are the ledgers?"

She released him and picked up one of the leather books. "Yes! These are the ones." She grabbed the other two, hugging all three to her chest. "Let's get out of here."

"What's that?" he pointed to something under the last book she'd picked up.

Her fingers deftly reached in and scooped it up. She held it up for him to see, turning it over. "An old 3.5 hard disk like they used to use in the nineties."

"Let me see it."

Rain fell, coating the window near the door. Handing the disk off to him, she held onto the ledgers as she grabbed the backpack and dumped them inside.

Nelson ran his fingers over the hard square of plastic. On the label, there was no name or list of files it contained, only a sticker of the solemn face of the Virgin Mary. Was she a good luck charm to keep whatever files were on the disk safe?

His search for missiles had been a bust, but maybe Sophie had just found something more interesting. He pocketed the outdated disk. "Help me put the cover back on."

Together, they returned the carrier of gemstones to its hiding place and secured the plastic case back on the base of the terrarium. Nelson made a quick scan, double-checking that everything had been returned to normal. Then, they snuck out the door.

They were drenched in a matter of seconds as they made their way to the guest house, sticking to the shadows like before, and avoiding the compound's patrols and cameras.

Inside the apartment, Sophie was nearly giddy. She dumped the backpack on a chair, wet strands of hair hanging around her face where they'd broken free of her ponytail. Her pants were soaked and had adhered even closer to her shapely curves. She shucked off her wet sweatshirt, and as she did so, the shirt underneath also rose, giving Nelson a view of her smooth, tanned skin, and the briefest glance of her lacy, black bra.

God help him.

He was standing there in his own puddle, eyeballing the generous outline of her breasts through the thin, wet material of her shirt, when she caught his gaze and sent him a scathing glance as she flicked water from her fingertips. "Could you grab some towels, please? I don't want to get the ledgers wet."

Towels. Right. He jerked his gaze away and went to the bathroom for towels.

Coming back, he tossed one to her. She dried herself quickly, then removed her ponytail and wound her hair in the towel. With deft fingers, she unzipped the backpack, removed the ledgers, and headed for the kitchen table.

Nelson toweled off, relieved they finally had what Sophie wanted, but frustrated he had no clue where the damn missiles were stored. He'd have to break into the house and scan it tomorrow. Maybe even check the staff house.

The missiles, Chica Bonita, keeping Sophie safe. His jobs were piling up fast.

Removing the disk from his pocket, he realized there was no way to see what was on it. Sophie didn't have a personal laptop, and even if she did, it would take a vintage 1980s computer to read one.

A loud, "Goddamn!" rang out from the kitchen interrupting his thoughts. It was followed by a sharp *smack*, like the sound of a book hitting the wall.

He tossed the disk on the coffee table and hustled to the kitchen. When he saw Sophie, his stomach sank to his knees. She was sitting at the table with her head in her hands, a look of total defeat in her slumped shoulders. One of the ledgers lay open on the floor near the doorway.

Yep, she'd thrown it against the wall.

"Tell me those aren't the wrong ledgers."

She shook her head without looking up at him. "They're the correct ones."

If those were the right ones...oh, hell. Had she discovered something bad about Angelique? Something even worse than being sold into slavery? "What is it?"

"I can't read them."

"Come again?"

"I can't read the damn ledgers."

He bent down and lifted the book from the floor. "Why not?"

She raised her head and he saw tears streaming down her face. "Because, after all this, all these months and years of searching for her, she's right here and I can't...I can't understand them."

"But you know Spanish."

"They're not just in Spanish."

She pointed at the book in his hands and Nelson glanced down at the lines of handwriting.

His brain couldn't make sense of them, even though he knew a good deal of Spanish too. What was written on the page looked like his mother's native tongue, but the sentences were a gobbly-gook of mixed up words. "What is this?"

"They're in code, Nelson." Her eyes were disheartened. "A code we can't begin to cipher."

Code? Shit.

"Sophie." He started to move toward her.

She waved him off with one hand as she dashed at the tears on her cheeks with the other. "Don't. I know what you're going to say and I don't want to hear it. This was my chance to find Angelique, to find some kind of trail. I have to turn these ledgers in as evidence now without knowing what they say. The Bureau will decode them, and eventually I'll find out if she's mentioned, but it could take months, maybe longer."

She took the ledger back and closed it, gently caressing the leather cover. Her voice dropped a notch. "All this time, I thought I was finally going to find out what happened to her. I would finally have a lead or at least some closure. But no. The Morales cartel has outfoxed me yet again."

The pain in her voice was too much for him. He went to her anyway, bending down next to her and rubbing her back. "It's a setback, I won't argue that, but it's not the end. We'll find her, one way or the other."

"We?" She chuckled without humor. "There is no *we*, Nelson. I told you that before. You crashed my operation, yes, and although it pains me to admit it, you've been very helpful and useful. But when this is over, you'll go back to the taskforce and I'll go back to the Bureau. Once more, it will be up to me, and only me, to find out what happened to my little sister."

He had to do something. Had to convince her that she wasn't alone in this. He moved his hand to the back of her neck and massaged the tight knots there. "I'm not giving up on finding her. Whether it's tomorrow, or the next day, or next year, I will help you find Angelique, and if possible, bring her home."

Sophie's dark eyes slowly shifted to his. Tears once more filled them, but a spark of hope glistened there as well. "Why? Why would you do that after the way I've treated you?"

Her vulnerability was so rare, so raw, he had to glance away for a second and recover. Clearing his throat, he shot her one of his famous heart-melting grins—the one most women melted over—and tugged her braid. "We're partners now, remember?"

The spark of hope dimmed. "Partners, right. Like the last time."

"You weren't my partner then, Sophie. You sabotaged my operation to save your own."

"Which totally backfired on me and I ended up as empty handed as you when Ciro Morales caught on that I was undercover inside his human trafficking organization and shut it down. Oh yeah, and then after he went lights on with Chica Bonita, you left me."

Left her? "You lied to me, seduced me, and then told me to get the hell out when I tried to help you pick up the Chica Bonita trail again."

She sighed as if too tired to fight. "I was afraid, okay?"

"Afraid? Of what?"

A long, heavy pause weighted the silence. When she finally spoke, it was a soft whisper. "You."

She looked away.

His gut tightened. "Why the hell would you be afraid of me?"

Her gaze snapped back to his. "Nelson Cruz? The top ICE agent in the land who was handpicked to be on Victor Dupé's Southern California VC Taskforce? Do you know what I would give to be on an elite taskforce like that?"

Dupé's taskforces ran lean and mean. To date, there were only three of them on the west coast, each team consisting of five to seven agents from various government alphabet agencies. Each agent was handpicked by Dupé for reasons no one quite understood, but Nelson suspected it had something to do with a group's viability. Any agent with a big ego or their own agenda would never get an invite. Each member had to have experience and expertise in certain areas. When put together on a team, those experiences and skills formed a complete taskforce that could take on special missions. The SCVC taskforce had an eighty-five percent success rate at closing cases. The highest of all the taskforces, but the others weren't far behind.

"Wait a minute." Thinking about the experts on his team, Nelson suddenly had an idea. "Let me see that ledger again."

He stood and opened the book to a set of pages. Taking out his phone, he snapped a picture of the coded words.

"What are you doing?"

"Bobby Dyer, one of the guys on my team, is an expert at everything. Computers, creating backstop identities, anything involving communications. Maybe, just maybe, he knows how to decode these ledgers."

That earlier spark of hope reignited in her eyes. She touched her mouth with her fingers, trying to suppress a smile. "Seriously?"

Nelson attached the picture to an email and quickly typed a note to Dyer. "Worth a try, right? And if he doesn't know how to decode it, I bet he knows someone who does."

A small shot of glee came from Sophie, and she jumped up, throwing her arms around Nelson even before he'd finished sending the email. She showered his cheeks and neck with light kisses. "*Gracias*, thank you."

Catching her up in his arms, he lifted her for a second and set her back on her feet. She would actually make a great taskforce member, except for one thing. "As far as being on the VC Taskforce, I bet Dupé would love to have you. You have the skills and experience, but..." Her brown eyes were so trusting, so happy at the moment, he hated to state the obvious. "You're not exactly a team player, Soph. Dupé knows that. Hell, everyone knows that."

She released him and tried to step back, but he didn't let her go far. "I know, but...I couldn't be a team player before now."

She glanced away, still caught in his embrace, but searching for emotional distance. "All these years, I've been chasing Angelique. Not every assignment was about her, of course, but somewhere in the back of my mind it was. Everything I've done, including all the cases I've worked, I've been trying to make up for letting her down. Not just her, either. I want to save all the girls like her. I let my mother and my grandmother down by not keeping Angel safe. If I could save anyone, any young girl, I took the case, but my entire focus has always been on finding Angel. I didn't have time to be a on a taskforce. A partner would only slow me down, get in my way."

He drew her close again. She had to tip her head back to look at him. "And now?"

Her hands came up to rest on his upper chest, palms open. The heat of them seared him through his dress shirt. Here he was again, in the same situation as before. She'd lied to him, and now she was seducing him into helping her find her sister. Now that they'd failed, he expected she would kick him out.

Instead, her gaze dropped to his lips, and she whispered, "Are you going to leave me again when this is over?"

A part of him knew it was true, he *would* leave her. She was obsessed with finding her sister. She was FBI to her bones. She had no more time for a long-term, romantic relationship than she did for a partner. "Are we talking about finding Angelique? Or are we talking about...us?"

He waited for her to say, "there is no us", or something to that effect. Her lips parted, then closed. On a heavy sigh, she admitted, "Our jobs are not conducive to a relationship."

There it was. Finally, she was telling the truth.

"But..." She rose up on her tiptoes and brushed his lips with hers. "We do have tonight."

Nelson loved the feel of her lips. The taste of them. They were soft and warm and tasted like cinnamon.

The floral scent of her perfume drifted to him softly, her damp hair carrying the smell that rocked him back on his heels. He shouldn't do this, take advantage of her when she was emotionally vulnerable.

He checked himself as Sophie's tongue teased his lips open. Who was taking advantage of who?

He moved her around, dragging her into the living room. As he cupped her ass cheeks, she split her legs and he raised her off the floor, those sexy legs of her wrapping around his hips.

Her body locked against his, arms around his neck, her pelvis rubbing against his erection. Their tongues collided in the dance they both knew all too well, teasing and exploring each other's mouths.

The bedroom was out. He wasn't going to make it that far. Breaking the kiss, he placed his mouth against her neck and ran his tongue up to her earlobe. "Sophie? You sure about this?"

"Oh, God," she said, exasperation coating her words. "Of course, I'm sure. I don't kiss anyone I don't intend to get busy with. And just so you know, it's been a damn long time since I kissed anyone."

Like two years? It was unrealistic to believe this hot-blooded woman would be a nun, but at the thought of her sleeping with anyone else, a growl issued from his throat.

He kissed her, hard, wanting to erase the image of her in bed with another man.

Returning his kiss with ardor, she tightened her legs around him. He firmed a hand against the back of her neck and staggered to the couch. As he set her down, she gave him an evil grin, her hands removing her shirt in a quick and easy up-and-over motion.

Breasts. *Full. Display.*

Fuck. She was so damn beautiful.

The shirt landed on the floor and Nelson shoved the coffee table out of the way. The disk skidded off, landing on the floor.

Leaning down, he kissed her neck down to her shoulder. Her hands raked through his hair, down to his back, nails digging in as she pulled him closer and parted her knees.

"I've thought of this a hundred times," he said, eyeing her skin, her breasts, her flat stomach.

"A thousand," she moaned, sliding her hands under his shirt and impatiently unbuttoning it.

He straightened his arms and let her tug the shirt off, then dropped his mouth to one of her glorious nipples.

She arched into his mouth and moaned again. He moaned as well. So good. So sweet. So...

Hot.

His little firecracker.

Sucking harder, drawing the nipple out, he gently bit it. Her knees went wider still and she grabbed his ass, shoving his erection into the sweet spot between her legs.

Too much fabric. Between their pants, there was too much barrier.

He needed her out of her pants. Needed to be skin to skin.

ASAP.

Breaking away, he stood her up, switching gears so fast, she laughed and swayed on her feet. A quick zip and her pants were open. He peeled the damp fabric clinging to her skin down, down, down.

Baring her to him.

Oh, yes. This was what he wanted.

She was commando and the sight of her sex, engorged and ready for him, made him swear under his breath.

The pants pooled around her ankles and she kicked them off, then her deft fingers went to work on him.

Unbuckle. Unzip. *Whoosh.* Fresh breeze on his own commando parts and no more pants between them.

"Damn," she said, staring at his erection. "It's even bigger than I remember."

His ego caught fire, pride racing through him and making him jut out that much more. She licked her lips and smiled.

But if she did that again—that lip-licking—he was going to lose it.

She did him one better.

She moved forward and kissed him. Right. *There.*

"Mmm," she murmured.

Holy Mother of God.

Her tongue shot out and licked him. Just the tip, where her lips had just been, one of her hands tickling him from the underside.

Grabbing her by the hair, he eased her back. "Keep that up, *mi cariño*, and this will be over before you can blink."

She peered up at him, a wicked grin once more on her face. "As I recall, you have a remarkably fast reset button."

Only with her. Their one night together, he couldn't get enough of her. He'd been like a rabbit mainlining Powerade. "You do that to me. Make me want it over and over again, as much and as fast as I can get it."

With another of those lascivious licks of her lips, she arched back, raising her chest so her breasts pointed up at him. She spread her knees so her sex was on full display as well. "Take it. It's yours. As many times and as hard as you want it."

Fuck me. Fifty Shades of Sophie all over again.

She stretched out on the couch, wiggling her fingers at him. "Let's see if you're as fantastic as I remember."

He needed no further invitation. Climbing onto the couch, he grabbed her hips and positioned her the way he wanted her. With a quick jerk to elevate her pelvis, he drove into her.

She cried out, her slick folds accepting him, hips bucking to meet his thrusts. He watched her throat work as she said his name over and over again, watched her beautiful, full breasts rocking with the rhythm.

Wild. Unbidden.

It's yours.

He let go. Let himself fall into her heat and her wildness. In order to do that, he had to let go of the past and only focus on the here and now.

On Sophie.

The storm gathering inside him was building too fast. He couldn't hold back...couldn't...

Both of Sophie's hands slapped his butt cheeks and she arched, crying out as the orgasm struck. He slowed her, milking her, but his own release was following quickly on the heels of hers. He had to buck, had to move hard and fast again.

As if sensing his need, she increased the pressure on his ass and started undulating once more under him. "More," she ground out. "I want more."

Happy to accommodate, he rode her, gathering speed and building the momentum again. Their bodies, locked at the hips, couldn't possibly have gotten closer, but it felt like it to Nelson as she met him thrust for thrust, begging in Spanish for "more, more, more!"

The momentum hit the wall and Nelson froze, his erection spasming deep inside her. Over and over, he came in a blinding force of heat, Sophie consuming him.

His release caused another orgasm inside her, the tight walls milking him. Rubbing against him, she mewed, pressing down on him until he thought she would push both of them right through the bottom of the couch.

The couch held, and in the aftermath, as Nelson's arms gave out and Sophie pulled him close, he sank into her and knew he was gone. He would never feel this close to another woman again.

CHAPTER EIGHTEEN

Sophie woke to a rumble that wasn't thunder. The spot between her thighs ached and she rolled over and stretched languidly.

The noise was coming from downstairs. She patted Nelson to see if he heard it too, only her hand hit air and then the sheet where he'd slept next to her, making love to her all night.

The rumbling grew louder. Hastily, she dressed, throwing on a pair of jeans and a long-sleeve shirt before raking her hair up into a ponytail. Forgetting shoes, she hustled out of the apartment to see what was going on.

The rain had stopped, the early morning still and dark. At the bottom of the stairs, on the patio, sat a motorcycle.

The rider, dressed once more in his biker gear, killed the motor and tossed her a helmet. The horizon was lavender, no clouds or fog this morning.

Nelson's face was deep in shadows, but she felt his gaze slide over her. "Let's go."

A shiver ran down her spine at the sound of his voice. Or maybe it was caused by the memory of him doing wicked things to her all night. The damp, cold concrete made the bottoms of her feet itch. "Where?"

Nelson glanced over his shoulder, scanning the grounds for guards, she guessed, before facing her again. He lowered his voice. "The pill mill. You said it's about eight miles from here, right? I want to check it out. Will anyone be there this time of the morning?"

She racked her brain to remember the warehouse schedule. "The employees work from seven at night until three in the morning. They box everything up from three to four a.m. and the truck picks up the merchandise at four a.m. sharp. What time is it?"_

"Close to five. Let's check it out. I want to see if there is anything besides drugs there."

He was still looking for the missiles. She tossed the helmet back to him, and turned for the stairs. "Let me grab my shoes and a jacket."

A minute later, she stood beside him, eyeing the bike. The backpack with the ledgers was dangling from her hand.

The bike was black with silver chrome, running with a low, growly rumble. A track of black dirt cut through the garden. Rodrigo would have Nelson's head for that.

A bumper sticker was plastered to the leather seat where her butt was supposed to go. "My other ride is an army tank," it read.

Was she really going to do this? Climb on the back of his motorcycle and let him take her off into the night?

Well, technically it was morning, but still. She'd never been on a bike in her life. Bikes were dangerous, wild. Little Gran had always warned her against them and the boys who rode them. What if he lost control and the two of them went down in a cloud of dust and chrome and broken bones?

Nelson was staring at her. "Are we going to do this today?"

Sophie swallowed. Inched her foot closer. Stared at the bumper sticker. Did they have to take the bike?

She was about to ask the question out loud when she saw Nelson grin from the corner of her eye. He leaned forward, caught her around the waist and brought her close.

Wrapping a hand around the back of her neck, he pulled her head down so he could speak in her ear. He smelled like fresh air and dirty bars. Old leather and bike fumes. His hair tickled her nose.

"Scared?" he muttered in her ear over the roar of the bike. His lips grazed her earlobe, his breath hot and seductive against her skin.

Oh, yeah, she was scared. Nelson Cruz and a motorcycle the devil would love. What woman in her right mind wouldn't be terrified?

Except fear was one thing she never gave into. Ever.

Nelson drew back, eyeing her, and gunned the motor, making her startle. His grin grew into a challenging smile. "Store the backpack in the saddle bag."

She narrowed her eyes. Freedom beckoned with that smile of his. Eight miles of empty desert roads to the warehouse on a bike with a man who'd once again stolen her heart. Made her believe she wasn't alone on her quest to find Angel and bring down Morales.

The weight of the past on her shoulders, taking up so much mental space, suddenly lifted. It wasn't the freedom in his smile seducing her onto the bike, although that was hard to resist. It was the freedom of moving on with her life.

Yet, somehow, climbing onto that bike meant giving up something buried deep inside her. The thing that had been driving her all these years. The warehouse held no clues about Angelique. Going there wouldn't decode the ledgers or offer up any fresh evidence against Morales. Her case against the drug cartel leader was already solid.

Yet, Nelson hadn't hesitated to go to the snake pit and help her find the ledgers. The missiles weren't crucial to her operation, but they were crucial to *him*.

And right now, he was all she cared about.

She jammed the backpack in the side saddlebag.

Her foot moved of its own accord, her hand landing on his shoulder for balance. Pulse jumping, she swung her leg over the seat, planting her butt on the worn sticker.

The bike vibrated under her and she caught Nelson's smile in the rearview as it turned, knowing. He'd known she'd rise to the challenge.

But she wasn't doing it to prove anything to him. She was doing it for her.

He handed her the helmet again. The Savages logo was on both sides, reminding her once more that her whole life was about lies and subterfuge. Undercover ops and false identities.

Who am I?

She didn't want safety. Didn't want the damn helmet. She wanted freedom and danger and a new life free of the past.

A new life with Nelson Cruz.

Stop it.

Getting on this bike with him did not constitute a new life. But for a few more hours, it would be just the two of them. That was enough.

Tossing the helmet aside, she leaned into his back and wrapped her arms around his waist. "What are you waiting for?" she said over the growl of the bike.

And then as they shot out of the garden toward the compound gate, she laid her head on his back, enjoying the way the muscles there flexed as he steered them for the open road.

The guard at the gate didn't stop them, Nelson giving him a wave as he didn't wait for the iron gates to open fully before gunning the bike and jetting through.

They rode away from the compound, Sophie's hair blowing around her face and streaming behind her in the wind. The ground was wet from the previous night's rain, night-blooming flowers dotting the landscape here and there.

The beauty of the Morales acreage was soon left behind. On the outskirts of the city, they passed outcroppings of homemade lean-tos surrounded by mud. The sun-lined faces of old ladies already up and cooking over open fires turned toward them when they heard the rumble of the bike.

Somewhere in the midst, Sophie knew Rosalie was counting

her winnings from the previous day and dreaming of a new life in America.

The lavender sky turned dusky pink, then peach, as they drove east toward the desert, the miles licking away under the bike's wheels. The two-lane highway was empty except for an occasional truck heading toward Tijuana.

Another mile and Sophie saw the first rays of true sunlight break over the horizon. Tucking her legs closer to Nelson's, she watched the passing air dance in the curls of his hair, let her gaze linger on the back of his deeply tanned neck. What if they were just a biker couple off on an adventure? They could just keep riding, go wherever they wanted, stop whenever they grew tired.

They topped a hill and she saw the glint of the warehouse roof in the distance. The thrill of freedom and the little daydream she'd been entertaining dissolved like the fog burning off from the rising sun's rays.

The warehouse was of cheap construction, half-hidden in a valley and faded from the sun. A part of her wanted to ignore it, pretend she didn't see it, so they could keep riding.

Was this how Angelique had felt when she'd run away from home? The freedom, the anonymity? The ability to disappear and reinvent your life?

Just like Angel, Sophie couldn't outrun her grief. Her sister had ended up in the hands of a human trafficker, and while Sophie knew that wouldn't happen to her if she kept going on this road with Nelson, at some point, the bike would stop and her responsibilities would come crashing down on her.

"Is that it?" Nelson's voice was a loud wakeup call.

Sophie nodded, then realized he wasn't looking at her in the side mirror. He couldn't see her nod. She pointed over his shoulder at the building and gave him a thumbs up.

"Guards?" he said. "Cameras?"

Product was never left in the building during the day. "No

cameras," she called over the bike's noise. "No guards, except when workers are present so they don't help themselves."

Still, as Nelson pulled the bike off the road and onto the sandy ground, Sophie scanned the area for anyone hanging around. The sun continued to rise in the east, illuminating the tops of the low-lying hills. The warehouse lay in shadows.

Being on the noisy bike and approaching the warehouse head-on made her feel exposed. A target. Only Nelson's presence—his shear confidence—kept her from cowering behind him. On his bike, he was her shield. A warrior that knew fear but gave it no heed. She was used to being that person; that morning, it was nice to lay her armor down.

Dust rose around them, the desert ground already dry. No shots rang out, no men appeared. A wire fence ran around the perimeter with signs in Spanish and English warning intruders away. Red-brown rust edged the bottoms of the building's walls, a disease eating the warehouse from the ground up.

Nelson slowed the bike to a crawl. Sophie felt the low rumble more acutely in her blood, her bones, as they crawled across the sand than when they'd flown down the highway doing eighty.

The gate was chained and padlocked. No surprise. Nelson wheeled the bike around to the north side of the building and into the deeper shadows. He cut the engine and Sophie's ears rang with a phantom vibration.

Nelson waited for her to get off the bike before he dismounted. His boots crunched the rocks under them as he walked the side of the fence. "Doesn't seem to be electrified," he murmured, all business.

Sophie decided she was the only electrified thing in the general vicinity. The boots, the biker jacket, the fact she'd just rode over eight miles with her arms around his waist...it left her on edge. What was wrong with her? She'd rode with her head on his shoulder, and all of her female parts vibrating to the rhythm of his bike, wishing for a life that would never be hers.

Memories of the previous hours in bed with him had been playing through her head the whole time.

And now he strutted around the warehouse toward the front gate as if he owned the place. She followed on trembling legs, trying to tame her anxiety and wild thoughts.

I'm losing it.

His muscled arms jerked on the padlock. It didn't give, so he continued to the south side of the fence. Looking for holes? A back way in?

She stopped at the corner where Nelson was surveying the loading dock. An old army truck was backed up to the building. One of its tires was flat. Two windows, high up on the building, were caked with dust.

Nelson glanced back and motioned her over. "Come on," he said, lacing his fingers together to make a stirrup with his hands. "I'll boost you up."

"You're kidding, right?"

He grabbed the fence with one beefy hand and shook it links. "It's not electrified. We can climb over."

There was no barbed wire at the top either. Didn't mean she relished climbing the fence and hopping over to the other side. "It's at least ten feet tall."

"So?" He glanced at the top of the fence, back at her. "Don't tell me you're afraid of heights."

First a bike ride, now fence climbing. She'd been undercover with a dangerous cartel leader for nine months and, in all that time, she hadn't felt as wild and daring as she did right now. "I wouldn't have made it past Quantico if I were afraid of heights."

Ignoring his offer of help, she rubbed her hands together, grabbed the fence, and started up.

His soft chuckle settled her nerves. The fence shimmied as he began climbing as well.

Once he'd cleared the top, he dropped to the ground. Sophie was not so adventurous. She climbed halfway down the other side before letting go.

Strong hands gripped her waist at the same time her feet touched the ground, keeping her from losing her balance. She started to turn, but his hands held her hips in place. He pulled her back against his body, his mouth going just above her ear. "Look at that sunrise," he said.

Really? He was taking time to watch the sunrise?

But then she looked, and yes, indeed, it was a stunner. Streaks of vibrant peach and pink spread from the golden globe breaking over the hilltop. Long bars of sunlight striped the land and bathed her face in warmth.

The feel of Nelson's strong body against her back, supporting her, and the weight of his hands on her hips, gave her a sense of peace. Lifting her chin and closing her eyes, she let the feeling wash over her along with the sun's warmth. Her body relaxed against his and she drew in a deep breath. "It's beautiful."

Nelson's chest vibrated as he spoke soft and low in her ear. "So are you."

She turned in his arms, rose up on her toes, and kissed him gently. He snugged her into his body and kissed her back, a slow exploration.

Warmth that had nothing to do with the sun flushed her skin. It made her part her lips and allow him access.

She was strong on the outside, but not all the way through. All it took was a touch from him, a smile, and she was toast.

The pull of what he had to offer was strong. Too strong. But she couldn't completely lose focus. Not until she finished this operation and found the truth about her sister.

"Nelson." She broke the kiss, hating herself, but knowing this…this…whatever it was she had with him…was not real life. It was a product of the long, lonely hours she'd spent undercover. The long, lonely life she'd lived. She still had a job to do and so did he. "We better look for those missiles."

He laid his forehead against hers, eyes half-lidded. "You make me want to forget all of this and run away."

The words caught her off guard. Her throat closed up. It was as if he'd read her mind.

But only because he, too, had to know that regardless of what had happened earlier, when this operation was over, so were they.

The light filtering through the dirty windows was dim. Nelson found a switch on the wall and, a moment later, industrial lighting overhead flooded the warehouse. Rows of work tables took up the center of the concrete floor, each work station equipped with a light, a magnifying glass bolted to the table top, a box of latex gloves, thin metal blades for cutting the product, and cutting boards. At the front and back, raised walkways allowed guards to watch the workers and guard the product.

On the north side was one long, open shelving unit, flat boxes, tape, and other supplies jumbled on it. There were no other rooms, not even a restroom. The ceiling was open to the rafters.

Dollars to donuts, there were no missiles, hidden or otherwise.

Sophie circled the room, appearing to look for them anyway. She'd suddenly turned all business and now was keeping her distance.

One minute, she was a controlled and disciplined FBI agent, the next, a minx in his bed. And as soon as he showed her the tiniest amount of emotion, she turned tail and ran.

What did you expect? This was her modus operandi. He'd been through this same scenario before, yet, here he was again, falling for her body while he didn't understand her mind.

Yet, he was getting closer to figuring her out. Anyone who'd ever cared about her had died or left her. Coming from a close family like he did, he couldn't imagine what that was like.

While his mother had passed a few years ago from a heart attack, his father was still alive and kicking in New Mexico. Nelson saw him and the handful of siblings living close to their childhood home a couple times a year. He and his sister, Brenda, were the only two in California. Both of them had been less traditional than their counterparts and wanted more than a white picket fence and two-point-five kids. Brenda had wanted to be an actress. She'd moved to L.A., done the normal waitressing gigs, and even found an agency to represent her. One walk-on role in a film had landed her a commercial. She'd believed her career was taking off.

Then she had a one-night stand with a fellow struggling actor and no condom and that was all it took. Fiercely independent, she struggled hard to give Carly the best life she could have. It was difficult on a bank teller's salary, and Nelson secretly picked up some of Carly's medical bills so Brenda could pay her rent and utilities. One of the specialists Carly saw had suggested a service dog to help out. One trained to warn Carly, Brenda, and Carly's other care givers when she was about to have a seizure. Brenda had taken on some part-time typing projects at home to pay for one, but at the rate the fund was growing, Carly would be grown before they could afford it.

Sophie was proud and independent like Brenda. Nelson knew she'd turned her grief, guilt, and loneliness inside, locking her ragged emotions away. Normal relationships were alien to her. The moment she started feeling something for him or anyone else, she panicked.

He watched her checking every table and every corner of the room for possible hidden doors or clues as to whether or not the missiles were nearby. While her back was turned to him, he admired her sweet backside.

Suddenly, as if she felt his eyes on her, she whirled. "My ass may be big, but I assure you, it's not big enough to hide missiles."

Busted.

"Your ass is perfect, and it's a lot more interesting to look at than this ugly pill mill." He took the stairs up to one of the guard walkways. "Tell me what goes on here."

"Oxycodone and other narcotics shipped to the local low cost clinics are intercepted and brought here. They're mixed with a new designer drug that comes from Mexico City. The oxycodone is broken down, half of it replaced with inert ingredients like baking soda and repackaged for the clinics. The other half is mixed with the designer drug and blended with sugar or sea salt, then repackaged as bath salts. It's hauled across the border to America where it's sold."

Nelson felt two pieces of his brain snap together. "Project Bliss."

"What?"

"The taskforce has been working undercover on tracking down the source of an influx of designer bath salts for months. They're close too, but they don't know it's Morales."

"There are probably several Mexican suppliers, not just him."

He fumbled in his back pocket for his phone. "Still, I better call Coop."

"Did you hear anything back from your other guy about the ledgers?"

In fact, he had a text from Dyer. He hadn't noticed because it had come in when they were in transit on the bike.

Call me was all the text said.

Could be good, could be bad.

Dyer or Cooper, who should he call first?

Sophie was staring at him with her windblown hair and dark, shining eyes.

Dyer it is. "A text came in from him a few minutes ago. He wants me to call him."

Her face brightened and she moved close as he dialed. Dyer answered on the second ring and Nelson put him on speaker. "Sorry, man. It's a no-go on decoding that text. If it were computer code, I might have been able to figure it out, but a code written in Spanish is just gibberish to me."

Sophie dropped her head back looking at the ceiling. Her whole body screamed defeat.

Nelson wasn't accepting that. "Don't you have a buddy somewhere in the bowels of the government or some backwoods bar that could have a look?"

"Better than that. I forwarded it to Sara Rios."

"The fugitive apprehension agent? Why?"

"She's former CIA. An analyst. Years of experience decoding messages and other intelligence lingo. And…she just happens to be in your neck of the woods at the moment."

Sophie's head snapped back up. She lifted her dark brows at Nelson.

"Rios is in Tijuana?" he said.

"With Coop."

What the hell? Nelson turned off the speaker, bringing the phone back to his ear. Sophie watched him carefully. He turned his back on her and walked a few feet away. "What's going on? Did Bliss go sideways?"

"Nah. Ronni, Thomas, and Mitch Holton have that covered for now. Dupé has them laying low until Coop gets back to town."

"Why is Harris here?" *He better not be thinking he's dragging me back to San Diego.*

"Coop got new intel on Chica Bonita, something Dupé deemed more critical to check out. Seems someone is using the place again to traffick girls. They're showing up with forged papers and being placed with families who aren't actual blood relations, although their papers claim they are. The girls appear to be orphans and runaways, no one on the Mexico side who even knows they exist, hence why they're being picked up.

"We don't know how many have made it through, but the CI who talked to Coop had heard about three arriving in the past month. They're all underage, all of them with horror stories of past abuses by cartels around Mexico City and farther south. If they escape and make it to Chica Bonita, a couple women take them to a safe house along the border where they're given a set of papers. Later, another woman takes them into a tunnel that runs under the border crossing, and they're placed in a new home in America. They get enrolled in school and are officially adopted by their new family."

An underground railroad for illegals. Not the first time he'd heard about one, but this was unusual.

"Since you're tied up with Agent Diaz," Dyer continued, "Cooper took Rios and Holton with him to check it out. Dupé thinks it's bogus, that the girls are still drug mules and these so-called families are part of a larger operation. He wants Cooper to track down the women running the railroad and find out who's providing the papers for these girls. They're good, these papers. Looks like a real professional."

"A government agent?"

"Most likely that or a former agent with experience creating fake IDs."

The back of his neck tingled. He took a second to process what Dyer had just told him, because the images pinging around in his head weren't good ones.

"Nelson?" Sophie's voice cut through what Dyer was saying about catching up with Cooper and letting Sara Rios look at the ledgers. The soft brush of fingertips down his back alerted him to her very near presence. "Is everything okay?"

He turned slowly to face her, knowing that the fake Sophie, the one who pretended to care about him when all she really wanted was for him to drop off the face of the earth and not screw up her operation, was the one touching his back.

"I'll catch up with you later, man," he said to Dyer, moving away from those lying fingers as he hung up. Dyer was still talking, but Nelson didn't care. He couldn't focus on anything right now except the hollow ringing in his ears.

"This CIA analyst can't decipher the files, either, can she?"

Sophie's sad smile and deflated shrug seemed genuine. "It was a long shot, but thank you for trying."

He sent a text to Coop. *Where are you?* Then motioned at Sophie. "Let's get out of here."

His abrupt turnabout didn't seem to faze her. They snuck out the back door, locked up, and went over the fence. He was climbing on his motorcycle when his phone buzzed.

Cooper. His reply text was an address, one Nelson knew well. A biker bar two miles down the road from Chica Bonita where the Savages hung out.

Sophie's arms slipped around his waist. *Be there in thirty,* he texted back. *I have information you need to know.*

He pocketed his phone, started the bike, and shot down the highway.

CHAPTER NINETEEN

Sophie hopped off the bike. Her stomach was rumbling, calling for breakfast.

The helmet she'd tossed earlier lay in the mud. She waited for Nelson to shut off the bike's engine but he started backing it up, heading away.

"Where are you going?" she called over the din of the motor.

He stopped backing up the bike, head down. Why wasn't he looking at her?

Finding out that Nelson's team couldn't decipher the coded ledgers had been the last straw. When the time came, she would turn them over to the FBI with the rest of the evidence she still had in her possession. Like she had explained to Nelson, it would take months before someone in the Bureau figured out everything written in them, but she had no other choice now.

Nelson killed the bike's engine. He glanced around, keeping an eye out for security, until finally his gaze landed on her.

Not her face, though. He was staring at her kneecaps.

His voice was low, quiet. "I have to go meet someone outside of town. Stay here. You'll be safe."

"You're leaving? What if Guido or one of his men shows up?"

"At five-thirty in the morning? Guido's still in his pajamas and his men are sleeping off last night's party. I have the security team here up to snuff. Stay inside these walls, stay inside your apartment with the door locked. I won't be gone long."

He still hadn't looked at her. "What is this about?"

"My other operation. Chica Bonita." Ever so slowly, his gaze rose to hers. "There's been a new discovery. My boss is in town to check it out."

Her stomach suddenly did a nose dive. There was no point in asking further questions. She could see by the set of his chin he wasn't going to answer anything. In fact, he looked like he was about to haul her upstairs, handcuff her to the bed, and start asking *her* questions.

"I'm coming with you," she said, heading for the bike.

He backed up another foot, keeping her at a distance. "No you're not."

She kept charging. "Maybe I can help."

Another foot. He held out a hand to stop her. "You can't."

"How do you know?"

His mouth twitched as if he were subduing a smirk or maybe a curse. "Because I know."

What was he hiding? "Either you take me, or I'll get one of your security goons to drive me."

"You don't know the address."

"There aren't that many places outside of town where you would meet someone. I'll go door to door until I find you."

The smirk broke free. "Goddamn, you're stubborn."

"Little Gran said it was a gift."

"Little Gran was a good cook but she was crazy."

She slapped his arm. "She was not."

He chuckled, then grew serious again. "I'm seeing my boss. You go with me and he might force you to go back to America before we get Morales."

Sophie leaned forward and patted his cheek. "Oh, Nels, haven't you learned by now that no one forces me to do anything I don't want to do?"

Before she knew it, he grabbed her wrist. "You need to trust me and sit this one out, Soph. I'm not kidding. Let me go see my boss and find out what's going down with Chica Bonita. Then I'll be back to finish this op with Morales."

Trust him. After the past twenty-four hours, it should come naturally.

It didn't.

She wanted to—*God how I want to*. She'd trusted him with her body. Trusted him with the truth about the ledgers.

But could she trust him not to blow her operation? Not just Morales but the lost girls too? "What's going on at Chica Bonita that would bring him down here when we're ready to arrest Morales and end it anyway?"

"I can't share that."

"Of course you can't. Let me play devil's advocate here, though. What happens if your boss decides to shut down whatever's going on at Chica Bonita before I arrest Morales for the rest of his cartel dealings? What then, Nels?"

He pulled her closer, turned her hand around and kissed her palm. "I won't hang you out to dry, I swear." His eyes were earnest, his tone sincere. "No matter what happens with Cooper Harris and Chica Bonita, I will be back to help you take down Morales tomorrow."

She believed him. The realization came like a roller coaster, building, building, building and then winging over the crest. Her stomach went into free fall. A sweet lightheadedness made her head swim.

I trust him.

A new form of hope sang in her veins. Sophie gave his hand a hard squeeze, then stepped back, her fingers sliding through his ever so slowly as he reluctantly let go. "Thank you, Nels."

He opened his mouth as if he were going to say something else. Then he shut it and released her hand fully. For a long moment, he sat staring at her. Quiet. Resolute.

"Hurry back." Sophie blew him a kiss and watched him ride away.

Thirty minutes later
Outskirts of Tijuana

Cooper heard an approaching bike.

He'd heard bikes come and go all night from the apartment above the bar. The place rented by the hour, but for him and Agent Rios, he'd cut a deal. Twenty-four hours and silence about their presence in exchange for a sizable wad of cash and the promise he would overlook certain abuses of the law going on downstairs.

He didn't want to arrest anyone; this was Mexico after all. Not his jurisdiction. But he had plenty of contacts and friends, in low places as well as high, that could make the owner of the bar's life hell if he chose to get in touch.

Glancing out the upstairs window, he saw the wild hair and the vest and knew it was another Savage. Not just any Savage, though.

Nelson Cruz had heard he was in town.

The bike pulled up out front and Cruz dismounted. He looked up, caught sight of Cooper in the upstairs apartment window. Cooper motioned for him to come around back.

Cruz took something out of the motorcycle's saddlebags, then hoofed it around back. Ten seconds later, there was a knock at the door.

"Yo," Cooper said.

Cruz entered, a leather bound book in his hands. "Couldn't stay away, huh, boss?"

If only. "If you'd done your job and taken out Chica Bonita like you were supposed to, I wouldn't need to be here."

Cruz knew he was kidding and the two did their normal manly hand grasp, half-pat on the back hello. Dust rose from Cruz's vest where Cooper slapped him.

"Dyer said you brought Rios with you and you're looking into some underground railroad?"

Cooper returned to his post at the window. The sandy area around the bar was so dry, it was hard to imagine it had poured last night. "The papers the illegals are carrying are quality stuff. ICE and the Bureau believe there may be a dirty agent down here helping these women with the paperwork."

There was a long pause as Cruz stared him down. "You're looking for a dirty agent?"

Cooper stared back. He needed coffee.

Cruz folded his arms over his chest. "What branch? FBI? ICE?"

That was the dig. "Could be any of them. Agent Rios is in town right now asking around about runaway girls. Where they go, where they hang out, where they disappear to. She's pretending to be looking for her little sister's friend who ran away from home and is determined to get to America after a drug cartel killed her parents. I'm hoping Rios can infiltrate this underground railroad and figure out who's in charge."

"Damn." Cruz smacked the book down on the table. "I was hoping she was here."

"Why?"

"I need her to look at this ledger. The entries are written in code. Dyer said Rios could probably figure it out."

Cooper cocked his chin at the book. "Something in particular you're looking for in that one?"

Cruz's silence told him all he needed to know. Agent Sophie Diaz was the one interested in what the ledger said, not Cruz. "How is your charge? I'm surprised you didn't bring her with you."

"Diaz? Fine."

"Ready for the sting tomorrow?"

"Chomping at the bit."

"She willing to share with the CIA?"

"Not on your life. She's worked this operation for nine months and now the CIA is going to blow in and take the credit."

"All they want is this European dealer. I'll make sure Diaz and the Bureau get Morales."

"Morales's little sister is home from Mexico City. We need to make sure she's safe before, during, and after this thing. She's only eleven and she's blind. She seems to have no idea her brother is a drug lord."

Every member of Cooper's taskforce had a conscience. It sometimes caused problems, but it made each of them better agents. "I'll do everything in my power to make sure the girl is safe."

"Agent Diaz will appreciate that, and so will I."

"Rios will be back in a little while." Cooper went to the wooden table and pulled out chair. "Meanwhile, I need to put eyes on Chica Bonita and figure out how these women are getting the girls through there."

He sat and showed Nelson a simple sketch he had of the property's layout. "You know the grounds and the building itself from your raid two years ago, right? You've been inside." He handed Cruz a pencil. "If you were using the place to run a smuggling operation, how would you go about it?"

The agent resisted sitting for a moment until Cooper shoved the chair across from him out with a kick of his booted foot. "Sit. I need help with this. You can get back to Agent Diaz in a few minutes. I assume you left her well-guarded."

"She's safe." Cruz dropped into the chair. "There's something else I need to tell you."

Cooper listened as Cruz explained about the warehouse where Morales manufactured his drugs. "Agent Diaz says by her calculations they're shipping out a hundred pounds of bath crystals every week, all headed to Southern California."

Morales was supplying bath salts to Southern Cali? Cooper's day just got brighter. "So at least one of our major suppliers could be out of business by Monday morning. If he's the only supplier, we can shut down Project Bliss."

The guy's knee bobbed up and down with nerves. "Possibly."

"Nice job, Cruz."

"I still didn't find those missiles."

"While I'd like our taskforce to get credit for finding them, that's not our gig. The CIA is in charge of those damn missiles. They should have done more to get eyes on them before tomorrow. But as long as Morales brings them to the drop point, and all goes as planned with the takedown, they'll be out of commission shortly."

Cruz tapped his thighs with his thumbs, looking at the table. "And what if the takedown doesn't go as planned, Coop?"

His agent new something he wasn't sharing. Had to be something with Agent Diaz again. "What are you worried about specifically?"

He shrugged, trying to look nonchalant. "There are too many players. Too many agendas. Maybe I've been under too long, but I got a bad feeling about this CIA thing."

Cooper did, too, but knew it was as much a part of his competitive nature as it was about worrying about the op blowing up. "None of the agencies play well with each other. That's part of the point of our taskforce, to create stronger bonds and reinforce solid communication. When Agent Rios gets back, I'm sure she'll have insight for us into the CIA's perspective."

Cruz didn't look like he cared about the CIA's perspective, but he picked up the pencil and started making notes on the sketch. "This is not an entrance. There's a service door back here. Under the platform is a hidden metal door to the basement. Like a storm cellar. If the women are using Chica Bonita for smuggling, I'd lay odds, this is where they're entering and leaving."

As he went on, giving Cooper a detailed account of the building's layout and the best spots for surveillance, Cooper sat back and listened. Whatever Cruz was hiding, he was still a damn good agent.

Cooper hoped Agent Diaz wasn't about to cut him off at the knees.

CHAPTER TWENTY

Sophie still hadn't gone inside. After Nelson had ridden away, she'd sat at the patio table, sending a text to Wanda Kohl in the States and watching the peacock and other birds make their way into the garden. So much had changed in the past few hours. *She* had changed.

Yes, she still wanted to know what had happened to her sister. She still wanted to shut down the Morales drug cartel and make sure Lexie had somewhere safe to go when Rodrigo landed in federal prison.

Then there were the girls she'd been helping sneak into America. She'd been over it and over it in her head, and there was no way she could continue helping Yolanda transport the Chica Bonita girls across the border. The upside was that once she put Morales out of business, he would no longer be able to use Chica Bonita for human trafficking or anything else, if he was indeed resurrecting it.

Another cartel leader would surely come along and Yolanda and her crew would renew their efforts to transport the lost girls into safer territory where they had a fighting chance to get a good education and live with a supportive family. There have been times in the last few months when Sophie had fantasized about leaving the FBI and devoting herself to the same cause, only from the right side of the law.

That was a fantasy. The only way she could bring about true

change and shut down the criminal enterprises involved in human trafficking was to stay in the Bureau.

Her phone buzzed with an incoming text. Wanda at Child Services. *Looking into an option for you to gain temporary custody of the girl until a permanent home can be found. I'll know more soon.*

Sophie sat back. Her take care of Lexie? Out of the question. She adored the girl, but Lexie shouldn't be forced to live with the undercover agent who had taken down her brother, and there was no way the Bureau would let Sophie do such a thing.

The fantasy about leaving the FBI flashed through her mind again.

Don't be ridiculous. The Bureau is all you have.

Except maybe she had Nelson too.

Nelson and Lexie all in one package. Now *that* was a fantasy.

Stomach grumbling and ready for some strong coffee, Sophie pushed out of the chair and went upstairs to her apartment.

Right as she opened the door, the hairs on the back of her neck stood straight up. Someone was inside.

Holding her breath and going completely still, she started to ever-so-slowly release the doorknob and step back when the door was jerked out of her hand and a man she hated stood in front of her.

"Sophie, you little minx. Where the hell have you been?"

He was ten pounds heavier than the last time she'd seen him and he was failing to grow a beard. Deep creases lined his forehead and the bags under his eyes sagged like weighted hammocks.

If there was a hell, the CIA was the devil. "Get out of my apartment, Agent Blue. You shouldn't be here."

"Where did you and your bodyguard go this morning?"

She shoved him backward and shut the door behind her, fearing that some guard might come by and overhear them. "None of your damn business."

"Not my business?" He pushed her up against the door, held her there. "This whole operation from front to back is my business. Now where's your bodyguard? I'd prefer he not walk in on us and try to kill me."

"He wouldn't be my bodyguard if it weren't for you and your stupid idea to take out a hit on me, *Guido.*"

The undercover operative who'd wormed his way into the Morales cartel five-plus years ago scratched his scraggly beard and chuckled. "I had no idea who he really was when I hired him to kill you. Although, I did think twice about hiring him at all, since he looked like he might actually be able to get the job done."

"Lucky for you, he's not a real Savage."

Blue leaned closer, his breath smelling like tequila at seven in the morning. "Lucky for *you*, you mean. Who does he work for? Is he one of you?"

"You didn't run his face through the CIA database in your spare time?"

"He's Agency?"

"Immigration, but he's better at his job than you are at yours."

"Is that why he's not here right now? He left you all alone when there's a hit out on your life? Doesn't seem too swift to me."

"He knows I can take care of myself."

For emphasis, she kneed him in the balls.

He was half a second ahead of her and managed to deflect. She still made contact with his thigh, causing him to flinch and grunt. That was all the opening she needed. Using her elbow, she landed a hard jab into his diaphragm and sent him down on his ass.

"Now tell me what the hell you're doing here," she said.

"God, you're a bitch." He gained his feet, chuckling and rubbing his sternum. "Did you find those ledgers?"

She wasn't the only one who wanted them. The details they provided were of interest to him and the CIA as well as her and her agency. One of the reasons he had infiltrated the cartel was because the CIA was suspicious of Ciro Morales's possible involvement with a Cuban Marxist group who had been funded by the Chinese government to gather intel on America's missile program. The CIA believed there were details of top secret information in those ledgers, as well as Ciro's contacts in the terrorist world.

Agent Blue thought Sophie was going to turn those ledgers over to him when she found them. In exchange, he'd offered to help her with the paperwork for the lost girls. She'd never planned to give the ledgers to him; he'd been unable to find them when he worked for Morales and then had gotten himself fired when Ciro had died and Rodrigo had taken over the reins. She may have wanted the ledgers for a different purpose, but they belonged to the FBI now.

"I don't have them." Thank goodness she had taken them with her that morning and then forgotten them in the saddlebags on Nelson's bike. Time to throw him off that bone. "Do you know about the exchange tomorrow?"

"Yeah. Agent Borcillo thinks he's going to finally nail this European asshole he's been chasing for the past sixteen months, but there are no missiles. I told Borcillo that a dozen times. I never saw any in the five years I worked for Ciro and you can't hide something like that. Whatever the kid is bringing to the table tomorrow, it ain't missiles."

"Rodrigo claims he's buying another exotic snake."

"Fucking nutcase. I hate that kid."

Suddenly, Sophie remembered the floppy disk Nelson had found in the trays of uncut diamonds. What was stored on that disk?

A new thought made her take a step back. Blue was right; there weren't any physical missiles.

Only the technology to *build* them.

"You need to leave," Sophie said, hustling him to the door. "Don't come back here again. I have less than twenty-four hours to finish this mission and I don't need you or anyone else, regardless of your agency credentials, blowing it for me. If everyone does their job, we'll all get what we want tomorrow."

"I need those ledgers," he snarled before backing towards the door. She liked the fact that he didn't feel safe turning his back on her. "If you screw this up, Agent Diaz, I will bring the full force of the CIA, and the president himself, down on your fat ass. I know all your dirty little secrets and I'll be happy to tell the Bureau every last one of them."

Sophie had never responded well to threats, or anyone calling her curves fat. This time was no exception. "Don't forget, I know a few of your secrets too. If I go down, you go down with me, Agent Blue, or whatever your name is."

He opened the door and shook a finger at her, but before he could say anything, a young girl's voice interrupted.

"Maria-Sophia? Are you up there? We came back early!"

Lexie.

"Shit," Agent Blue said. "Tell me that isn't who I think it is."

"It is." She shooed at him with her hands and lowered her voice. "You have to get out of here. Now. Rodrigo can't find you here."

"No problem. Let me just blink my eyes and turn invisible a second, 'cuz now instead of a seven guards to avoid, there are twice that many if Morales is back."

Sophie wanted to punch him. Her brain spun in chaotic circles. "Go out my window, shimmy down the trellis and make a run for it. I'll draw the guards to the front."

He warmed to the idea almost immediately "Maybe I should rough you up, first. Make it look like I was here to kill you."

Bastard. That would get Nelson in trouble for sure. "Try it, and you'll be the one who gets roughed up."

He bared his teeth, reached for her as if her challenge meant nothing.

"Maria-Sophia?" The girl's footsteps echoed on the stairs. "Are you home?"

"Damn kid," Blue swore under his breath.

Home. She didn't have a home. Hadn't in a very long time. Too bad this small space with Nelson had started to feel more like a home than a layover point.

She shoved Blue toward the window. "You're on your own."

He followed her, then whirled around at the last second. "Sorry, sweetheart. This is going to hurt."

She saw it in his eyes—he wasn't sorry at all as he struck her hard across the face. The force snapped her head back and she hit the edge of the couch.

"In case I get caught," he said, shoving the screen off the window and swinging his leg over the ledge. "I need to make sure Morales believes I came to kill you."

Reeling from the blow, she nevertheless flipped him the bird.

"See you tomorrow," he said, swinging the other leg through and disappearing.

"Maria-Sophia?" Lexie appeared in the open doorway with her dog. "Who were you talking to? Is Nelson here? We came back early. I didn't want to stay there any longer."

Sophie heard yelling down in the yard. She started to rush out, to create the distraction she'd promised, but then she heard gunfire. Grabbing Lexie, she hustled her inside. "Hey, I'm so glad to see you."

"What was that noise?" Lexie asked. "The sound was like firecrackers."

"Just a truck backfiring." Digging out her phone, Sophie pulled up Nelson's number. She needed to warn him, hoping against hope he would check his phone before he headed back to Casa Morales.

No matter how she spun this, he was going to be knee-deep in shit.

Better for him if he stays away.

Sophie typed the message, hit send, her cheek stinging like a son-of-a-bitch. "How was the beach?"

"Wet. And cold." Lexie stroked Harry's head. "Harry got sand in his fur. I had to brush it out. It took forever."

163

A second later, Rodrigo Morales burst through the door. He breathed a sigh of relief when he saw Lexie was safe.

Had his men caught Agent Blue?

Rodrigo's gaze snapped to Sophie's. His jaw tightened when he saw her red cheek. Blue had probably left a handprint there. "Where is your bodyguard?" Rodrigo demanded.

I'm on my own again, Sophie thought. *Better make this good.*

Nelson was ready to get out and head back to the Morales compound when Sara Rios returned.

"No luck," she told Cooper. "One person I spoke with said to go by the bingo hall in Old Tijuana later today, though. Said she's heard things about a women there who might have connections."

Nelson's throat suddenly felt tight. He cleared it. "What kind of connections?"

"Good to see you again, Agent Cruz." She shrugged off her jacket and tossed it on a chair. "Connections to Morales and Chica Bonita."

"You get a description of this woman?"

Both Harris and Rios shot him a suspicious look.

"What?" He shrugged. "I've been there with Sophie. I might have seen the gal."

"Where is Agent Diaz?" Rios asked.

"Back at the compound."

"Ah."

There was a lot unspoken in that simple "ah."

She'd brought coffee in Styrofoam cups up from the bar. She handed one to Harris, offered the second to Nelson.

He shook his head. He wanted the coffee, but Rios hadn't known he was there. If he took her cup, she'd be without.

She took off the lid and blew on the liquid. "The description my informant gave sounds like ninety percent of the women in Tijuana. Mixed Hispanic, medium height, twenty pounds overweight, dark hair and eyes, lots of jewelry. But she's apparently a regular at the hall and can be quite a…grumpy person. Everyone knows her, my contact said."

Jewelry. "Like bracelets?"

Rios jiggled her arm where a set of three metal bracelets clanged together. "Every woman around here wears bracelets. I'll go play bingo later today, and if she's as popular as my informant claimed, I should be able to find her."

"Did your source say anything about friendship bracelets? You know, the ones made of thread."

Harris was studying his map. "You taking up a new hobby, Cruz?"

Rios smiled at the joke. "Is that something I should keep an eye out for?"

He wasn't sure. "Nah, never mind." He handed her the ledger. "Can you look at this? It's a ledger Ciro Morales recorded a lot of important information in, but it's in code. Dyer thought, with your background in analysis, you might be able to crack it and tell Sophie what it says."

She thumbed through the pages. "Are you looking for something in particular?"

"Anything about the girls who came and went from Chica Bonita during the time period April to June of 2005."

Harris looked up. "What's so important about that?"

"Maybe nothing." He did not want to tell them, but he didn't really want to lie either. "It's a lead on a separate case that Agent Diaz is following. I told her I'd help her out."

Harris had just been preaching interagency cooperation, which seemed to work in Nelson's favor. He grunted his approval and went back to his map.

"I read the jacket on Rodrigo Morales on the way down," Rios said. "There's something I wanted to bring to your attention."

"What's that?"

She pulled out her phone, tapped the screen a couple of times, and showed Nelson a picture.

"This man. Do you know him?"

Bald head, tear drop tattoos. "Guido Ruiz. Rival of Morales and the one who put out the hit on Sophie."

"He's CIA."

Harris looked up. Nelson felt his insides crawl.

Rios showed the photo to Harris. "Did you know?"

Harris shook his head. "Hell, no. You sure?"

"I don't know him personally, but my source inside the Agency confirmed it." She tapped the screen again and brought up another photo, this one an official government one. "George Blue went undercover five years ago to try to recover advanced weapons technology the CIA believed had fallen into Ciro Morales's hands. HUMIN is his specialty."

Human Intelligence. The CIA had learned a hard lesson on 9/11 that drones and satellites couldn't replace on-the-ground operatives going undercover and gathering intelligence in person.

Nelson stared at the second photo. While Blue was younger and clean-shaven, the eyes were the same as Guido's.

Damn.

"He got in deep with Morales Senior and the cartel," Rios continued. "Even though he still hasn't recovered the weapons technology he originally went under for, the Agency has left him there to see what else he can find. He's been feeding credible intel back to the US since which has helped the Bureau, the Agency, and Homeland."

"What kind of weapons technology?" Harris asked.

"Specs for highly specialized missiles that went missing. Specs that had to be rebuilt from scratch. The US fears the missing intel is now in the hands of China or North Korea, but it may well be that Ciro died before he passed them on. They may still be in his son's possession."

"I'll be damned," Nelson said. "We were told Rodrigo might be exchanging missiles tomorrow for diamonds, but I can't find missiles on his property or at his warehouse."

Rios sipped coffee. "My source claims the operative tracking this European buyer insists Rodrigo has physical missiles."

"Well, if he does, I can't find them. Why the hell would Agent Blue put out a hit on Sophie?"

"Doubtful he knows she's an agent, and, well, he doesn't play by the rules."

Did anyone these days?

Harris blew out his lips and sat back. "What exactly are you saying?"

Rios set her phone on the table. "He's brutal. A killer. Even if he does know Agent Diaz is FBI, he wouldn't hesitate to get rid of her if his cover was in danger of being exposed or she got in his way."

"The CIA condones this?" Nelson asked.

"That's why he's good at cozying up to cartel leaders, but unfortunately, his integrity has been in question for quite some time. The Agency wanted to pull him out back when I was still with them. Blue was uncooperative. I don't know the details, but they decided to keep him under and use him best they could."

Inside his vest pocket, Nelson's phone vibrated. He drew it out, saw there was a text from Sophie, and turned his back on the others.

Morales is back early. I found your missiles.

Holy crap.

He paced to the window, hung an arm on the ledge, and stared out at the dusty parking lot. Morales coming back earlier was bad news. How was he going to explain his absence?

Rios sidled up next to him. "How are things working out with you and Agent Diaz?"

He shifted to be sure she couldn't see the screen on his phone. "Fine."

Subject closed.

Rios stared out the window. "She's a lone wolf. Protecting her can't be easy, since I'm sure she doesn't think it's necessary. From my own experience, I'd say she's like the hurricane currently moving up the coastline…she leaves a lot of debris in her wake."

He'd been part of that debris before. Maybe Rios knew that. Maybe she'd been left in the wake of Hurricane Sophie herself. Right now, he didn't give a damn.

Pocketing his phone, he gave Harris a nod and headed for the door. "Got to get back. I'll check in with you as soon as I can."

"Watch out for this Agent Blue," Harris said.

Nelson was more worried about Morales. "Send me that photo, will you?" he said to Rios. "The official version."

She nodded and he gave a wave over his shoulder, jogging down the back stairs as fast as he could go. His phone buzzed again in his hand.

Morales is raging that you're not here. I'll cover for you but stay away. I've got this.

Walking, talking Jesus, what had he gotten himself into?

…she's a lone wolf.

For half a second, he wondered if Morales was truly back and upset that his head of security was in absentia.

I've got this.

Was it possible that Sophie was trying to edge him out so she could take the credit for Morales's arrest the next day?

Things are different between us now, he reminded himself. *She wouldn't screw me over.*

As he hopped on the bike and gunned the motor, he prayed his trust in her was about to be rewarded.

"Rodrigo, please." Sophie eased away from the ice pack Morales held to her cheek. "I'm fine."

Still in her apartment, she sat on the sofa, Rodrigo across from her, using the coffee table as a chair. The cartel leader had seen his sister back to the main house and was now nearly breathing fire as he examined Sophie's injuries, but his touch was gentle as he wrapped a hand around the back of her neck and held her so he could lay the ice bag against her swelling cheek and fat lip. "No one invades my home and hurts someone I care about without repercussions."

She had to turn this around fast. Agent Blue had endangered them all. *Bastard.* "You care for me?"

She widened her eyes slightly and searched his face as if truly needing his confirmation.

His gaze dropped to her lips, rose slowly back up. "Lexie and I both have come to feel you are part of our family."

Dangerous territory ahead, the old cliché rang in her head.

But if it kept Rodrigo focused on anything besides his anger at Blue and Nelson, she had to plunge forward. "I feel the same."

His stare was long and dominating. Sophie forced herself to look down and away, her stomach revolting.

Rodrigo adjusted the bag. "I will kill Nico for leaving you alone. That was his main job, to keep you safe."

Back to that. "He received a tip that someone was hanging around the warehouse. I insisted he check it out. He didn't want to go, but... Rodrigo, we can't lose that warehouse. It's fifty percent of your income."

A muscle in his jaw jumped. "The warehouse was a decoy to get Nico to leave you."

"It was my call. I didn't give him a choice, and I felt safe here with all the new security. Guido claimed he got in by bribing a guard. Besides, he didn't come for me. You're right; the warehouse was a decoy, but not in the way you're thinking."

Morales cocked a brow. "How so?"

Sophie was glad for an excuse to draw free of his hand. She

crossed the room to the TV stand and shoved it out of the way. Dropping to her knees, she lifted the metal off a register that hadn't forced air through it in ages. Dust particles floated in the air as she lifted the grating and set it aside. Plunging her hand into the dark cavern under the floor, she felt around until her fingers touched cool plastic.

She'd retrieved the disk Nelson had confiscated from the pit and dropped it in there in preparation for the story she was about to tell. "When Guido and I scuffled, he dropped this. I kicked it away and he dove after it, but it fell into this register on the floor under the TV stand and he couldn't reach it." She blew off dust and dirt from its surface, then got up and closed the distance to Rodrigo. "The alarm was raised and he knew he had to run or get caught. That's what he hit me over—I ruined his plan."

She held out the disk and Rodrigo's body stiffened as he figured out what was in her hand. He dropped the ice bag. "How did he get that?"

She shrugged. "I have no idea. What's on it?"

His long, thin fingers brushed hers as he took the disk. "Something everyone wants. The thing my father died for."

"I thought your father died from a heart attack."

Morales stared at the disk as if it were a snake that would bite him. "He was poisoned, which led to the heart attack. Over this."

Now she was really confused. "Poisoned? By whom?"

Slowly, Rodrigo raised his face to look at her. "Guido Ruiz"

"What?"

"He took my father from me and now he wants the business too." Rodrigo's free hand balled into a fist. "I hate him. He can fucking have all of it. I don't want this life anymore."

He whipped the disk across the room, and *smack*, it hit the wall and dropped to the floor.

Sophie froze. She glanced at the disk, hoping against hope the impact with the wall hadn't damaged it. The green plastic looked the same.

Rodrigo rose, whirled on her. "Did he have anything else? Books?"

The ledgers? "Nothing that I saw," Sophie reassured him. "The only thing was that disk."

He breathed a heavy sigh. "Tomorrow, after the buy, Lexie and I are leaving for Europe. Call it…an extended vacation." He grabbed Sophie by the hand and pulled her to him. "Come with us."

He was taking a vacation after tomorrow's exchange all right. One to the federal penitentiary. "Lexie will be thrilled. She's told me many times that she wishes the two of you could spend more time together."

The urge to jerk her hand away and step back warred with the knowledge she had to play this out. "You don't need me tagging along. I can handle the money transactions from here, keep an eye on the business for you. You don't want to make a hasty decision about giving up everything your father worked so hard to build, do you?"

He took her other hand, successfully trapping her. "I don't want the business. I never did. I know what I want now. I'm taking Alexa away from all of this and we're never looking back. A new life waits for us in Europe. Have you ever been?"

Sophie shook her head.

"I want to take you, there. Show you everything. And not as my accountant, Maria-Sophia."

God, he was going to kiss her. She tried to prep herself, to stay still and let him, but…

"Sophie?" Nelson burst into the room, stopping abruptly when he saw her standing there with her hands in Rodrigo's. The corners of his eyes narrowed almost imperceptibly as he noticed her cut lip and swollen cheek. "What happened?"

Morales dropped her hands, straightened to his full height. "Fucking Guido Ruiz happened. Explain yourself. You defied direct orders and Maria-Sophia was injured."

Nelson's massive chest seemed to grow even wider. He strode toward them. "Yeah, about that…"

Oh boy. One pissing match coming right up.

Sophie braced for a punch. Nelson certainly looked like he wanted to hit something.

Instead, he held out his phone with a picture of a man on it. "I have some news you're going to want to sit down for, sir. Maybe we should go to your office."

Rodrigo didn't look at the phone, kept his angry gaze focused on Nelson's face. "Tell me here, and make it good, or you'll be visiting my friends at the pit."

Sophie sucked in a breath.

Nelson simply smiled and continued to hold out the phone. Sophie glanced at the face in the picture. The photo was a portrait of a man in front of an American flag. He looked familiar.

Was that…?

Rodrigo finally glanced at the picture. "What is the meaning of this?"

"Your arch rival, Guido," Nelson said. "He's CIA, sir."

CHAPTER TWENTY-ONE

Get back to Sophie.

It was all Nelson wanted to do.

He'd done the unthinkable and outed an Agency operative to save his own skin, but it had worked to appease the cartel leader and take the heat off of him. Sophie's operation was still intact. Nelson was still head of security.

Better than being snake food.

The downside was he'd had seven men to interrogate in order to find out which one had allowed Guido—Agent Blue—onto the grounds.

They all denied any wrongdoing. Nelson had gone through the security tapes, and low and behold, discovered Guido had gotten in with help from the outside. Chavez.

"He had the codes," Nelson reported to Morales. "I change them daily, and no one knew this morning's codes but me. I left to go check on the warehouse without sharing them. Chavez must have an electronic clone on the security system."

The man sat at his desk, scowling. His gun—the one Nelson had taught him to shoot accurately—sat on top of the desk. Morales stroked it. "Maybe you gave him the codes. Maybe you're a liar and a thief."

He was both, but not this time. No way he was taking credit for something he didn't do. "I would never do anything to harm Maria-Sophia. I shouldn't have left her alone, granted, but I

173

hate Guido as much as you do. I'd kill my mother before I helped him with anything."

"Did you not check for a clone?"

"I did but didn't find anything. It must be damn sophisticated technology, perhaps from the CIA?"

Morales seemed agreeable to the idea. He rocked in his chair. "Find it. Then report back to me."

"Yes, sir."

Nelson hustled down the stairs and outside. *Get to Sophie.*

She must have seen him crossing the grounds to her apartment because she met him at the door a minute later. "What the hell, Nelson?"

"Come here." He pulled her to him, hugged her tight, and kicked the door shut behind them. "Tell me you landed a shot to Guido's balls."

"Don't worry." Her tense body relaxed a smidgeon inside his arms. "I landed a few good shots. He'll be sore tomorrow."

Nelson drew back and cupped her face with his hands, examining her bruised cheek and cut lip. "I'm still going to kill him."

"Be my guest. I hate the guy. But I think you already signed his death certificate by outing him to Morales. What were you thinking?"

"I was saving my backside, and from all accounts, the guy is a douche bag. A very clever, heartless douche bag. Did you know?"

She moved away, suddenly engrossed in watching something outside the window. Her fingers twisted strands of her hair with nervous, jerky movements.

Nelson felt his insides dip. She'd known but hadn't shared the information with him. Why did it surprise him? "Morales wanted to know why a CIA operative was after you," he said quietly. "I told him the truth…I have no idea."

Eyes shuttered, she continued to keep her face half-turned away from him. "The CIA wants the ledgers. They believe there is top secret information in them, and terrorist contacts that

Ciro Morales made over the years. I agreed to find the ledgers in exchange for Agent Blue helping me with a few things while I was undercover."

Sophie would never turn over the ledgers to the Agency, even if she got what she wanted out of them first.

Unless she was getting something big in return.

"I told Morales the CIA probably wanted to turn you into an asset for them in order to get something on him." He took a couple steps toward her, watching her carefully. "What kind of things is Agent Blue helping you with?"

Her face was sad as she stared out the window. Nelson wondered what she was seeing. Not the grounds, he would bet. Maybe her operation going up in smoke? All the lies she had told coming back to bite her in the ass?

He wanted to call her on it…her duplicity. But she faced him again, hands on hips, once more in agent mode. "How did you find out about Blue?"

"Agent Rios. She's a former spook who's now FBI. She saw his photo in a file my boss gave her and she filled me in. According to her, Blue would throw is grandmother under the bus in order to keep his cover intact. I'd like to know why the hell he took out a hit on you, knowing you're FBI."

Her gaze cut away from him and she folded her arms under her breasts. "I told him Rodrigo is attracted to me. He was hoping to make him more protective so that he would open up and invite me to stay inside his house. Blue was convinced the ledgers were hidden there even though I told him I already searched the house."

"You sure Blue wasn't simply trying to get you out of the way? He's had a sweet gig down here for a long time. I don't doubt he wants those ledgers, but I'm not sure he's ready to give up the cartel life."

She ignored his questions and posed one of her own. "How did you convince Rodrigo that his arch rival was Agency? I'm sure he asked how you knew such top secret information."

The Alaskan tundra had nothing on Sophie Diaz at that moment. In her quest to keep his interrogation focused on everything but her, a cold determination had turned her eyes, tone, and body language into ice.

"I told him the truth," Nelson said. "That I knew a fugitive recovery agent in the area who happened to have crossed paths with Agent Blue and had first-hand knowledge of his association with the CIA."

Her laugh was devoid of humor. "I still don't understand why you would do such a thing, even if the guy is a douche bag."

"He took a hit out on your life, Sophie." He pointed to her red cheek. "He punched you in an effort to cover for himself."

"Blowing another agent's cover…it's the most unprofessional thing you could ever do."

"That's rich coming from you."

She sucked in her cheeks. "I didn't reveal your identity with the Chica Bonita operation. You blew that op the first time around all on your own."

Yeah, by sleeping with you.

They'd had two days together. Two nights. Once she knew he was ICE and closing in on Chica Bonita, she'd panicked and tried to steal some files. The next thing he knew, his op was over. She'd barely made it out without getting caught and her risk-taking brought the whole house of cards down. The files were bogus; nothing could be proven on the human trafficking ring, and nothing led back to Ciro Morales or any other cartel. Ciro wasn't stupid, however. He shut down CB in a matter of hours.

Nelson didn't want to talk about the past, and he didn't want to fight. His arms ached to pull her close and hold her.

But there was no getting past her icy armor. He needed to be all-business too. "You said in your text that you found the missiles."

"There are no physical missiles. The disk we found has the

missile designs on it. I'm sure of it. That's what everyone is actually after."

The specs Rios had told him about? Most likely. In one fell swoop, they could take out a drug cartel, wrap up Project Bliss, and recover those specs. "Where's the disk now?"

"I gave it back to Rodrigo. It was the only way I knew to explain why Guido was here but didn't kill me. I told him Guido dropped the disk making his escape." She waved that away. "What's important now is that we get the ledgers back to their hiding place before Rodrigo retrieves his go bag."

That could be a problem. "You think he's going to take off?"

"Tomorrow after the exchange, he and Lexie are going on a"—she made air quotes—"vacation."

"You think it's a permanent one."

"Before you got here, he told me Guido can have the business. He's fed up. He wants out."

Nelson scrubbed his eyes. "Yeah, but now he knows Guido is actually Agent Blue who is CIA and not interested in taking over the business. He's switched gears and now has a boner for the feds. He wants to stick it to the U.S. and the Agency."

"Can you blame him?"

He was exhausted from trying to work all of this out. "I don't really give a fuck as long as our covers are still in place, but I need that disk."

Her lips thinned. "I'll see if I can get it, but I bet Rodrigo is keeping a close eye on it if he's changed his mind about staying here. Can you get the ledgers back to their hiding place?"

"Sort of. I left one of them with Agent Rios to see if she could decipher the code. If Rodrigo discovers they're gone, just tell him Guido stole them."

"No, no, no." She paced two steps one way and then two back, her eyes snapping. "We have to get that ledger. Immediately. I told Rodrigo that Guido *didn't* steal them."

Well, great. "I have the other two and I can get them back into that bag. I'll contact Rios and have her bring the third one and slip it in somehow. Meantime, I have to figure out how Chavez, and in turn, Blue, got the code for the gate. A sophisticated CIA clone is my guess. Is Chavez Agency as well?"

Sophie stiffened slightly. "Not that I know of."

Didn't mean it wasn't so. From her body language, he guessed she still wasn't telling him everything. *What's new?* "I'll be back in a few minutes. Sit tight."

"I'm tired of sitting on my ass." She blew by him and grabbed the door handle. "I'm going to see Lexie. It's the last day I have with her."

"Cortana is going to visit her auntie," Lexie said, feeling around inside the dollhouse with one hand as she balanced the doll on her legs with the other. "She needs to pack a suitcase of her favorite outfits and books."

"Oh, of course." Sophie handed her a small, plastic case. "Where does her aunt live?"

"San Antonio, in America."

"Texas, huh?"

"Yes! Cortana wants to see the cowboys and buy a pair of red leather cowboy boots!"

Sophie helped Lexie and Cortana, her doll, pick out several outfits and pack them. "Have you ever been to America?"

"No, but when I grow up, I want to live there with my auntie. She's just like Cortana's."

Sophie paused in sorting clothes. "Your aunt?"

"Aunt Margo. She lives in San Antonio. I only met her once when I was a baby, so I don't really remember her, but my mother told me all about her. She was my father's sister and she liked horses. She left the family, so they sort of forgot about her. She owns a dude ranch. When I'm older, I can work for her and ride horses every day."

Brain cells fired. Ciro Morales had three sisters. Two were still in Mexico. One had died. None of them were named Margo. "Why did she leave the family?"

"She didn't like it here anymore, Mama said. She argued a lot with her father, my grandpapa, I guess. Mama said it was business stuff." Lexie shrugged, carefully running a brush through her doll's hair and caressing the hair with her other hand. "My grandfather wanted her to go into the family business and she didn't want to. She loved horses and wanted to have her own ranch. He told her to leave and never come back. Mama really liked her, she said."

"That's sad." Sophie's pulse raced. "So she lives in Texas, now, huh?"

"*Si.* She changed her name and everything. Mama said we would visit her someday, but we never did."

A ripple of excitement made Sophie's fingers twitch. "What was her name when she lived here?"

Lexie held up the doll, a huge smile on her face. "Cortana. I named my favorite doll after her."

Cortana Morales. The dead sister.

Who wasn't really dead, if Lexie was to be believed.

Tears stung Sophie's eyes. The girl was so precious, and she'd just given Sophie a means to save her. Leaning over, Sophie gave Lexie a hug. "What a beautiful name. I bet your aunt will be thrilled to see you when you make it to San Antonio. She'll be honored to know you named your favorite doll after her."

Lexie giggled and reached for the dollhouse again, her short, chubby fingers searching for something once more. "How should we do her hair? Up or down?"

Sophie handed her a miniature hair clip and wiped away the tears threatening to fall down her cheeks. Once more she was ever so grateful that Lexie couldn't see her. "I think either way, she's as beautiful as her name."

CHAPTER TWENTY-TWO

Morales was out for blood. Specifically Agent Blue's.

Nelson did as instructed with the gate. He took apart the electronic panel and went over it with a more critical eye.

Sure as the Pope had a cross, the box hid a tiny, cloning Wi-Fi device no bigger than his thumbnail. Whoever had installed it had stuck it behind a tangle of rainbow colored wires.

Why did he have the feeling, it wasn't Chavez or Agent Blue who had stuck it there?

But if Sophie had done it, why hadn't she fessed up?

Nelson removed the device and made a pit stop to see the snakes. No one was around. The caretaker had been their earlier and no one else seemed psyched to hang out with snakes. Not even Rodrigo himself.

Imagine that.

So even though it was the middle of the day, Nelson managed to return the two ledgers to their hiding place without an issue.

Next, he took the clone to Morales. As he hit the top of the stairs heading to Morales's study, he heard the sound of laughter coming from Lexie's bedroom. While Sophie was surely dying inside over betraying the girl, she was making sure Lexie had one last good day.

Morales kept Nelson waiting in the hall for twenty minutes. Pissed, Nelson leaned against the wall and tuned into what

Sophie and Lexie were talking about, concentrating on the fact that this time tomorrow, he was out of there.

The two females seemed to be playing with dolls. Lexie insisted on Sophie's doll and hers being sisters—a game Sophie could probably enjoy.

A text buzzed his phone. He pulled it out and saw it was Agent Rios. He'd texted her earlier about the ledger.

Where do you want to meet?

Damn. He needed that ledger but he was stuck here until he checked in with Morales. *Change of plan. Hold tight. Will meet you as soon as able.*

A moment later, she confirmed.

The study door opened and Morales's bodyguard, Sanny, motioned him inside.

"Nico, what have you brought me?" Morales said without looking up from his desk.

Putting his phone away, he sauntered across the floor. Nelson grabbed the cloning device from his pocket and tossed the no longer functioning thing on the blotter. "This was inside the security gate's main box. It's probably been there since your father was in power."

"Is there anything else I should know about?"

Nelson paused for half a second. "Sir?"

Morales raised his gaze. "Is the warehouse in need of more security?"

Oh, right. His excuse for leaving the compound. "A single chain-link fence is hardly a security measure. Your workers, and the product they're making, isn't safe."

"A good place to draw Guido into, then, *si?* To cut him down?"

Morales had mentioned this idea of trapping Guido, aka Blue, and killing him, to Nelson at their earlier meeting. The cartel leader, regardless of what he'd told Sophie, was no longer making plans to leave Tijuana. Deception was always a strong motivator for revenge.

Even with the sting looming on the horizon, it was important to stay in character. "He doesn't know that *we know* he's CIA, but he does know I'm working for you instead of him. That can't set well with him. He probably wants my head on a plate. Why don't we give it to him?"

The green disk sat off to the side of the desk. Morales eyed it. "You want to be bait?"

"Why not? I'll head into town later and act drunk at one of the bars. Leave myself vulnerable. We'll see what it nets us."

Morales tipped his chair back and steepled his fingers in thought. "You'll kill him if he comes after you?"

I'd love to. He deserved at least a sound beating for hitting Sophie. "Absolutely."

"Maria-Sophia and my sister will be safe here with you gone?"

Nelson pointed at the clone. "No one's getting in again. I've tightened security yet another level inside and out."

That was a partial lie. There wasn't much more he could do with security unless he put Morales in a bunker.

"I have business in town tonight. While I attend to that, you may go to the bar. We'll see what happens."

"Sounds good."

"Meet me out front when night falls."

With that, Morales waved him out the door and went back to his work.

When Sophie arrived at her apartment, her fingers itched to dial her friend in child services. She needed to do it quick before Nelson got back and overheard her.

Why don't you just tell him?

Because he already thinks I'm a pushover for the girl.

Why was that so bad? Sophie wasn't sure, anymore. Nelson

knew her weaknesses, knew she felt guilty betraying Lexie.

Old habits died hard though, and she wasn't sure this lead would pan out. She'd covertly pumped Lexie for more information while they played, and if Cortana Morales had changed her name, Lexie didn't know what her last name was anymore.

The woman had a 140-acre dude ranch in San Antonio. She had moved to America around the time Lexie turned five. It wasn't much, but Sophie had found people with less. She hoped Wanda could do the same.

Inside, she threw off her shawl. The soft sound of running water made her swear under her breath. Nelson was already there and in the shower.

Checking the bathroom door was closed, she pulled out her cell phone and headed for the kitchen.

It was after hours. Wanda's phone went to voicemail and Sophie left a detailed message about everything Lexie had told her. While she did so, she surveyed the interior of the fridge for dinner options.

And found something she hadn't expected.

A single pink rose sat in a juice jar on the top shelf. One from the climbing rose bush outside.

Nelson had brought her a flower?

As she finished her message to Wanda and ended the call, she brought the flower out and breathed deep. The light scent of the rose tickled her nose.

Such a small thing, but it made her heartbeat speed up in her chest. Nelson was amazing on so many levels. She felt terrible guilt for ruining his previous operation. Guilt for so many damn things.

Guilt was a useless emotion, though. Little Gran had taught her that. Every day was a fresh start. Better to keep moving forward and make the world a better place than to dwell in a past that could never be changed.

After giving the rose a special place in the center of the

table, she went to work making dinner. She was frying chorizo and thinking about the next day, when Nelson slid up behind her.

His big, strong hands gripped the top of her hips as he nuzzled her neck. The clean scent of his soap wafted around her, mixing with the spicy smell of the meat. She laughed despite herself as his lips nibbled at her earlobe.

An unsettling feeling took up shop in her chest. How was she supposed to deal with the operation at the same time she had to deal with the churning emotions Nelson evoked? One minute they were arguing over the case, and the next, they were screwing each other blind.

Worse, it was getting harder and harder to keep the two areas of her life separate. She couldn't get away from her thoughts about him by focusing on the case, because he was such a huge part of it now.

And when she caught herself daydreaming about a future with Nelson, the case—with the end only hours away—ruined it. There could be no future for the two of them. No serious relationship. They were both too dedicated to their jobs.

"Smells delicious," he murmured against her neck. His arms wrapped around her waist, his front pressing into her back. "How soon do we eat?"

Such a normal, homey thing to say as their bodies spooned over the stove. As if they were a real couple, married and already settled into a routine.

Sophie rested her free hand on top of his arms and closed her eyes for a second. What would it be like to have a normal relationship? One where she had someone to count on, to talk to, to love?

Resting her head back against his shoulder, she held onto the image a moment longer. He was shirtless, and she could feel the heat of his chest through the thin shirt she wore. If only she could stay like this forever, safe in the circle of his arms. "Five, six minutes, maybe."

He kissed her temple. "I need to make a call. Then I'll get us drinks."

He released her and, just like that, the idyllic, homey vision evaporated. The agent inside Sophie struggled to the surface, pushing aside the bitter stab of hurt. How ridiculous, to be hurt by Nelson exchanging her for a phone call.

She took a deep breath and focused on the frying meat. It wasn't Nelson's fault that she was having these stupid daydreams. "Who are you calling?"

"My boss," he said. "I have to go into town with Morales tonight. While he's busy, I want to talk to Cooper and Agent Rios. Update them on our situation. I can get the ledger back from her then."

"Oh."

Suddenly, Sophie felt the touch of his hand on her elbow. "You okay?"

No, I'm not okay. I'm freaking in love with you.

Making sure her calm, collected mask was in place, she pasted on a smile. "Go make your call. I don't want dinner to get cold."

Leaning forward, he gently kissed her lips. "It's almost over. You did it, Sophie. You did good."

He smiled and patted her cheek. As he turned and walked out of the kitchen, he was reaching in his pocket for his phone.

Sophie turned off the stove and moved the skillet off the burner. From the oven, she withdrew a cookie sheet of toasted tortillas. Trying to keep her mind blank, she began to build the dinner she had in mind. Her fingers shook as she scooped meat onto the tortillas and sprinkled them with different toppings. Her chest hurt, her eyes burned. Her stomach felt like a wet washcloth that had been wrung out.

Stupid heart.

Nelson's low voice murmured from the living room. Damn him for being so sexy, so loyal.

So good to me.

Heat flooded her cheeks. For a second, she felt woozy. Stumbling back, she found one of the kitchen chairs and sank into it. What was wrong with her? It was illogical for her to feel anything but attraction to Nelson, and here she was, confusing good sex with love.

Great sex, she corrected herself. *Amazing sex.*

But still. Sex didn't equal love.

And yet, her heart didn't seem to care about logic.

Her heart knew it wasn't about the sex. It was the fact that Nelson paid attention to her. Real attention. Not just to her physical looks. Crazy as it seemed, he understood her goals and motivations and was helping her close this case after nine long months of being undercover.

He made her feel special. Like she was his friend.

Her job had always been her lifeline. The only thing connecting her to a normal life. Working for the FBI gave her life purpose. Without it, she had none if she could not find her sister.

Which was looking like less and less of a possibility. She'd been fooling herself all these years, believing that if she found her sister's trail, rescued her sister from the life she'd fallen into, they might be able to become a family again.

She been fooling herself into believing her sister was still alive. Odds were, Angelique, like so many lost girls, had had her life cut short.

Even if she was alive somewhere, and Sophia were able to rescue her, she would most likely need a lifetime of therapy to overcome the atrocities she had lived through.

More damning, she probably blamed Sophie for everything that had happened and with good reason. No way she would welcome her big sister, the one who'd left her at a critical juncture in her life, back into her world.

With the Morales case about to wrap up and the possibility of finally finding out what had happened to Angelique within reach, Sophie wondered what she had left. Her job seemed less significant. She had no one to go home to. Truth be told, she didn't have a home. Before this case, she'd rented an efficiency apartment in L.A. Knowing she might not be back for a long time, she'd given up the lease and put her things in storage.

Although she'd been working, her time with Lexie had made her yearn to be part of a family again. The past few days with Nelson had made her yearn for a relationship.

She'd lost so many important people in her life, the thought of sharing anything—her heart, her past, her future—with anyone scared the crap out of her.

"Soph?" Nelson was standing in the doorway. A hunk of hair, still wet from the shower, hung down over his forehead. His dark brows were drawn, causing a crease between them. "You sure everything is okay?"

"Fine." Sophie started to rise, but the world, or at least the kitchen, tilted around her.

Her legs went numb, refusing to hold her. She fell back, hitting the edge of the chair and flopping sideways.

Strong hands caught her before she hit the floor. On a sharp inhale, she found herself in Nelson's arms.

"Fine, huh?" He stared into her eyes, the crease deepening between his brows. "You don't seem fine."

Hair stuck to her cheek and she brushed it away, finding a slight sheen of perspiration on her skin. "It's nothing. Just…"

She tried to finish the lie, but words eluded her.

"When was the last time you ate?"

At the mention of food, she realized he could be right. "I haven't eaten all day. Must be low blood sugar."

With great care, he eased her onto the chair, hesitating a moment to make sure she wasn't going to fall off again. Assured she was okay, he sauntered over to the refrigerator, grabbed a soda from inside and brought it back. The soda was in a glass bottle with a metal cap. He used the edge of the table and smacked the cap with his fist. *Pop!* The cap flew off. It landed on the tabletop and spun precariously close to the edge.

He handed her the pop. "Drink up."

The orange liquid fizzed on her tongue as the cap stopped spinning. It burned the back of her throat as she slipped, the warm sensation from the carbonation traveling all the way down her chest and into her stomach.

When she started to set the bottle on the table, Nelson stopped her with a finger on the bottom. He guided it back to her lips and tipped it up. "More."

After two more swigs, he seemed satisfied, and turned to inventory the progress of dinner. "What are we making here?"

"Mexican pizzas."

"Hmm." Without any instruction, he went to work, piling ingredients on the flat tortillas and bringing two to the table a minute later. Snatching up her pizza cutter, he sliced her round tostada into quarters, then did the same to his with a slight flourish.

He slid one plate toward her as he took a seat. Realizing he didn't have a drink, he tilted back in his chair until he could reach the fridge. Balancing the chair, he reached inside and grabbed a beer. Before the refrigerator door shut, his chair's feet hit the floor, and he popped the top on that bottle in the same manner as her soda.

He chugged the beer, set the bottle down, and eyed her as he bit into his mini pizza. Chunks of tomato, lettuce, cheese, and chorizo fell onto his plate. "Is this one of Little Gran's recipes?"

He was beautiful, even in the wane overhead light. She'd never before thought of a man as beautiful, especially not Nelson. Sexy as hell, yes. Brooding, cocky, sin on a stick, absolutely. The kind of man Little Gran had always warned her about.

As she sat across from him, drinking him in on their last night together at the same time she drank the orange soda he had forced on her, beautiful was the only word that came to mind.

His hair, now starting to dry, popped out in places from

where he'd slicked it back. The inkings on his smooth, tan skin emphasized his biceps and chest as he fed himself. His nearly black eyes watched her carefully from his side of the table, taking in every movement, even as he tried to act casual. He knew she hated being pampered or worried over.

"No," she answered. "This recipe is mine."

He nodded. "It's damn good."

A warm buzzing that had nothing to do with the soda set up shop in her stomach. "Thank you. If the chorizo isn't spicy enough for you, you can add hot sauce."

"I like it the way it is." His gaze was intense as he watched her take a bite of her own pizza. "It's delicious."

The warmth in her stomach spread and a light fluttering low in her belly made her flush. Suddenly, she was famished. She dug in, and their conversation came to a halt.

At least the verbal part. As Sophie downed her food, and Nelson inhaled his, she felt an electrical charge of energy flowing between them. He watched her eat, the crease between his brows disappearing and lust slipping into his eyes. As she finished her pizza, licking her fingers, he jumped up and brought her another.

His hand brushed hers as he slipped the pizza off the spatula and onto her plate. Another flourish of the pizza cutter and she had four neat quarters again. "Do you need anything else?"

Just you. "No, I'm good."

He heaped another tortilla round with ingredients, adding extra chopped jalapeños, and sliced it on his plate before sinking into his chair. His eyes slid over her again in a way that sent heat to the spot between Sophie's legs.

"Tonight is poker night," she volunteered. "Rodrigo never misses it. I'm surprised he's taking you though."

She bit into her pizza. The cool cheese and lettuce contrasted perfectly with the warm, spicy meat.

Nelson drank his beer. "He wants me to lay a trap for Blue."

"Tonight?"

189

"Don't worry about it. I'll play along, pretend to be trying to draw the man out. Tomorrow, it will be over."

"Especially for Agent Blue since his cover is blown."

"Blue will be fine. Morales isn't going to tell anyone between now and then. Think how it looks." He chewed on some pizza and swallowed. "Blue was an undercover operative in Rodrigo's father's cartel for years. Not the kind of thing you want to get out. Undermines business."

"Blue's days are still limited. Rodrigo will put out the word once he's in jail. At that point, he'll have nothing to lose."

"Unless the CIA uses Lexie as leverage."

The thought chilled her. "How?"

"If they want to keep Blue under down here, what better way to shut up Rodrigo then to offer refuge to his little sister? He keeps his mouth shut and she ends up in a nice, comfy home with a family who will keep her safe. If he talks, she goes to a Mexican orphanage."

"You've put her right in the middle of this by blowing Blue's cover."

He wiped his hands on a napkin. "She was already in the middle of this, Soph. The CIA isn't happy with me, but I spoke to Agent Rios a little while ago and she's working to cut a deal with them to help the kid out."

The orange soda burned in her stomach. She was never going to see Lexie again after tomorrow. "I made some calls. I already have someone working on a solution."

He stopped and stared at her. "Why didn't you tell me?"

His indignant tone didn't set well with her. "It was my problem. I didn't think you cared what happened to the girl."

"Of course, I care." He closed his eyes for a second and took a breath. Opened them again. "Look, I don't want to fight. I apologize for stepping on your toes if I did. I know you're attached to the girl and I wanted to help. That's all."

The irritation left her as quickly as it had come. "I didn't mean to snap at you or sound ungrateful. It's just... I'm not used to this partner thing. Sharing information goes against my grain."

"You like to be in control. I get it. Just know that when this is over, however things shake out, my boss has agreed to make sure the girl is okay. I've already talked to him and he's got connections. We'll figure something out, even if it's off the books."

"Your boss cares about an eleven-year-old girl caught in the crossfire of a cartel leader and the FBI?"

"Cooper Harris is a lot of things, but he's not an unfeeling ogre. Hell, he adopted a six-pound Chihuahua because his girlfriend told him to. Trust me, he's a marshmallow under his tough exterior."

Nelson eased back in his chair, taking his beer with him. "I convinced Harris that Lexie's important to you and you're important to me. He gets it. Hence, you have his support, and Agent Rios's. She knows more about the CIA and how to manipulate them than everyone on the taskforce combined. If we have to, we'll use the ledgers or our knowledge of Blue's crimes as leverage against them to make sure Lexie's taken care of while they're using her against Rodrigo."

Words again defied her. She took a second to digest what he'd just said. *I'm important to him.*

Important could mean a lot of things, yet… "You did all of that for me?"

His eyes had taken on that lusty edge again. He set the beer on the table, came around to bend down in front of her. His strong hands grabbed the sides of her chair and turned it so she faced him. "I would do anything for you, Sophia."

She loved it when he used her given name. She was tired of being undercover. Tired of being Maria-Sophia.

Tired of not being herself.

The warmth of his hands on her ankles startled her, sending a jolt of longing up her inner thighs. The soft cotton of her skirt tickled her skin as he inched the fabric higher and higher, grazing her calves. Cool air swept over her knees as he peeled the fabric back, his palms brushing against her sensitive skin.

"When you're done with this assignment, are you going home to Los Angeles?" he asked.

She'd been so focused on his hands and the sensations he was setting off in her body, she barely heard the question. "What?"

He was peering at her underwear now on display. "L.A. and San Diego aren't that far away from each other."

Was he saying he wanted to see her after this operation was over? "I'll be in town for a while. Depends on how fast the Bureau and the Justice Department get this through the courts."

Leaning down, he placed a soft kiss on the inside of one of her knees. "And then you'll be off on another undercover assignment?"

She really didn't know, and at that moment, she didn't care. Her voice came out husky, dry. "Why?"

His lips trailed kisses up the inside of her thigh, his warm breath sending goose bumps over her skin. "Would you like to see me again? After this if over?"

He made it to the juncture of her thighs but apparently didn't like the lack of access. He grabbed her hips, scooting her forward on the chair. Her legs fell open. "For sex, you mean?"

"And other things." His lips nuzzled her panties. "I'd like to make you dinner one night. Hit a movie. Go bowling, or whatever you like to do when you're off work."

She didn't "do" anything when she was off. A book, a glass of good wine, and a bowl of popcorn were the highlights of any night she stayed home. And then she went to bed early.

Tipping her face down, she watched him lick her through her panties. Under his warm tongue, a shiver started low in her belly and spread. "I'm a thrill seeker," she lied. "Sky-diving, mountain climbing, white water rafting. You name it."

His dark eyes rose to hers. "I can keep up."

Oh, she bet he could. "You'd distract me. Get me killed."

Eyes never breaking contact with hers, his long, thick fingers moved her panties aside. "More like save your ass." His hands pushed her legs wider, baring her sex to him. "What do you say?"

Breathless, she whispered. "I might let you tag along."

He took his mouth to her, lips sucking, tongue stroking. Throwing her head back, she moaned, and in response, she heard a low, guttural growl come from his throat. It vibrated past his lips, registering deep inside her.

Moving rhythmically against his mouth, she loved the bite of his hands locked onto her hips, urging her on. Loved the way his tongue flicked at the top of her sex, then plunged deep, only to return to lick up and down again.

Over and over, he tortured her until his dominating lips and tongue did the trick. The kitchen titled on its axis again, but this time, she didn't fight it. The hot rush of orgasm tore through her body, nearly lifting her out of the chair.

Mindless on the wave of desire, she let go, let Nelson ease her back so the chair supported her once more. Floating, floating, floating. Only here, in the aftereffects of his lovemaking, was she free.

Bliss. There was no other word for it. She didn't want it to end.

As if reading her mind, and eager to please, his hands lifted her blouse, his wet mouth trailing kisses over her stomach, up to her breasts. "Let's get this off," he murmured against her skin as he tugged the blouse gently over her arms and head.

The next thing she knew, he was lifting her, turning her to bend her over the table. Her bra and panties went the way of the blouse, and only the skirt, shoved up around her waist, remained on her body.

Her breasts swung free as she braced her hands on the table and looked back. He'd ditched his pants, his erection proudly jutting toward her. His hands ran over her shoulder blades, around her sides, up to her breasts. Cupping each of them, he kissed the back of her neck, nibbling at the tendon running from neck to shoulder. A shudder ran down her spine.

He used his knee to spread her legs wider, whispering in her ear. "Just how much risk are you willing to take, Sophia? I want more than tonight. More than a dozen nights with you. Can you stand the heat?"

"God, yes," she panted, dizzy with lust. "I can take anything you dish out, Agent Cruz."

He entered her fast, making her cry out. Pumping into her, he made the table scoot forward on its legs—screech, screech, screeching across the floor. The bottles fell over, the plates scattered, the remnants of their dinner went flying.

Bracing against the onslaught, she pushed back, their bodies slapping together in perfect rhythm. Deeper, harder, faster, until her arms trembled from the weight of him, from the sheer mass of him. Glancing over her shoulder, she saw the corded muscles of his upper arms, the veins in his neck standing out. Saw his hair falling over his face as he watched himself pump into her.

The second orgasm hit with the ferocity of the Santa Anna winds, making her grip the edges of the table and shout his name. Her arms finally gave up the fight, succumbing to the force known as Nelson Cruz, and she slumped forward as he continued to punch into her, once, twice, three times, before he threw his head back, his nails digging into the flesh at her hips, and she felt him explode inside her.

The table stopped screeching. The world fell away once more, her vision going soft and fuzzy. Her hearing tuned out the sound of everything but Nelson's breathing as he slumped over on top of her, his chest solid and warm against her back. She closed her eyes and smiled, her sweaty body stuck against the laminate, Nelson's hard weight pinning her down.

In essence, Nelson had fed her, made love to her, and made sure the little girl she was desperate to save had a fighting chance tomorrow. What more could she ask?

She was about to drift off on that thought when the man in question pulled out of her, and carefully, gently, lifted her off the table and carried her to bed.

194

CHAPTER TWENTY-THREE

Staring up at the night sky, Nelson listened to the sounds of nocturnal insects softly echoing through the trees. In the distance he heard an owl hoot. The image of Sophie, lying in the bed fast asleep after another round of lovemaking, had imprinted itself on his brain. He would never forget it. Never forget her.

No matter what happened tomorrow, she had ruined him for all other women.

Didn't that thought make his sack tuck up.

It also made him smile, the feeling so deep, so absolute, it went all the way to the marrow in his bones. His cells vibrated at a higher, more alive frequency.

If his sister were here, she'd tell him not to screw it up, and two seconds later, she'd be hauling his ass to a jeweler to make him pick out a ring.

Damn, he was so gone.

He could imagine it though, this domestic life shit with Sophie. If things were different, if their careers were normal ones, they could make it work. Her cooking for him; him laying her out on the kitchen table like he'd done after dinner. Her wanting kids; him ready to take care of a big family.

The night was clear but another dousing of torrential rain was predicted. He leaned on the black SUV, savoring a few moments of twinkling stars and thoughts of engagement rings while waiting for that motherfucker Morales.

This had become the man's game...making Nelson wait for

him. As if he were passive-aggressively punishing Nelson for leaving Sophie alone and allowing Guido—Agent Blue—access to his compound.

Nelson didn't need the punishment. He was still mentally beating himself up over his failure to find the cloning device as well as for leaving Sophie without his protection. If he could have physically beat himself up, he would have.

And he wouldn't have blamed Morales if he'd taken a pot shot at him. Wouldn't have stopped him. Might have even welcomed the pain.

But Rodrigo wasn't a fighter. He'd probably never struck another man in his life. Even if he had been one to use his fists, he instinctively knew that initiating three rounds with Nelson would have ended badly for him, and Morales was all about protecting himself.

Nelson had learned in his lifetime that there were men who weren't afraid to get in your face with their fists and there were men who preferred to keep things less personal, so they used guns or other men to take you down. He preferred the first; any man who came at him with fists would at least get a fair fight. He had no trouble going one-on-one.

Morales wasn't that kind of man. He had no issue with killing you, but he preferred not to get his hands dirty.

Blue on the other hand… The awful bruise on Sophie's face made Nelson want to hunt the CIA operative down tonight for real, and maybe he would. Give the man a taste of his own medicine. *Nobody touches Sophie.*

It was a ridiculous thought, but his heart and mind were in agreement. Yes, she was a trained federal agent with the capability of taking care of herself, but that didn't matter. Underneath that tough exterior, she was a wounded woman who needed care and love. Not more of this shit.

How many more hours did he have left with her? He felt hope that she'd agreed to see him after the op was over, but she'd been talking out of lust, not commitment.

The thought wiped away his light mood. He'd always wanted more of her. Even after she'd stabbed him in the back. He'd tried with other women, tried to wipe her from his memories, but it hadn't worked. One-night stands and relationships were both out because he compared every woman he hooked up with to her. She'd given him the ultimate screwing over—literally and figuratively—and sick bastard that he was, he only wanted more.

With her track record of changing her mind, he figured he had the rest of tonight and that was it. One last night, and here he was, spending it with a fucking cartel leader.

The man in question exited the side door of the mansion and made his way to the SUV. The driver was already inside and Nelson opened the door for Morales.

They drove off the grounds and towards town. Much of the night sky disappeared as the high rises of the city blotted it out.

"You have a plan, *si?*" Morales said from the backseat.

"Yes, sir. I'll notify you as soon as I have any progress to report."

Morales didn't speak to him again as the driver, who apparently was familiar with the poker night run, dropped Nelson off at a corner bar and drove off with Morales in tow.

The street corner smelled of stale beer and fried food. Women in tight spandex and ridiculous heels eyed him to see if he were hitting up.

The place was a hangout for Guido's men. Nelson thought about going inside and seeing if he spotted the bastard, but before his fists led the way, a nearby vehicle flashed its lights at him.

Nelson strolled down the sidewalk, saw the passenger side window roll down. "Get in," Agent Rios said.

He did, loading himself into the backseat.

Harris was driving. "Agent Diaz okay?"

"Except for the bruise on her face courtesy of Agent Blue."

Harris pulled the black Ford away from the curb and started driving. "What happened?"

Nelson gave them the rundown. Rios had no expression that he could see when he told her and Harris he'd outed the CIA operative in order to throw suspicion off himself and Sophie.

"Your ass is going to be in deep shit, amigo," Harris said. "Deeper than it already was."

Fuck that. The CIA didn't scare him. "There was only one way to keep our cover from being blown and that was it. Besides, Sophie says Blue wants the ledgers. That's all he cares about. He would have gladly sacrificed her, and any other operative involved, to get them."

"Speaking of," Rios handed him the one she still had in her possession. A piece of paper was rubber banded to the front. "I cracked the code. It's one the Russians used during the Cold War. The template is on that paper."

"No shit?"

Her slight smile in the dashboard's light was self-deprecating. "The CIA is definitely going to want to get their hands on those ledgers. But so is the Bureau, DEA, NSA, probably even the Department of Defense."

Nelson felt like saying 'no shit' again. "Important intel I take it?"

"The Department of Justice will have a field day with the amount of detail, not just about the Morales cartel, but about every cartel and international drug dealer, terrorist, and human trafficker that Ciro Morales ever had contact with. He may have built an incredible drug empire, but he brokered just about every illegal commodity you can name at one time or another. He had ties with Russia, China, Cuba, you name it."

"Was there anything about the girls who went through Chica Bonita in or around the summer of 2005?"

"I didn't see anything about the CB operation in this ledger. Maybe it's one of the others. Do you still have them?"

"Had to put 'em back. After Blue crashed the party, Morales told Sophie he wanted out. She was afraid he'd go to retrieve them and find them missing. That's why I wanted you to bring this one to me so I could replace it. Luckily, Morales decided to hang around to have me take out *Guido* tonight."

She scoffed. "Bad call on his part. Sneaking out in the middle of the night might have saved him a lot of prison time."

"He's one mixed up dude. Doesn't want anything to do with the business, but seems to have stayed out of honor to his family. He's planning to take his sister and head to Europe for a do-over."

Harris made a right turn. The city lights zoomed by. "Too late. He only ran the cartel for a short time, but he's the one who's going to pay the price for everything his father did."

"Any progress on keeping his little sister out of the goatfuck?"

"I've made some calls, but it takes time. Lot of hoops to jump through getting her into the US legally and into a supportive home."

Time was the one thing he didn't have. "I've got two, maybe three hours max before I need to report something to Morales. Where are we going?"

Rios turned to look at him over her shoulder again. "The bingo hall was a bust today, but I have another lead. A woman who claims she knows something about the underground railroad. I'm going to meet her now."

"We'll hang back," Harris said. "Maybe canvas the Savages bar for a while. Most of them know you." He glanced in the rearview at Nelson. "You can feel them out about Chica Bonita."

He'd rather be home with his own *chica bonita*.

Just then, Harris's cell phone buzzed. He answered while driving and pinned the thing between his ear and his beefy shoulder. "Yeah? Whatcha got?...Tonight? You're sure." A lengthy pause. "Shit, all right. We'll check it out."

He disconnected, slowed to stop behind a red Camaro at a stoplight and tossed the phone on top of the dash.

"What is it?" Nelson asked.

Harris looked over his shoulder and checked his mirrors before cranking the wheel right. "It's show time."

They were boxed in by cars. He wheeled into a parking lane and took the first turn, a couple horns blaring at him when he merged quite rudely into oncoming traffic. "The underground railroad is moving someone. Tonight."

The loud ring of a phone woke Sophie from a sound sleep. She fumbled her hand around on the nightstand but couldn't find it, slanted one eye open and saw it wasn't there.

Rolling over, she noted Nelson was gone—*poker night*—and that the phone was nowhere in sight.

Brrrring.

Where was her damn phone?

Living room.

Scrambling, she fought the tangle of bed sheets around her body. Nelson had done a good job of tying her up, emotionally and physically, with his lovemaking. He'd been sweet and gentle the second time around.

Almost as if it were their last time.

Maybe it had been.

Sophie's heart gave a lurch on top of the pounding it was doing thanks to being so rudely awaken. *This is* not *the last time*, she told herself. *This is just the beginning for us.*

She hoped.

Brrrring.

Her feet hit the floor and she pushed off the bed. What if it was Nelson? What if it was Wanda saying she'd found Lexie's aunt?

The sheet was still wrapped around one ankle and as soon as she started to sprint, she went tumbling. "Oof!"

Her hands smacked the hardwood floor, knees following. She

was naked, everything jiggling and giving a cry of alarm at the rough treatment. "Damn it!"

Quickly, she kicked off the sheet, gained her feet, and sprinted for the living room. Another ring split the air and the phone vibrated on the coffee table. She scooped it up without reading the ID and tapped the accept button. "Hello?"

"Tonight's package refuses to go," a woman said.

Yolanda.

Sophie rubbed the sleep from her eyes. "Why?"

"She lost her *amulets para suerte.* Claims she's not going without them."

Another curse issued from Sophie's lips. Rosalie and her damn lucky charms. "She has to go tonight."

"I told her that. She refuses. What do you want me to do?"

Rosalie wasn't a young girl. She wasn't particularly in need of a new life in America. Yet, Sophie wanted her to have a chance. The chance her mother never had. "Is she there? Put her on the phone."

"She left. Said to forget it."

Crap. "Was she going back to her place?" Her place being a tent on the edge of town. Sophie had followed her there once, and that had been the thing to convince her to approach Rosalie and offer her a way out.

"No idea," Yolanda said. "I have to go. There have been people asking around. A woman. I'm worried it is *la policia.* Time to lay low until you get back."

"No, we have to find Rosalie and get her into the system tonight."

Yolanda had a fierce determination to save young girls from a life on the streets, but part of her was scared of ending up there herself, or in prison. "I'm sorry. I cannot risk the whole operation for one person."

Then what are we fighting for?

Sophie couldn't blame her, though. Rosalie wasn't their normal rescue and if she didn't want to cooperate—would give up a life in America over a foolish lucky charm—then they couldn't force her to head north. "I don't know when I'll be back. You may have to continue the operation without me."

A stunned silence followed. Then, "How will we get the papers?"

Sophie didn't have an answer. Without Agent Blue, there were no papers for the lost girls.

There was no goodbye, no good luck, or take care. Yolanda simply sighed and disconnected.

The fact that Yolanda felt Sophie was abandoning her was all too clear.

Maybe I am.

Too many maybes.

Who was asking around about the underground railroad? Had to be Nelson's boss.

How could she get Rosalie to cooperate? Sophie set down the phone and chewed a nail. Time was up. She'd take one shot at getting Rosalie to the handler tonight. If she refused, there was nothing else Sophie could do for her.

That thought stuck in her chest, pinching it. In her mind, she saw herself standing on that street corner, waiting for Angelique all those years ago. Waiting for her sister to show up so she could take her across the border and bring her to America to live with her.

Angelique hadn't shown up. So typical of her, trying to show Sophie she was independent and didn't need her.

Sophie had waited an hour. Called her repeatedly and got no answer. She'd worried obsessively for the next few days, checking with the police, combing the local hospitals, asking around the places Angelique had mentioned in her letters. No one had seen her.

And then Rosalie had found her. Without a word, the woman had handed Sophie a simple woven bracelet, the threads broken as if it had been ripped off Angel's arm. Rosalie had told Sophie she'd seen Angelique outside the bingo hall, two men—

two Savages—accosting her. Later, when Rosalie left the hall, she found the bracelet lying in the gutter.

She wouldn't say more than that, but Sophie had followed the trail, going toe-to-toe with a few less-than-savory characters connected to the Savages who told her about Chica Bonita. About the Morales cartel. Sophie had done her best to track Angelique, but her trail was cold and Sophie wasn't an agent yet. She was still at Berkeley on a full-ride scholarship with no family and no resources to fight a cartel.

Rosalie. She couldn't leave the woman behind.

Going back to her bedroom, she threw on dark clothes and went to retrieve her gun from its hiding place behind the dresser.

Have to save her.

But the gun wasn't there.

She whirled around, trying to remember if she'd left it in its holster or somewhere else.

No, she'd put it back just like always.

Had Rodrigo searched her apartment?

Not Rodrigo. Blue.

Sophie swore. The CIA agent had made sure she couldn't get to her gun and shoot him on his last visit.

She didn't have time to worry about that now. Pulling out the top drawer, she scooted around scarves and earrings until she found what she wanted.

Her mother's good luck charm.

One of them, anyway. The tiny troll grinned at her, its blue eyes nearly rubbed off, chunks of its bright hair missing.

It wasn't Rosalie's lucky charm, but it was the best Sophie could do. Rosalie was scared, maybe had even pretended to lose her lucky charms as a form of self-sabotage. Sophie knew the addiction—she'd self-sabotaged a few times in her own life.

What Rosalie needed wasn't a silly plastic toy, but the empathy of another woman. Sophie would try to be that woman tonight.

Like her, Rosalie had no family. No support system. There was no one to share the happy times with, no one to lean on during the bad times. While Rosalie's life in Tijuana was a sad and lonely one after Ciro Morales had kicked her to the curb, it was less scary than the unknown of America.

Better the devil you know.

Pocketing the troll, Sophie left the apartment. She scooted across the compound to the garage. Inside, she flipped on the lights. A row of expensive cars sat in a line, the overhead lights reflecting on their shiny hoods.

Sophie walked down the line, letting her fingers trail over the hood ornaments. Mercedes, Jaguar, Porsche, Land Rover.

She could use something more nondescript, but nondescript was not a word in Rodrigo's vocabulary.

At least the Benz was black.

Climbing in, she found the keys hanging in the ignition. She punched the garage door opener and checked the time. It was earlier than she thought, a few minutes after eight. Getting past the guard at the gate was her only real challenge, and she had an idea for that.

The car started with a deep purr. Sophie played with buttons and knobs until she found the lights. Turning them on, she put the car in gear and drove out of the garage.

Along with all of the other cars in the stable, the Mercedes had an onboard computer system linked to the gate, signaling it to open as she approached. A light was on in the guardhouse, spotlighting the guard who was eating his dinner.

At her approach, he did a double take, his face immediately on display.

Xavier. Why couldn't it be Sanny or one of the others? Xavier was a cruel bully, and a massive one at that.

But then he shifted to his left and Sophie saw an opportunity. Kristine was in the booth with him.

The woman had a crush on him. She regularly brought him food. Tonight, with Rodrigo gone, she'd probably decided to bring him a special desert along with the main course.

Gotcha.

Sophie braked as Xavier flagged her down, stepping from the guardhouse to lean down and look inside the car. Fat drops of rain began to fall and Sophie only rolled the window down a crack.

Xavier addressed her in Spanish. "Where the hell do you think you're off to?"

She held up one of Lexie's bracelets. After playing dolls, the two of them had made several together. "Alexa made a good luck bracelet for Rodrigo tonight, but he forgot to wear it. The poor little girl is going out of her head. You know how she is, she is so scared of losing him after what happened to her mama and papa. She swears he's going to be killed in a poker game if he doesn't have this bracelet on. I told her I would take it to him."

Xavier refused to speak to her in English. "It is not safe for you to leave the compound, especially without a guard."

Sophie answered in English; she could be stubborn too. "Once I'm at the bingo hall, I'll text Rodrigo's bodyguard to come out and get it. I won't even leave the car."

"I must have authorization in order to let you out alone."

"Are you sure about that? You want to bother Rodrigo during poker night when you know that if it involves Alexa and her happiness, he's going to insist one of us brings this bracelet to him." She purposely looked over at the guardhouse and Kristine. "Your dinner is getting cold, and I have nothing better to do tonight, but if you want to be the one to drive into town and take this to him, by all means."

She held out the bracelet through the crack in the window.

Xavier hesitated. His gaze darted to the guardhouse where Kristine waited, then back to Sophie and the bracelet. Sophie's heart fluttered inside her chest, pulse thrumming under her skin, as Xavier took a full sixty seconds to decide what he was going to do.

He knew it was a risk, and it took everything inside Sophie not to keep talking, to try to convince him. She bit her lower lip in an effort to stay silent. Xavier was old-school Mexican; the harder a female pushed him, the more likely he was to push back.

Just when she was about to give up and hit the gas pedal—consequences be damned—he took a step back and put his hands on his hips. He cocked his head and jutted out his chin, motioning for her to go. "Don't damage the car."

No surprise that he was more worried about the vehicle than about her, but she didn't need to be told twice. In English or Spanish.

Pulling the bracelet back inside, she punched the gas and sailed through the gate.

Eight minutes later, she hit the outskirts of the city. The squatters' houses were a conglomerate of lumps against the hillsides, no streetlights in the vicinity, and a steady rain drenching their fires in the fire pits.

It certainly wasn't the neighborhood for a sleek Mercedes-Benz, and Sophia slowly edged the car down the barely wide enough footpaths, searching for Rosalie's tent.

Her lights flashed over a garden gnome with a faded red hat. Bingo. Parking the car, she got out and made her way to the makeshift door. "Rosalie? It's Maria-Sophia. Are you home?"

She heard grunting from inside; Rosalie lifting her body off a chair? Several seconds later, the flap opened a few inches.

Rosalie screwed up her face as if she'd chewed on a jalapeño. "What are you doing here?" she said in Spanish.

Sophie didn't reply. She only held up the troll.

The woman's face softened. Her gaze dropped to the ground. "I cannot go."

"You can. No one is stopping you, except for yourself. But it *is* your choice. I'm only here to tell you that I understand. Whether you stay here or go to America, the decision is life-changing. Scary. I know because I've been in that situation. I just wanted you to have this."

She handed the troll to Rosalie. "It was my mother's. Her favorite. He brought her a lot of good luck." Until it didn't. Until nothing about her mother's life was lucky. "I don't need it anymore, but I think maybe you do."

Rosalie took the troll and hugged it to her chest, eyes closed. "You have done too much for me already. Save someone else."

"I will help plenty of other women, I promise." And in that moment, Sophie knew it was true. "But those papers are yours, Rosalie. No one else can use them, just like no one else can live your life for you. You have the means to save yourself, right here, tonight. There are people waiting to help you. You have people in America who want you to come and live with them, work for them as their nanny. All you have to do is give yourself permission to accept that help. Accept the love we're all trying to show you."

In the dim illumination from the car's headlights, Sophie saw tears tracking down Rosalie's face. She wanted to grab the woman and tell her goodbye, but she knew it was better for both of them if she kept her distance. Otherwise they would both be crying.

Taking a step back, she started to turn around, those tears she didn't want to cry burning in her eyes. The steady rain had drenched her, so no one would see them if they did fall.

She took two steps, then couldn't stand it. Whipping back around, she closed the distance to Rosalie, shoving the curtain aside and throwing her arms around the woman.

One bear hug later, Sophie released her, and without another word or look, jogged toward the car. She'd just reached for the door handle when she heard a yell.

"Wait," Rosalie called.

Sophie turned.

Rosalie still held the troll. She heaved a giant breath and wiped at the tears on her cheeks. "My bag. I need my bag."

Sophie watched her disappear into the shadows of the tent. A minute later, she reappeared, bag and troll in hand. With one last look back, she waddled to the Benz, head down as the rain poured down.

CHAPTER TWENTY-FOUR

Chica Bonita was dead. As in, dead-end.

Surveillance was nearly always a long, drawn out affair. Tonight, the minutes ticked by like a clock caught in syrup. Nelson's ass ached, his eyes were dry from straining at the dark cluster of rundown buildings inside the fence, and the rain hitting the roof was making him sleepy.

Three hours had passed since they'd camped in the alley across the street from Chica Bonita. Not one car had driven past. Not a soul had entered the area. One warm body had left— probably a vagrant—crawling under a large gap in the fence and disappearing into the long alley that ran behind the buildings and ended in a vacant lot. Harris had given chase, but ended up empty-handed. Rios had tried her contact, calling and texting, and ended up with the same. No answer, no response to voice mail.

Harris had contacted whoever had called him in the first place and double-checked their intel. Yes, they were sure the underground railroad was moving someone tonight. The meet was the same: Chica Bonita.

So they sat and sat some more, barely able to keep up a decent surveillance because of the heavy rain.

"I hate to break up the party," Nelson said, not hating it at all as he checked the time, "but I've got to touch base with Morales and tell him I failed to catch Agent Blue."

And then I can get back to Sophie. He had plans for her tonight.

Plans that involved waking her up and making sure she stayed naked until sunrise.

"No one is out in this weather," Rios said. "Maybe if it clears off before morning...?"

Harris rubbed his close-cropped hair with a beefy hand. "Who else is working undercover in this area? Any ideas?"

"Agent Cruz, Agent Diaz, Agent Blue." Rios shrugged. "That's all I know of."

"The papers are legitimate documents. The real thing. No one but a federal employee would have access to them."

"Well, it's not me or Sophie." Nelson yawned. "And Agent Blue doesn't seem like the bleeding heart type to help a few young women jump the border."

Harris started the car, shaking his head. "Has to be someone, maybe not an undercover operative. Someone with connections in town. We need to check with all the federal agencies and come up with a suspect list."

The words came out of Nelson's mouth before he realized how weird it was that he—an ICE agent—was saying them. "Do we really care? A couple of girls get into the US with legal-looking papers. Are they terrorists? Drug dealers? Gun runners? No. Most likely they're mules but it's not like they're carrying enough product to keep major dealers in business. We have bigger fish to fry right now, don't you think?"

Harris grunted. "Not my call. Orders from Dupé are to flush out whoever's helping these women get into the States with legit papers that technically aren't legit, and shut them down."

The windshield wipers flipped up and down, making no dent in the water streaming down the window. Harris put the SUV in gear and started to pull out of the alley when car lights suddenly swept around the corner of the block.

Jamming the SUV back into park, he cut the motor.

A dark sedan crawled down the street as if lost. The three of them inside the SUV ducked as the cars headlights grew closer. Nelson held his breath as the vehicle drove past them and kept going. He peeked over the front seat and watched the taillights as the car drove on.

Harris was watching too. "That's the first car we've seen in this neighborhood since we arrived."

"No one in a Mercedes Benz comes to this part of town at this time of night," Nelson stated. "Unless it's a drug dealer doing a drop."

"Or a CIA operative doing one," Agent Rios added.

Harris eyeballed her. "You think it could be Blue?"

"It's not Blue," Nelson said. The car's brake lights flashed as it turned the corner at the far end of the block. There was a sticker on the back bumper, and although he couldn't read it with the dark and the rain, he didn't need to. It was a Holy Francis sticker. The convent where Lexie went to school. "That car belongs to Rodrigo Morales."

"What the hell is he doing out here?"

"He's not. He's still warm and dry at the poker game." Nelson had seen the outlines of two people in the front seat. While one of them was tall and heavy, the driver had been petite. He'd seen the outline of her face in the dash's illumination, the dark ring of a bracelet circling her wrist as she kept one hand high on the steering wheel.

But it had taken his poor brain several seconds to catch up. "Maybe one of his off-duty guards is taking the boss's car for a little outing."

"In this neighborhood?" Rios asked.

He wasn't about to jump to conclusions. He also wasn't about to wait here any longer. He was crawling out of his skin. "Take me back. I'll look into it."

Harris started the car again. "What about Morales and his orders for you to trap Blue?"

Nelson dialed the cartel leader's phone. His call went to voicemail. "Hey, boss. Blue is laying low. I can't get any bites from his men or any leads on him. I'm heading back to the compound. I've snagged a ride."

He disconnected and nodded at Harris. "Let's go."

En route, Harris's phone buzzed and he put the caller on speaker. "Yeah, Thomas," he answered. "What is it?"

"Mitch and I traced that last shipment of bath salts to a warehouse in Oceanside. We found bodies."

"Shit. How many?"

"Two dozen. But they're not human."

"What? Our connection is bad. Sounded like you said they're not human."

"The connection sucks, but you heard me. The bodies we found... They're snakes, Coop."

Harris was silent for a moment. "What's the punch line, Mann? What the hell are snakes doing at the warehouse?"

A new voice came across the airwaves. Mitch Holton. "They've been gutted and tossed in a heap, sir. There are rat carcasses with 'em. My guess is that they're mules."

"Drug mules?"

"Yes, sir. These are no ordinary garden snakes, either. They couldn't have crossed the border without proper documentation covering exporting and importing exotic pets."

Nelson sat forward. "What kind of snakes?"

"Big-ass ones," Thomas answered. "A couple of six foot anacondas and several more I'm unfamiliar with."

Rios shifted to look at Nelson. "Doesn't Morales deal in exotic snakes?"

"Collects them. And gemstones," he told her as Harris turned onto a main street and merged with one-way traffic. The brighter lights here were still not enough to attract anyone in this storm. "According to Agent Diaz, Morales is an expert with diamonds and shit."

Rios nodded. "He studied gemology at university according to his file."

"I've seen some of the uncut stones and they look just like the gravel on the bottom of the cages." Nelson stared out the window, lost in thought. "What if the snakes weren't carrying drugs? What if they were transporting uncut diamonds, both in their habitat and in their bodies?"

"Have the snakes tested," Harris told the two agents on the phone. "For drugs and for…whatever the hell you test for when it comes to diamonds."

"Yes, sir," Thomas said.

"We'll keep you posted," Mitch added.

The line went dead.

"The exchange tomorrow," Nelson said. "It's under the guise of Morales obtaining some new exotic snake, but maybe it's more than that."

Rios nodded. "It may have nothing to do with missiles either."

"Transporting uncut diamonds in snakes?" Harris blew air through his lips as they hit the highway. "And I thought I'd seen it all."

Nelson sat back in his seat. "But Morales isn't interested in expanding into the U.S. He keeps talking to Agent Diaz about Europe."

"Which is why he's meeting with the European dealer," Rios said. "He's looking for a new transporter."

"That son-of-a-bitch." Nelson scrubbed his face, an exhaustion that had nothing to do with the long night, gripping his bones. "He's not getting out of the cartel business and going legit. He's switching his product."

When the Morales compound came into view a few minutes later, Nelson told Harris to pull over and let him out. He didn't want the vehicle to be seen by the guards. Besides, he needed to clear his head, even if it was raining like a banshee.

He stuck the ledger under his coat and zipped it to the top to keep the thing dry. "I'll walk the rest of the way."

Harris pulled to the side of the road and shot Nelson a hard look over the seat. "Keep your head down and don't rock the boat tonight, Agent Cruz. The CIA will take down Morales at the exchange tomorrow, and then you can help Agent Rios and

I find the person responsible for the Chica Bonita underground railroad."

His voice and his gaze brokered no argument, so although Nelson had promised Sophie he'd make sure she got her man, he decided it was better to lie than disagree. "Roger, that, boss."

Nelson got out of the car and started walking. Head down, he tromped through the rain, his gut cramping. He knew exactly who was responsible for the underground railroad.

And he was about to spend one last night with her before he had to arrest her for breaking the federal immigration laws.

CHAPTER TWENTY-FIVE

Yolanda wasn't there.

Sophie parked two blocks away, the windshield wipers fighting furiously to keep the rain at bay and failing. Her pulse beat right along with them.

When Yolanda was at Chica Bonita and had determined the coast was clear, she always hung an orange rag on the front gate. Wind could have blown it off in the storm, or perhaps Yolanda had suspected someone was watching them.

Who in their right mind would be out in this weather? And no one knew what they were doing here except those directly involved.

Sophie texted the woman and waited.

"What is wrong?" Rosalie asked.

She didn't dare tell her, not after making it this far. "Nothing. This is how it works."

Since Rosalie only knew the bare basics about the operation, she didn't know that anything was amiss. "What happened to your face?"

Sophie touched her cheek. "I fell."

"Hmm." Rosalie's tone told her she knew Sophie was lying. "You should be more careful."

Sophie's phone vibrated with an incoming text. Yolanda.

I couldn't wait any longer. Kids home alone and scared of storm.

Crap. Now she was on her own.

Rosalie is with me. How do I get her to Juan and Martha?

Juan and Martha Ramirez were the next stop. Each person or couple involved with the lost girls only knew a limited amount of information. No one had the complete details in case any one of them got caught.

The reply text was an address north of town. Sophie was slightly surprised Yolanda would give it up that easily, but perhaps the woman sensed this would be their last transport.

Plus, while Yolanda didn't particularly like her, Rosalie had helped them find the lost girls, and Yolanda, as well as Sophie, knew they owed her this chance.

Pocketing her phone, Sophie smiled at Rosalie and put the car in drive. "We're all set."

Slowly, they drove through the storm, winging their way north with the hope of freedom in both of their hearts.

In recent years, human trafficking had become the fastest growing activity for criminal organizations around the world. Sex slaves, forced laborers, commercial sexual exploitation, forced marriages, organ harvesting...it all added up to billions of dollars in crime.

When Sophie came through the door just after midnight, Nelson was waiting for her on the couch. He'd been working on deciphering the first ledger, using the code decryption Agent Rios had provided him. He'd found several logs of Chica Bonita's trade of human beings.

"Oh," Sophie said, pulling up short inside the doorway. "You're back."

She didn't sound happy to see him.

Nelson didn't reply, refocusing on the ledger. The entries did not include the girls' names, but he'd found a physical description that resembled Angelique. Sixteen year old Mexican-Caucasian female. Long, straight brown hair. 5'7".

One-hundred twenty pounds. An asterisk had been placed by the color of her eyes: Green.

Green must have brought more money.

But in the six years Chica Bonita had been trading in girls, Angelique couldn't be the only one to meet that specific description. Nelson hated more than anything to get Sophie's hopes up.

So he didn't say anything.

Sophie hung up her jacket, kicked off her shoes, and shook out her wet hair. "How did it go in town?"

"Fine."

Although illegal, human smuggling was not the same thing as human trafficking. The women Nelson suspected Sophie was helping across the US border were not forced into slavery. They weren't drug mules. They were on a quest for a better life, trying to escape poverty and persecution while securing more opportunities for themselves and possibly their families back in Mexico. They sought higher education, better living conditions, jobs, and healthcare.

Who could blame them?

But there were laws in place to assist those seeking a new life in America. Nelson was the first to admit the system was flawed, and often took years for processing and approval for many who applied. The girls in Sophie's care probably didn't have years. Some of them might not have even had months, weeks. She wouldn't break the law for just anyone. These girls reminded her of her sister, and to get involved in this operation of human smuggling, he imagined Sophie knew the girls were destined for human trafficking.

Didn't make it right, but sometimes the heart trumped rules and regulations.

"Where have you been?" he asked without looking up.

She told the same lie she'd told the guard whom Nelson had questioned the minute he got back. "...and I couldn't get a text through to Rodrigo's bodyguard, probably because of this *awful* storm, so I had to park the car and go inside and wait. The doofus running the poker game wouldn't let me in and he wouldn't interrupt it to tell Rodrigo I was there. No one ever came out, and finally, I gave up." She gave a full body shake. "I'm chilled to the bone. I need a cup of tea."

She escaped to the kitchen.

In the past, human smuggling rings had been done by small entrepreneurs. Since Nelson had been with ICE, human smuggling had become big business. Entire syndicates had arisen to meet the need, some networks spreading across multiple countries. Smuggling routes weren't limited to two countries anymore either. Some routes took the person in question through multiple places before ending at their final destination.

Nelson focused on the details of the possible Angelique entry again. If he was deciphering the code correctly, she'd been sold to someone in the US as a child bride.

He double-checked the formula Rios had provided. Scanned the ledger notation. Sex slaves were coded with the number 33. There was a similar number system for a different group of girls, but these appeared to be "models". For commercial pornography, if Nelson's guess was accurate.

From the kitchen, he heard sounds of Sophie moving around, filling a tea kettle, setting out a mug.

Forced marriages, while much fewer than the other two, were coded with an alpha-numeric listing. Probably because the clients didn't require more than one to fill a need. Unless the marriage didn't work out, or the bride ran away.

In Nelson's experience, those forced to be brides were treated no better than those sold into the sex trade or labor force. In fact, many ended up as both porn star and maid to their husband.

Sophie appeared, hurrying through the living room only to disappear into the bathroom. She emerged a moment later with a towel, and as she dried her hair, she hustled back to the kitchen, never looking at him. She hadn't even noticed the ledgers.

He needed to tell her about this entry. Needed to question her about Chica Bonita. Yet, he sat on the couch, his mind a tangle of past and present.

A few hours ago, he'd been stupid enough to think about a relationship with her. Now, here he was, racking his mind for a way to get her out of the deep hole she'd dug for herself, and knowing there wasn't a way out unless he turned his back on her.

He either had to turn her in or completely forget about the bracelets and the lies she'd been telling him.

God, he wanted to save her. *Had* to save her. He couldn't arrest her, no matter what she'd done.

But if he didn't, and the truth came out that he knew she was leading the smuggling operation, he'd lose his job and do prison time.

While he was stewing, she appeared in the doorway holding her cup of steaming tea, the towel now draped around her shoulders. "Do you want anything?"

He marked the page with the bracelet Lexie had given him and closed the ledger. It was now or never. How she played this out would tell him what he had to do. "How about the truth, Soph? I'd like some of that."

Her brows dipped and she gave him an incredulous smile. "About what? And what are you doing with Rodrigo's ledgers again? I thought you put them back."

Yep, he should have known. Denial, distraction…two of her favorite avoidance weapons. "Don't worry about the ledgers. Tell me about Chica Bonita and your underground railroad of human smugglers."

On a sharp inhale, she stepped back, eyes wide.

He waited for the denial. Steeled himself for the lies about to come out of her mouth. Forced himself not to jump up and shake some sense into her.

As he kept his gaze locked on hers, he gritted his jaw. His heart was shredding. His pride as well.

And then her shoulders fell. The smile drooped. She shut her eyes, pressing her lids tight as if she could erase him from her vision. "How did you figure it out?"

Whoa. Wait. Was she coming clean?

"Little things." He pointed at the friendship bracelet on her wrist. "The bracelets, the kid at the bingo hall. I saw you driving the Benz tonight. Harris, Rios, and I had the place staked out. They don't know it was you driving that car, by the way."

Silence stretched. He saw her throat constrict with a tight swallow before she finally opened her eyes and spoke. "I screwed up, Nelson, but…"

"Screwed up? Honey, you didn't just screw up. You set fire to your career. Hell, you're putting *my* career in danger."

Her chin rose a notch. "You don't have to stay."

"Goddammit, Sophie." Anger, sharp and biting, shot through his limbs. During his teenage years, Nelson had been a lifeguard. The first rule in lifeguarding was to utilize any means possible before actually jumping in to pull someone out of the water. Even though you were a strong swimmer and the person you were trying to help was half your size, a desperate person could drown you in their efforts to survive.

Drowning with her was better than living without her. He had no choice but to jump into the water and try to save her.

Unable to sit any longer, he jumped up and gripped her by the shoulders. "Of course, I have to stay. I care about you, don't you get that? Still pisses me off that you've put yourself in so much danger and broken every law in the book to boot. What were you thinking? This isn't like you."

She put her hands on his chest and pushed him away. "Wrong. This *is* like me. All I've ever wanted was to do is the right thing. Make everyone happy. Always the good girl who followed the rules. Well, not anymore. When a young girl needs help, I'm going to help them. I'm not letting them be kidnapped and sold off, or even killed, because I did my job instead of doing *the right thing.*"

Used to be those two were synonymous.

Her eyes snapped. "Believe it or not, what I've done here? I'd do it all over again. Losing my career, losing you... I know what's going to happen and it sucks, that's for damn sure. I'd do anything to keep my job. Anything to keep you. But if helping those girls across the border costs me everything I hold dear, it was still worth it. To give them a new life, new hope. I had to help them, Nelson. They've lost everyone they care about. They have no future here. And even when I'm back in the States, I don't intend to quit helping those in need, either. Even if it means writing letters from jail."

In that instant, his heart melted. She stood before him, barefoot, still wet from her trip to save the goddamn world, and sporting that bruise on her cheek. She was every bit the warrior he'd first fallen for, and while her shoulders were slumped from exhaustion, her back was straight. There was no wavering, no hesitation.

He loved her for that. Loved her for what she was doing, even though it was illegal, and God help him, he was going to do everything in his power to protect her from the US government.

Definitely drowning with her.

Forcing himself not to open his mouth and yell at her for being so fucking wonderful and stupid at the same time, he went to the bathroom and grabbed the jar of wild yam cream, came back, and patted the seat next to him. "Start at the beginning. Tell me everything."

She eyed the spot, stayed where she stood. "What are you up to? Getting me to confess my sins so you can put it all in your report tomorrow?"

The back of his neck heated. "Sit down and tell me about the operation. I want the details so I can figure out how to save your sorry ass."

Her brows shot up to her hairline. "You're serious?"

He just looked at her.

She shook her head. "No one can implicate you if you don't know the details."

He reached out, grabbed her empty hand, and dragged her to the sofa. Taking the cup from her, he set it on the table and began dabbing her cheek with the cream. "My mother was an illegal."

"What?"

"My dad married her to keep her from being deported. Luckily, they fell in love and had a happy marriage. Thirty-three years, in fact."

She was staring at him. As if she wondered why he was telling her this.

"If she hadn't taken a chance, risked life and limb to enter America, I wouldn't be here. I think of that every time I have to arrest an illegal and send them back home."

"Why did you become an ICE agent then?"

Her skin was smooth and cool as he gently doctored it. "I wanted to fix the system, and my specialty has always been counterterrorism and violent crimes, not deportation. That's why I'm on the taskforce as an undercover operative. Doesn't mean I don't come across plenty of illegals, but they aren't my primary concern."

"What are you going to do about me?"

"I'm going to help you."

Her whole body sagged. She bent forward, knocking his hand away, and hugged her knees. Her voice was muffled, but the sheer exhaustion in her voice was still clear. "You can't help me. Nobody can help me."

He replaced the cover on the jar. "You're undercover, and making decisions based on your mission. I'm not your boss and I'm not your judge and jury. My job here was to protect you, so that's what I'm doing."

"And tomorrow, when my operation is over?"

"We'll play it by ear. I'm the only one who knows you're involved in the smuggling ring. If I keep my mouth shut…"

Straightening, the incredulous look returned to her face, this time for real. "That's why I didn't tell you, you know. About all of this. I didn't want you implicated when the shit hit the fan."

Even with their past history, he believed her. "Who provides you with the papers? Agent Blue?"

She nodded. "It was part of our deal. If I hunted for the ledgers and turned them over to him, he provided legitimate papers for the lost girls."

"Lost girls?"

"That's what we call them."

"Who did you help tonight?"

"Her name's Rosalie. She worked for Ciro Morales as his accountant before me and it didn't end well for her. She lost her daughter, her home, everything she had. Her daughter was thirteen."

Nelson's stomach burned. "What happened?"

"She wouldn't tell me the details about her and Ciro, but she obviously crossed him—or possibly Blue when he was still working for Ciro. One of the Savages kidnapped her daughter when she was walking home from school. Rosalie saw it; she was walking to meet her at the ice cream shop that Lexie loves. She knew all about the Savages and sending girls to Chica Bonita, so she confronted him. One of Morales's bodyguards beat her to a pulp, broke her arm, wrecked a couple discs in her back. Her daughter's body turned up a few days later. Rosalie's house was burnt to the ground, all her belongings and what little cash she had, destroyed along with it."

Sophie's voice was raw with emotion. "Rosalie ended up in one of the squatter tents on the edge of town. I saw her at the bingo hall and heard her story, and knew I had to find a way to help her. She'd lost everything, even her dignity, but the one thing she had was anger. She wanted revenge and I couldn't blame her, but I wanted to give her something more. I wanted her to feel needed again. Necessary. That's all any of us ever really wants, isn't it? To know we can make a difference in this ugly world?"

"So you recruited her to help with the underground railroad."

"More like she recruited me. She and Yolanda, one of the other leaders of the network, already had most of it in place. They got a couple of girls across the border, but the paperwork never held up under scrutiny and several had been deported back here. Blue was pressuring me to find the ledgers, so I cut a deal with him."

Smart girl. "Speaking of." Nelson tapped the ledger. "I found three years' worth of entries for Chica Bonita."

She did another hard swallow. Her voice was barely more than a whisper. "Angel?"

"I've been decoding as fast as I can, but haven't found anything definitive on her yet. From what I can tell, the girls were processed and entered into this system by physical description rather than names. There's at least one that matches Angelique around the time of her disappearance."

"Show it to me."

Side by side, they sat on the couch and he walked her through the code and the entry he'd found that matched Angelique's description. "How do we figure out where she ended up?" Sophie asked.

"That's what I've been trying to figure out." He pointed to a column at the far right. "The decryption code doesn't work on these entries. Number, number, letter, number, number, letter, number. Five numbers, two letters. I don't know what they mean."

Sophie studied them and worried her bottom lip with her teeth. "I don't know either, but there's something about them that looks familiar."

"Have you seen something like this in your books?"

"Maybe." She fought a yawn, blinked a couple of times. "Would help if my eyes weren't blurring."

"You're tired." He brushed the side of her hair with his hand. "And I need to get these back to the pit before Morales gets home from his poker game."

"He'll stay in town all night."

Nelson tugged the ledger away from her and took a screen shot with his camera of the page with Angelique's description. Setting the phone on top of the closed ledger, he took her hands and drew her upright. "You need some sleep so you're ready for tomorrow. Go to bed. I'll put the ledgers back and join you in a few minutes."

"I'm too worked up to sleep."

She was dead on her feet. "Take a hot shower. It will help."

He walked her into the bathroom, kissed the top of her head, and shut the door behind him on his way back out.

Before he left, he heard the sound of the shower. Picking up the ledgers, he concealed them in Sophie's backpack and slipped out into the night to get rid of them.

CHAPTER TWENTY-SIX

Sophie couldn't believe Nelson hadn't arrested her on the spot. Standing under the hot spray in the shower, she closed her eyes and slicked her hair back from her face. A face with a big smile on it.

She'd managed to get Rosalie to safety. Thanks to Nelson and Agent Rios, she had a possible lead on Angelique. While she'd been in the kitchen fixing tea, Wanda had texted to say she found Lexie's aunt in San Antonio. She planned to meet with Cortana the next day to explain what was going down, after she received word from Sophie that Rodrigo was under arrest, and see if Cortana would be willing to provide a home for the girl.

Everything was going to work out. In a few hours, she would make the bust of her career and send Rodrigo Morales to prison. Once she had Lexie safe and secure, she would continue her search for Angelique.

Hang in there, sis. I won't let you down this time.

The image of the column of letters and numbers flashed through her brain. Maybe it was wishful thinking, but she was sure she had seen something similar recently. In the morning, she would take one last look at the books she had taken over from Rosalie. Maybe something in them would jog her memory.

With any luck, Nelson would help her track down Angelique. He'd promised he would, and Sophie believed him.

The problem would be keeping him out of the fray if Agent Blue decided to blow the whistle on her. With the SCVC Taskforce hot on her trail, and Blue's cover possibly blown to hell, he had little incentive to keep her illegal scheme a secret. He didn't seem to care about breaking the rules—he hadn't gotten in trouble yet for doing so—but he might decide to pay her back for Nelson's double-cross.

Sophie hung her head, water running down the back of her neck. After all Nelson and done for her, she couldn't let him take the heat over the lost girls. Ruining her career was one thing, ruining his as well was not an option.

Climbing out of the shower, she toweled off, pulled on a tank top and pj bottoms and slipped into bed. Fatigue consumed her.

If Agent Blue kept his mouth shut, they were safe. If he didn't…

The only way to protect Nelson was to send him away.

Rock meet hard place.

He wasn't going to like her cutting ties with him. He'd already told her he was going to help. While she enjoyed that fantasy, what choice did she have? His taskforce was investigating her human smuggling operation. Yes, it was about to go dormant for a while, but if they ever traced it back to her, and she was having a relationship with Nelson, he was going down in flames with her.

After all he'd done for her, she couldn't let that happen.

No longer smiling, Sophie pressed her thumbs into her temples where a headache was already pounding. In a few hours, it would all be over.

The only question left was who was she taking down with her?

Sometime later, Sophie woke with a start. Flashes of light bounced off her eyelids. She sat up too quick, and the room, illuminated every few seconds by lightning, took on an eerie, disco ball effect. Her hand snaked out and she patted Nelson's side of the bed.

Empty, the sheets cool to the touch. Did the man ever sleep?

The red numbers of her alarm clock blurred, but seemed to read shortly after three a.m. Slowly, she raised herself into a sitting position and scooted to the edge of the bed.

Rain beat against the side of the apartment, wind howled. Another damn storm. Would the hurricane ever leave them alone?

As the room seemed to contort and fade before coming into bas-relief again, Sophie pinched herself to make sure it wasn't a vision. Sometimes, it was hard to tell, especially when the shadows seemed to be reaching for her.

The pinch hurt, and her view didn't change. Her temples still pounded from the earlier headache, probably causing the vertigo. She hadn't slept enough and the storm's pressure system was also contributing to her wooziness. The errant and bright lightning acted like a disco ball as she moved across the room.

There were no lights on in the apartment, but the chaotic lightning did a fine job of showing her the way. A body stood in front of the living room window, looking out.

"Nelson?"

He didn't look at her. "We need to leave."

"What?"

His gaze was pinned on the night outside the window. "I don't trust Blue. He could go to Morales and rat us out. We should leave tonight."

"If we leave, we could blow the whole operation."

His body was rigid, hands on his hips, jaw muscles jumping. "The FBI has their warrants. They can swoop in anytime and arrest Morales. If Blue tells Morales you're a Fed, your life is in serious danger."

Her head was in danger of exploding, not just from the headache but by his one-eighty. "I'm not letting anyone else arrest him. It's my job and I've worked damn hard to keep my cover intact and gather all of that intel on him. Nobody is stealing this case from me."

Nelson was silent, his strong cheekbones and square jaw beautiful in the shadows.

"Besides," Sophie mumbled, rubbing her aching head, "I have to be here for Lexie."

He set a fist against the window edge, bowed his head.

"Nels?" She moved closer. "What's this about? You're not yourself."

Thunder rumbled. Nelson raised his head. "Something's not right with any of this—Morales, Blue, Chica Bonita. I feel it in my gut, just like I did when we worked together before. Even without Blue, Cooper Harris is looking into your operation. Things could go south for both of us in a big-ass hurry."

He had the jitters. Maybe it was because of the storm or the fact she'd put him in the line of fire over the lost girls. She got the jitters the night before every big arrest, too.

But they couldn't bail now. At least she couldn't. She touched his arm. If she could get him back to bed, let him sleep, he'd feel better come morning. "We can't leave in this storm, and Blue and Rodrigo are stuck in town while it's raging, so they can't get to us. How about we go back to bed and get some rest? We can leave at first light if you're still feeling anxious."

He finally canted his head and looked at her. "Two taskforce members discovered the corpses of large, exotic snakes and half-digested rats in a warehouse in Oceanside. A warehouse similar to the one Morales runs here. The evidence suggests the snakes were transporting something in their stomachs."

"Besides rats?"

He nodded.

"Drugs?"

"Remember the uncut gemstones we found in the pit?"

The realization struck Sophie with the same speed and intensity the lightning outside was arcing through the air. "Diamonds? He's selling the snakes with diamonds in their stomachs?"

"Exotic snakes like the ones in the pit are worth a lot of money, right? Does it make sense to use them as mules?"

"The gemstones could be worth two to three times as much as the snakes, and like I mentioned before, they're lightweight, easy to hide, easy to move."

"So it *is* possible."

"Yes."

His gaze switched back to the window. "But he'd need the right paperwork to get the snakes across the border, or he'd need an underground railroad like your smuggling ring. Which do you think Agent Blue is supplying for him? Fake papers or the same underground you're using?"

Her stomach dropped to the floor. "You can't be serious. You think Rodrigo and Blue are working together?"

"After learning what we have about Blue, you don't think it's a possibility?"

Her legs trembled and she fumbled her way into a chair. In an instant, Nelson was there, like he had been earlier that day when she'd nearly fainted in the kitchen.

He ran his palms up her thighs, down her arms, his eyes searching her face. "I take it from your reaction, that it makes sense?"

His touch and the concern etching deep lines on his face made her want to fall into his arms and never leave. The precursor to the visions was often as bad as the aftermath. "I don't know. I have a headache from this never-ending storm system, and it makes it impossible to think straight."

"Let's get you back to bed. I'll rub your temples for you."

Before she could protest, he scooped her up in his arms and carried her across the floor. A massage sounded like just the thing to help her.

She cuddled into Nelson's warm embrace, ready to ignore his theory on Rodrigo and Blue, when without warning, a vision—brutal and unsparing—bitch-slapped her

CHAPTER TWENTY-SEVEN

Sophie's body went rigid in Nelson's arms.

Her jaw clenched, her breath came in gasps, her lips moved but no words came out. Her eyes were open, but unfocused, and she twitched as if someone were prodding her with a branding iron.

"Sophie!" He made it to the bed and gently laid her down. Her body spasmed, as if she were having a seizure, and he wondered if he should find something to put between her teeth so she didn't bite her tongue.

Her chest heaved; she arched her back. "No," she cried.

Helpless, he didn't know what to do. He grabbed her hands but she didn't grip him back. Her index fingers stuck straight out, rigid. The others curled into her hands.

He took her by the shoulders and gave her a light shake. "Sophie, what's going on? Do you need medical attention?"

Like she could answer him. He wasn't even sure she knew he was beside her.

And then, as fast as the episode happened, it disappeared.

A giant gasp left her mouth and she sat straight up, nearly knocking him backward. "Nelson." She shook her head as if to clear it. "What happened?"

"You tell me. You were fine one second and the next, you were having some sort of seizure."

She gripped her head with both hands, all her fingers working now, and squeezed her eyes shut. "Oh, hell."

"What? What happened? Do you have epilepsy or something?"

"Or something."

He needed to touch her, so he rubbed one of her thighs. "Do you need to see a doctor?"

Her eyes opened and her hands fell into her lap. "A doctor can't help me."

A shot of pure fear shot up the back of Nelson's neck. "What aren't you telling me?"

"You won't understand."

"There are a lot of things about you I don't understand, but I accept them anyway."

She cut her eyes to him, then chuckled out of the blue. "You won't believe me even if I tell you."

"Try me."

"All right, but don't say I didn't warn you." She sighed loudly. "Recipes aren't the only thing Little Gran shared with me."

"Okay," he said hesitantly. "What else?"

"You're going to think I'm a freak."

Her reluctance didn't help his unease. "Soph, just tell me what it is. I won't think you're a freak."

"I have…" She dipped her head, staring at her hands as they played with the hem of her pajama top. "I see things. As in…the future."

His mind repeated the words. Once. Twice. Three times. "You see the future."

She nodded.

"Like as in, you can predict it?"

"You think my near-perfect arrest record is all due to hard work and nothing else?"

"Um, yeah?"

She released the edge of her top and sighed. "It is, actually. The only other times I've had visions while working are when I've been near you. You wanted to know how I knew you were in the pit getting beat up? I had a vision and saw you there.

Why do you think I always work alone? I have to. Just in case I *do* have one. How would I explain these episodes—my visions—to a partner?"

Between the wild storm outside and the unnerving revelation going on inside, Nelson had the sudden impression he'd landed in the Twilight Zone. "Why do you only have visions when you're around me?"

"I used to have them about my family. Growing up, Little Gran said it was because I loved them, and that made their link to me stronger."

Nelson sat back. This was some kind of craziness all right. "So you...?"

"Love you?" Sophie tilted her head back on her neck and let go of a heavy sigh. When she finally righted herself, she locked eyes with him. "Do you think I'm a freak?"

He needed to choose his words carefully. "Of course not. It's just, I've never encountered anyone with the gift."

Her posture softened. "That's what Little Gran called it too. A gift."

He was no longer as freaked out about her visions as he was about the other thing she'd said. "So are you?"

"What?"

He gave her a small grin. "In love with me?"

There was a long, heavy pause. She stretched it out, making him wait. Torturing him, and then...

"It's a possibility. The visions are never about anyone but those I care for."

"A possibility?" Wow, she knew how to get a guy's hopes up and then leave him hanging by a thread. "Would you say it's a *strong* possibility?"

Her lips broke apart a bit with the hint of a smile. The storm had moved off and lightning flashed softly in the distance, casting a lovely spotlight on her high cheekbones. She stuck her tongue in the tiny gap between her teeth and gave a deep-bellied laugh. "*Si.* A strong possibility."

He leaned in. "So what did you see?"

Her smile vanished and she closed her eyes. "I'm not sure. It seemed to be the same vision I had of you in the snake pit a few days ago, only I heard screaming. A woman's screams, not yours."

"Did you recognize the woman?"

"No." She opened her eyes. "Maybe it was only an echo of the first vision. It seemed like an almost exact replica."

"Has that ever happened before?"

Solemnly, she nodded. "With Angelique. I used to have the same vision over and over. She was struggling against a pair of men dragging her into a van."

Nelson drew her into a hug, shifting his body around so he could rock her. Minutes passed and he stroked her hair, whispering platitudes in her ear. She loved him. It was more—much more—than he could ever hope for.

After a while, he felt the shift in her breathing, saw the soft rise and fall of her chest. He waited another few minutes until her sleep deepened, and then he left her in bed to go call Harris and tell him he was hunting down Agent Blue.

"The tropical storm has been upgraded to a hurricane." Harris said. "It's turned inland again." Static crackled across the airwaves, his voice cutting in and out. "No one's going anywhere tonight. Hunker down and cinch up. We're riding this one out."

Nelson tightened his hold on the phone. Two hours until sunrise and he was outside on the porch, watching the garden next to the apartment take another beating as a fresh wave of wind and rain pummeled it.

The storm was bad, but in his mind, this was the perfect time to strike. Neither Blue nor Morales would be moving around.

He had to raise his voice slightly to be heard over the sheeting rain. "I think Blue and Morales are working together to get those snakes across the border."

Harris said something that came across garbled. Then the connection cleared. "...makes you think that?"

He couldn't exactly tell his boss about Blue forging the papers for Sophie's lost girls, so he didn't. "Call it a hunch. I've been turning it over in my mind all night. I think Blue threatened to expose Ciro Morales at some point, and Ciro kicked him out. After he died, Blue cut a deal with Rodrigo. They kept their official cover as enemies intact to keep suspicions off of them, and meanwhile, they've been shipping everything from bath salts and diamonds to sex slaves into America. The drugs and girls make them money, but it's the rocks that secure their future."

"That's a serious accusation, Cruz. What does Agent Blue gain out of all of this?"

"He knows the Agency isn't going to leave him down here forever, and the day will come when his little enterprise ends. If he goes back to Langley, he could get benched for the crimes they've been letting him get away with, or worse, they could offer him up and send him to jail. The CIA has left him alone, not because he's feeding valuable intel back to them, but because if they don't, he might blow the covers off a lot of other agents in this area."

Nelson snuck back into the apartment, closing the door softly behind him. Now he lowered his voice. "My guess is he's been planning his retirement carefully for the past couple of years and when he found out about Sophie's operation, he kicked it into high gear. He and Rodrigo are both planning their escapes to go underground. The gemstones are easy to hide, store, and retrieve. Between the two of them, they could have millions waiting for them in America when they pull the plug down here."

There was a long silence from Harris's end and some

background talk with Agent Rios. Harris came back on the line a moment later. "Is the meeting tomorrow with the European dealer still a go?"

"As far as I know, but with the hurricane stirring things up, it could get cancelled or postponed. We can't take that chance. Blue could disappear on us, or Morales could get wind we're onto him. We need to shut down this operation asap, starting with our CIA friend."

"Agent Rios says Blue is still pretending to be Guido—he was in the bar last night with a few of his men—and no one has outed him that we can tell."

"That's because Morales doesn't want to out him. Sending me after him tonight was for show. For all I know, Blue has told Morales about Sophie and me, and we're dead meat come morning."

Another long pause. Harris was a thinker, which made him good at leading the taskforce, but he was also a doer. The men and women under him respected his brains *and* his brawn. "I'm all for an exfiltration, but neither Morales nor Blue are at the compound, so the biggest threat to your safety at this moment is Mother Nature. Rios and I can keep an eye on both men and notify you of their movements should they decide to venture out in this storm."

Damn it. He walked on silent feet to a spot where he could glance into the bedroom. Sophie was sleeping deeply. Lowering his voice even more, he said, "One call to Morales's men and Sophie and I could be in deep shit."

"Agreed, but you've outwitted those chumps before. You can do it again. Stick to your orders. Keep Agent Diaz safe and bring her home in one piece. I'll leave it up to you to decide when to exit the city. Give me a heads-up if you need help."

Harris's faith in him was good for his ego, and it wasn't misplaced. He could outwit Morales's men if need be. Pacing into the kitchen, he ran a hand through his hair. "I'll take care of Sophie, but just so you know, if Blue comes anywhere near her or this compound before we leave, I will disable his ability to walk and talk."

His boss didn't try to argue with him, but his tone was less than happy. "You're walking a fine line and you're already in trouble with Dupé. You get yourself in trouble with the Agency, I may not be able to bail your ass out."

The Agency was the least of his worries. If anyone found out he'd covered for Sophie, his ass was going in a deep, dark hole that not even Victor Dupé could bail him out of. "Understood, sir. And…"

"What?"

"Thank you. It's been a pleasure working with you on the taskforce."

"What aren't you telling me, Cruz?"

"Let me know if you see movement out of Blue or Morales," he said and disconnected.

Sophie was still sleeping, which eased the ache in his heart a bit. He wanted to crawl in next to her, but he was too keyed up. Grabbing his jacket—which would do him absolutely no good—he decided to go check the house. He needed proof that Blue was working with Morales, and somewhere inside that mansion might be the key to piecing all of it together.

The normal fifty-second walk to the house took him nearly five minutes. He could barely breath, the onslaught of rain and wind so great. When he finally made the west side and let himself in by overriding the security system, he found a dark house. Alexa was hopefully in bed, but her caretaker was probably awake, keeping an eye on the storm and her charge.

The first place to start was the study.

It would have been nice to have Sophie there to watch his back, but she needed the sleep after her vision or whatever the hell that was. He didn't really believe in visions or psychics or any of that stuff, but he'd grown up in a family who did.

The only thing he was sure of was the fact Sophie had definitely experienced something that had upset her. If she claimed it was a vision, then so be it. There were things in this life he'd never be able to figure out or understand. What he *did* know was that underneath his inept cartel leader persona, Rodrigo Morales was one slick son-of-a-bitch.

Nelson picked the lock to the office and made his way inside. He didn't dare turn on lights, so he pulled out his flashlight. The beam glided over the desk, gemstone display, and snake terrarium. The desk seemed like the most obvious place to find what he was looking for, but he pointed the flashlight at the gemstone display and let it linger there. The glass was built into the bookcase with an LED light strip and was about the same size as the snake terrarium. He didn't know much about diamonds, but he didn't have to be an expert in rocks to know that the value of what was contained in the case was probably more than five years of his paychecks. Maybe ten.

Nelson ran his hand along the edges, looking for a way inside the cabinet. The display appeared to be completely sealed, but there had to be a door or hatch to access the gemstones. Nelson dropped into a crouch and felt the underside of the bookcase shelf. At the far back, his fingers touched metal; a lock.

He craned his neck and shined the flashlight on the metal. A brass lock and two hinges winked at him in the light.

Thanks to his lock pic, thirty seconds later, the bottom of the case swung open. Flashlight in hand, Nelson aimed it up and saw something stored underneath the single layer of gemstones.

What was this?

He took out a small, red book and flipped through it.

Ledger. There were two more tucked inside.

More fucking ledgers.

The handwriting inside was delicate, careful, loopy. Page after page listed diamonds, rubies, emeralds. Morales's collections, what he'd bought and sold, the dates, and to whom.

Like father, like son.

The next ledger contained names. Not of people.

Of snakes.

Along with the name was the type of snake, where the animals were bought and sold, dates, and suppliers. Some were in South America and Africa. Others were in the good old U.S. of A.

None of the logged names were Agent Blue, or his alias, Guido.

Didn't mean there wasn't a connection.

"Rigo?" Lexie's voice startled him. A sweep of his flashlight showed the girl standing in the doorway, her dog next to her leg. "Is that you?"

Returning the ledgers to their place, he hastily closed up the case. "It's me, Nico. Your brother isn't here."

She held out her hand to hand. "Nico? Where's Maria-Sophia?"

"Sleeping." He crossed the room and took her hand. "Which is what you should be doing. I came to check on you and make sure the house was safe. Let's get you back to bed."

"I can't sleep. The storm makes so much noise. I wish Rigo was home."

"Where's Kristine?"

"She said she had work to do and that I need to stop being such a baby."

What kind of work did Kristine have to do at this time of the morning?

"Will you stay with me?" Lexie asked as Nelson guided her out to the hall.

Where was Sophie when he needed her? "Let me finish up here and I'll be right there."

Seemingly satisfied, Lexie headed toward her room at the other end of the hall. Nelson heaved a sigh, giving the office one last sweep of his flashlight. The snake tank was still an option. He'd check that after he got Lexie in bed. If he didn't find anything there, he'd go through the desk.

Turning to follow the girl, he pulled up short when he caught sight of a shadow from the corner of his eye. A shadow that shouldn't be at the top of the stairs.

"Fancy meeting you here," Agent Blue said. His voice was low, his skin a sickly yellow in the glow of the beam from Nelson's flashlight.

He motioned at Nelson to head back into the office. "We have a few things to discuss."

At the far end of the hall, Lexie heard Blue's voice and turned back. "Who's there? Are you coming, Nico?"

"I'll be right there, kid."

Blue took a step toward him. Water droplets beaded on his forehead. "Isn't that sweet. The big, bad immigration agent taking care of a cartel leader's little brat sister."

Nelson didn't back up. "How did you get into the compound? I destroyed that little piece of technology you were using to clone the security system. Which one of the guards did you bribe?"

"Didn't need to bribe a guard. The housekeeper likes me."

Kristine. No wonder she'd left Lexie alone. She was waiting for Blue to show up. "What does she get out of this?"

"Besides my awesome presence? She has two kids at home. Instead of being with them, she's stuck here taking care of Rodrigo's little sister. She has no loyalty to him. This is a job, plain and simple. I drop by occasionally, make it worth her while. Tonight, after she let me in, I sent her on her way. The rest of your measly security team has bailed as well."

"What do you want?"

Blue swept his jacket back, resting his hand on his waistband. The action showed Nelson the semiautomatic hanging in a holster under his arm. Nelson also noticed the man was wearing black gloves. "Heard you outed me to Morales. I had to take immediate action to control the damage. Thought you should know, he's turning himself in first thing tomorrow morning. Cutting a deal with the Attorney General."

"Right. And I'm the pope. There's no way he would do that."

"Sure he would. He gives up his network of suppliers, and in return, all he'll get is five years, minimum security. Paperwork is being drawn up as we speak."

"Bullshit. He's planning an escape, his swan song, to get out from under this mess. You're helping him, and my guess is, you're bailing too. Got a nice little cache of gemstones waiting for you in the States, don't you?"

Blue rocked back on his heels. "My, my, you're a clever one, aren't you?"

"If Morales turns himself in, why not finger you and sweeten the deal even more? You won't let that happen. So even if you *did* convince him to cut a deal with the AG, you're going to kill him before he sees the sun rise."

Blue removed the gun from its holster, let it hang at his side. "I suppose you shared this theory with Agent Diaz?"

The gun meant only one thing.

Let him try to kill me. "She knows nothing." He had to keep her safe if at all possible. "I shared it with people higher up on the food chain, though. My boss, his boss, the CIA. Killing me won't stop the fire and brimstone about to come down on your ass."

Behind Blue, Nelson thought he saw movement on the stairs. Sophie? One of Morales's security guards? Kristine?

"The Company doesn't care what I do," Blue said. "I'm immune to the laws that govern you and your bitch because I get results where others can't."

Nelson couldn't shine his flashlight on the stairs in case it was Sophie. He had to keep Blue's attention on him. "Nah, the game's almost up. My source inside the CIA says they're gunning for you as soon as the deal with the European buyer is over at noon. But you know that, don't you? You've suckered Morales into believing he can cut a deal with the AG, and meanwhile, you're going to take the diamonds and make a run for it. You'll have a sweet, easy new life while he rots in prison."

"Nico, are you coming?" Lexie called.

"In a minute, *chica.*"

Blue raised the gun and cocked it. "You really shouldn't lie to the girl."

"What are you going to do with her?"

One shoulder shrugged. "Collateral damage. I'll leave the weapon in your hand and make it look like you shot her, then killed yourself. The gun, by the way, is registered to your girlfriend."

Nelson braced, thigh muscles ready to jump at Blue. No way he was dying by a traitor's gun, and no way he was letting an innocent girl be taken down with him. "You're a disgrace to your country."

"And you're a"—

Bam!

The hallway exploded with a flash and a bang from a gun.

CHAPTER TWENTY-EIGHT

Blue's body arched toward Nelson, his eyes going wide as a dark, wet bloom of blood soaked through the front of his shirt. For a second, he seemed suspended, head thrown back, mouth slack. The gun fell to the floor, then he dropped to his knees and face-planted at Nelson's feet.

Behind Blue, it wasn't Sophie who stood with the weapon that had done the damage. It wasn't one of the security team or Kristine either.

As someone flipped on the lights and Lexie came running down the hall calling for him, Nelson felt his skin crawl.

There, with a sick smile on his face and his gun pointed at Nelson's chest, was Rodrigo Morales.

"Alexa," he said to his sister, "go back in your room. Nico— or should I say, Agent Cruz—and I need to talk."

There were two men stationed directly behind him, one on either side. Sanny and Xavier. Both glared at Nelson.

Lexie's voice was small and timid. She seemed to want to throw herself at her brother, and at the same time, run from him. "I don't understand. What is going on? Did you come home early because of the storm?"

Nelson tousled her hair. Under his fingers, he felt her shaking. "Nothing to worry about, kid. Your brother's home safe and he'll tuck you in after he and I are done talking."

She seemed to sense the lie. "I want Nico to stay and read

243

me a story," she said to Morales. Her tiny chin jutted forward.

Three inches from her feet, Blue lay bleeding out on the tile floor, his gun lodged half under his leg. Nelson was fast and pretty damn agile, but he couldn't risk Lexie's life by diving for the gun.

A shootout with Morales, he could win hands-down. A shoot-out with Morales *and* two of his goons? The outcome was questionable, and Lexie would end up the collateral damage Blue had meant for her to be.

Nelson also couldn't bring himself to take out her brother right in front of her, even if she was blind.

"Alexa." Morales's voice was sharp. "Go back to bed. Now."

"I want Maria-Sophia!" She stomped her foot, but then turned on her heel and headed for her bedroom.

Morales waited until she was out of sight, then pointed at Nelson. "Take him to the pit," he said to Sanny and Xavier.

As the first goon stepped over Blue's body, Nelson lunged for the gun. "Sorry fellows," he said, rolling and coming up with it on the other side. "I ain't doing that shit again."

He fired.

"Maria-Sophia!" Tiny hands slapped her cheeks. "Wake up!"

The vision hangover encased Sophie in a thick, heavy fog. But like a trained dog, her legs swung around and she was sitting up before her eyes were even open. She was tired of these rude awakenings, that was for sure.

As she blinked her eyes a few times, Lexie came into view. "Wha…what?"

The little girl was beside herself. "It's Nico. They took him to the snake pit. He made Rigo mad. You have to help him!"

Nelson, Rodrigo, snake pit.

Sophie's stomach dropped. She took the girl's hands. Lexie was drenched, her service dog as well. "Slow down. Tell me what happened."

The girl rattled off how she'd heard noises and found Nico checking on her at the house. Then another man had shown up, and she'd eavesdropped on their conversation. The man was going to kill her and Nico, but her brother had arrived and she'd heard a gunshot. Rigo had yelled and told her to get back in bed, then ordered his men to take Nico to the pit. There had been more gun fire and she'd covered her ears with her pillow. When she was finally brave enough to take the pillow off, everyone was gone.

Sophie threw on a sweatshirt, ignoring the throb in her right temple. Something bad had happened. She had to find out what. "Did your brother say anything about me?"

"No, why?"

She turned Lexie toward the door. "Let's get you back to the house."

"I want to go with you. I hate snakes, but I like Nico."

Sophie guided her out the apartment door, still open from her entrance. Lexie's service dog followed obediently. He had something in his mouth. "What's Harry got?"

"I think it's Nico's phone. I tripped over it on the stairs. It's been vibrating, but when I try to answer it, nothing happens. It keeps vibrating."

Gently, Sophie took it from Harry's mouth and wiped off the drool. If she could get in touch with Nelson's boss...he was in the area, right?

The touchscreen came to life with a picture of the Savages logo, asking for the password or fingerprint ID. She didn't know the password and she certainly didn't have the correct ridges and whorls for Nelson's fingerprint.

And her boss was three hours away in L.A. Longer, considering the storm would have shut down most traffic in and out of the city.

No help was coming from the outside. She had no weapon. All she had was her training.

And her intuition.

Shoving the phone in her jacket pocket, she put the hood of Lexie's coat up over her head. "The snake pit is no place for you."

"Because I'm blind?"

"Because you're eleven."

The wind and rain assaulted them and cut off further discussion. Sophie shielded the girl behind her body the best she could as they fought their way across the yard.

Lexie picked up her argument as soon as Sophie dropped her inside the house. "Take me with you. I don't want to stay here alone."

"Where is Kristine?"

"She let the bad man in. The one who was going to kill me and Nico."

Sophie's head spun. Who was this bad man? Why had Nelson been in the house in the first place? Had he really gone solely to check on Lexie?

She bent down to put her face close to Lexie's. "Okay, listen. Nico's in trouble and I need to get to him. Go to your bedroom and stay away from Kristine. Lock the door and don't let anyone in unless it's me or Nico, okay? I'll come back for you as soon as I know what's going on."

The girl went up on her toes and threw her arms around Sophie's neck. "I'm scared."

Returning her hug, Sophie's nerves nearly made her voice crack. She was scared too. "You were very brave to come and get me. Be brave for a few more minutes, okay? Head up to your room, lock the door, and I'll come see you as soon as I can." She brushed the girl's wet hair away from her face and told the lie Little Gran had once told her. "Everything's going to be okay."

Lexie released her and sank back down to her heels. "I'm not leaving this spot."

Such gumption, Little Gran would have said. Sophie squeezed Lexie's hand. "I guess that will have to do, but steer clear of Kristine."

Heart and head beating a death march in time with one another, Sophie headed back out into the storm.

CHAPTER TWENTY-NINE

A single black eye watched him.

The albino python slithered across the floor, fifteen feet of scales and muscle checking out its next dinner entree.

Nelson was pretty sure he was that entree.

He'd taken out Xavier, nicked Sanny with a bullet to his hip. The guy had appeared immune to pain, coming after Nelson and sending both of them tumbling down the stairs.

On the way down, something had snapped in Nelson's ankle when the meathead landed on it. He'd also received a nice blow to his head. At some point, he must have blacked out, waking up to a blinding headache and strapped to a chair in the snake pit.

As Rodrigo Morales did a good job imitating his freaky pet, circling Nelson and fingering a knife, all Nelson could do was think about Sophie.

The Sophie who cooked him meals and looked at him with those big, doe eyes from across the table and made his libido go Code Red. The Sophie who curled into him when she slept. The Sophie who handcuffed him to her bed and teased him with her lacy bras and garter belts.

The Sophie he'd once dreamed of being a daily part of his life if things had been different.

The amazing food and the kitchen table and the handcuffs paled in comparison to the other, very nontraditional Sophie who lived and breathed outside his dreams. Who, if he didn't turn this snake pit adventure around in the next few minutes, would be at the mercy of a sick, but very clever, cartel leader.

"When Guido—Agent Blue—came to me," Rodrigo said, "I didn't believe him. Maria-Sophia an FBI agent? You, an immigration officer?" He made a disgusting noise in the back of his throat. "All of you playing me? A joke, *si*?"

The disgusting noise morphed into a humorless chuckle. "My father was a smart man. He said I wasn't cut out for this business."

What had happened to Sanny? He was nowhere to be seen. The snake inched toward Nelson's leg. Blood dripped on the floor from a wound Morales had cut into his upper left bicep, pooling and drifting toward his front right foot.

Morales flicked his thumb across the edge of the knife's blade. "The business, however, has grown on me."

"Snakes don't eat people," Nelson said, even as the python flicked its tongue at him, seemingly sniffing at his pant leg.

Could he smell the blood? Did snakes even have the ability to smell?

Rodrigo wiggled the blade at the snake. "Technically the constrictor family can eat adult humans. Specifically, the reticulated python, African rock python, Burmese python, and the green anaconda. But even if they don't eat you, they constrict and kill you if they deem you're prey. I've raised mine to enjoy human flesh, and yet,"—he leaned forward and smiled a heartless smile—"it is the kill they seem to enjoy the most."

The snake's head slithered onto Nelson's lap, the heavy weight speaking to its massive size and strength. His balls shriveled up so hard and so fast, it nearly gave him a head rush.

The python's head angled to Nelson's right, where his cut bled, and coiled around behind the chair. Morales, enjoying the sight, sliced the knife through the air and took a chunk out of Nelson's left thigh.

The pain was intense. Blood soaked his wet jeans. The snake in the terrarium across from them hissed as it watched.

If it was just the two of them, Nelson could get the upper

hand. If the giant python got itself wound around him, he didn't stand a chance.

He couldn't stand up, but he could rock the chair over, maybe give the snake a dose of its own medicine and squeeze it. "Snakes don't scare me," he lied. Snakes absolutely freaked him out. "And neither do you."

He rocked to the left, or tried to. The damn snake's upper body had to weigh at least thirty pounds and stopped him from tipping. He felt it slide around his back as blood gushed from his wounds.

"Rodrigo!" Sophie suddenly burst into the room, throwing the door back on its hinges and wiping rain out of her face as she stormed inside. "What are you doing?"

Morales whirled, knife still in hand. "Maria-Sophia. Or should I say, Agent Diaz? So glad you could join us." He motioned her to come farther inside. "I promise I wasn't leaving you out of the party, but I have more…captivating…plans for you."

Morales winked, stroked his knife.

Nelson had to give her credit. Sophie didn't so much as flinch. "What are you talking about? Who is Agent Diaz?"

"The gig is up, as they say." He started for her. "Time for your friend to face the music. Or the snake as the case may be."

Her eyes darted to Nelson, then the snake. "Stop with the American sayings and tell me what you are doing. Why is Nico tied up and that…that…snake loose?"

For half a second, Morales seemed to sway in his conviction that Sophie was an undercover operative. "You know why."

"I'm sure I don't." She stomped across the floor to get close to Morales, ignoring the knife and jabbing a finger into his chest. "What I *do* know is you scared your poor sister to death. She heard men arguing, gun shots. She was worried sick about Nico and came out in this horrid weather to wake me. She insisted I find you and Nico. What in the world is going on?"

Morales was totally focused on Sophie. Silently, Nelson rocked to the right, using the snake's weight as leverage.

But there was too much of the extended albino body on the ground, countering his momentum.

Need. More.

Morales grabbed Sophie by the wrist, jerking her to him. Her chest bumped into his, one of her feet catching on the tail of the snake.

The python hissed and jerked its head, knocking into Nelson's injured thigh. Its tongue poked out and it turned its gaze on Sophie.

The distraction didn't keep it from continuing to enclose Nelson in its grip, however. Another slide of its massive body and it formed a complete circle around his ribcage, tightening, tightening, tightening…

"I offered you a life you could only imagine." Morales held Sophie tight. He bent his head and spoke close to her lips. "Twice. The world will be ours if you come to Europe with me. I will build a new empire and make you queen."

He'd switched gears on Sophie so fast, going from accusing her of being an agent, to trying to seduce her again, Sophie's head spun. Wasn't this his way, though? He never did what she expected.

The python was gaining real estate on Nelson's battered body. Someone had beat him up good. Blood ran over the floor, and Sophie felt sick. But her queasiness over the blood was nothing compared to how freaked out the snake made her.

Play along. She swallowed past her fear and derision. Pretended to be interested in Rodrigo's offer. "All I've ever wanted is a family."

"Alexa and I will be your family, and I will help you find

your lost sister. Alexa told me all about her. My father had many contacts throughout the world. All you have to do is come with me and I will put out the word on her."

She would do almost anything to find Angel, even trade her future.

But not to a man like Rodrigo.

With the ledgers, they had a good chance of figuring out where Angelique had ended up. She might not be there anymore, might even be dead. All Sophie could do was pursue the lead and see where it took her.

Rodrigo, however, wanted to be the hero. "You would do that for me?" she asked.

He smiled down at her, brushed her lips with his. "All you have to do is one thing for me."

The touch of his cool lips made her want to recoil. Out of the corner of her eye, she saw Nelson rocking his chair from side to side. She gripped Rodrigo's arms and held him in place so he wouldn't notice. "What?"

Rodrigo rubbed his cheek against hers. In a quick movement, he turned her around, bringing her arm behind her and pulling her back against his chest. She felt the sharp edge of his knife at her throat. "Prove your loyalty."

As Rodrigo shifted her to face Nelson, Nelson quit rocking his chair. The python had now coiled itself around Nelson's throat and its head bobbed next to his temple.

The tongue flicked out at her, and a shudder ran down her spine. From the scrunched expression on Nelson's face, he was losing the battle for air.

"Prove myself how?" she asked.

Rodrigo released the arm behind her back but didn't lessen the knife's contact with her throat. Her back was still against his front, and she felt a solid lump poking her in the back.

Eww. He had a hard on.

He handed her a gun. It must have been tucked in the back of his waistband. "Kill him."

Had he really just handed her a loaded weapon? Surely he knew better, even if he was holding a very sharp knife to her throat.

And then on the heels of that thought, came another. *Thank you.*

He'd just handed her the solution to her problem. She only hoped the gun held at least two bullets.

One for the snake and one for Rodrigo.

Clearing her mind of Nelson's red face and struggled breathing, she accepted the gun. "You promise to help me find my sister?"

"I promise." The pressure against her throat grew unbearable, the knife edge drawing blood. Rodrigo's breath was hot as it tickled her earlobe. "Now shoot him."

Nelson gave her a funny look as she raised the gun and pointed it at him. Or maybe that was simply the look of someone being strangled and crushed by a python.

Her headed pounded. The storm raged, battering the windows with rain and tree limbs. Sophie cocked the hammer.

Nelson's eyes widened. He shook his head and tried to speak, but all that came out was a muffled whisper. A whisper that sounded a lot like "don't."

The snake circled the front of his face, tightening its grip on his neck.

She would only get one chance to hit her target. If she didn't shoot the snake in the head, it wouldn't die instantly. It could still suffocate Nelson to death before she could save him, assuming Rodrigo didn't slit her throat the moment he realized she didn't intend to do as instructed.

But if she missed, she'd kill Nelson instead.

Taking a deep breath—as deep as she could with a blade cutting into her throat—she let it out halfway and held it. Eyed her target.

One.

Shot.

Nelson was gasping for breath and once again desperately trying to rock the chair. Rodrigo was holding her tight. Warm blood ran down her throat and over her collarbone.

Outside, the wind howled. The window panes shuddered.

One…

She put her finger on the trigger.

Shot…

The snake serpentined its head toward her.

Time stopped, noise and light and feelings fell away, her focus coming down to a single spot.

Sophie pressed the trigger.

Bam!

Her arm jumped, the knife sank deeper. A small hole appeared in the snake's head, the impact from the bullet propelling it backward where it hung, suspended for a second. It dropped like a cement brick, taking Nelson over with it.

"No!" Rodrigo shouted, but before he could slit her throat, she jammed her booted heel down on the top of his foot. His hold loosened. She dodged away from the knife and spun.

He was fast, grabbing her by the hair and jerking her off balance before she trained the gun on him. Fighting through the pain—*get to Nelson*—she reared back, Rodrigo's grip still firm in her hair, pulling it out at the roots.

One more shot!

She fired.

Instead of the sweet sound of a bullet exploding, all she heard was a click.

No.

She pressed the trigger again. *Click, click, click.*

One bullet. The fucker had only loaded it with one bullet.

Not so stupid after all.

The knife swung, burying itself deep into her side and cutting her down. She dropped to her knees, then fell sideways. Rodrigo's foot caught her in the ribs, struck again in the stomach, the groin. He threw down the knife and punched her face.

Head reeling, the room spinning, she coughed up blood. He shoved her onto her back and stood over her. "I could have given you everything."

She spit the blood from her mouth. "No, you couldn't. Because the only thing I want is…" Lifting a finger, she pointed at Nelson, still tangled up with the snake. Was he alive? "Him."

Rodrigo spit on her, then walked off. A moment later, she heard the motorized sound of a terrarium door opening.

Medusa. The anaconda. He was letting her out to play.

He walked past Sophie, careful to avoid stepping in the blood running from the cut in her side. "Enjoy a nice, slow death," he said before grabbing the black gemstone case and heading out the door.

She heard the lock click into place.

Locked in with a monster of a snake and bleeding out, sick laughter bubbled out of her mouth. *Nice job, Soph.*

Nelson still wasn't moving. Sophie flipped herself over and tried to stand. She couldn't even get to her knees.

Coughing up more blood, she reached one hand forward and started crawling.

At the same time, Medusa emerged from her cage.

CHAPTER THIRTY

Nelson came to with a suffocating weight on his stomach.

He sucked in air. At least he could breathe again.

Breathe he did. A heaviness rested on his chest, but it was no longer the vise grip it had been, and his throat was no longer being squeezed.

Air—oxygen—was good.

He was lying on his back, his hands pinned behind him, but seemingly not crushed. The python's body had cushioned the fall and the top of his body hung suspended a few inches above the floor.

He blinked up at the stark overhead lights and drew another sweet lungful of air. When he tilted his head to the side, he saw the dead snake's beady eye staring back at him.

Where was Sophie?

She'd shot the snake, and thank the Virgin Mary for that, but two inches from his head? *Jesus.*

"Sophie?" he called, but it came out hoarse, scratchy. His vocal chords refused to obey. Clearing his throat, he tried again. "Sophie!"

Better, but still not normal.

There was no answer and his vision was limited to what he could see when he lifted his head.

No Rodrigo, lots of blood, and… Oh, God. A body lying face down with one arm stretched out toward him.

"No."

His heart tripped over itself and he called to her again. She didn't answer and he zeroed his focus in on her chest. Held his breath, even though his body was still screaming for more oxygen.

There. Either his eyes were playing tricks on him—his mind refusing to believe she was dead—or he'd seen her upper back rise ever so slightly.

He wiggled harder, managing to shift the snake's body and letting gravity help. A meaty section slid toward the floor, freeing his chest.

As he shimmied his body, the blood that had seeped out from his arm and thigh lubricated the snake's skin. He felt the lower half shift and he jerked his legs as hard as he could. His ankles were still tied to the chair leg, but something sharp nailed him in the calf. The chair leg had splintered during the fall.

Using as much force as he could, he tipped his body to that side, putting stress on the chair leg until he heard it snap completely. His leg sprung free, taking a piece with it. A few more contortions and he was free of the snake.

And he was almost free of the chair when he heard the sound of something slithering up behind him.

He knew that sound, and once again, his balls shriveled up inside him. Ever so slowly, he picked up the busted chair leg and firmed his hand around it. Then he turned his head to look over his right shoulder.

Fuckin' A, I hate snakes.

Staring back at him not more than two feet away was the green anaconda.

CHAPTER THIRTY-ONE

When the anaconda lunged, Nelson jabbed it in the mouth with the sharp end of the splintered chair leg. The snake's head went up, its mouth opening wider, fangs on full display.

He wedged the bottom of the stick into its lower jaw.

With its mouth jacked open and unable to close, the snake reared back, shaking its head.

That should keep him busy for a few minutes.

Hustling over to Sophie, he gently turned her over to examine her wounds, keeping a close eye on her chest.

In.

Out.

That little bit of movement kept him from losing it.

She was a mess of bruises and sticky blood. He located the cut in her side and applied pressure.

"Stay with me, Soph."

Removing his T-shirt, he tore it into several strips. The snake was still busy trying to get the stick out of its mouth. One strip he folded into a bandage. The second he used to secure the bandage to the cut, tying it around her waist.

Her cheek was split and the previous bruise from Blue was lost under a new, fresh one. Nelson swore under his breath, vowing to kill Morales if it was the last thing he ever did.

Sophie's chest rose in a deeper breath. She blinked her eyes open. "Nelson?"

"You're going to be okay. I'm going to take care of you." He didn't know how exactly. Her wound needed stitches and she might have internal injuries. There was little chance he could get an ambulance here in the storm. Checking his pocket, he realized he'd lost his phone.

"Rodrigo?" she murmured.

"Gone to the house, I imagine, to get Alexa and leave."

"Go...after...him."

"And leave you? No way. He won't get far in this storm."

Her hand touched his arm. "Help me...up. Have to get him."

"Lie still. I've patched up the knife wound, but you need a doctor."

She angled her head and looked down at his handiwork. Blood was already seeping through the layers of cotton shirt. Her head dropped back and she looked at the ceiling. Then she seemed to catch sight of the anaconda writhing around on the floor to her left. "*Cristo!* I hate blood, and snakes, and..."

"Cartel leaders?"

"How did he know about me?"

"Agent Blue told him about both of us."

"Bastard."

"Rodrigo killed him."

"I figured as much from what Lexie told me. I can't say I'm sorry. Revenge for you outing him?"

"More likely to save his own skin. He claimed to have brokered a deal between Morales and the Attorney General. Morales was going to give up all his contacts in exchange for an easy sentence."

She cut her eyes to him. "Seriously?"

"Makes sense, but then Blue threatened Lexie, not knowing Morales was standing behind him."

"He would kill a child?" Her sigh was heavy. "What a...pig."

She cocked her chin toward the anaconda who was fighting a useless battle with the stick. "What did you do to him?"

"He's got a mouthful of chair leg."

"I'm glad you're...okay."

"Me, too."

"You have to go get Rodrigo. Make sure…Lexie's safe."

"I'm not leaving you."

"I'll be okay."

"That snake could still crush you."

Her fingers searched off to the side for something, found the discarded knife. "Not if I slit his throat first."

Nelson smiled at her bravado. "If you pass out from blood loss, you'll be easy pickins."

She leaned to her right and came up on her elbow, cringing and grabbing her side with her free hand. "Then we'll go together."

He put a hand on her shoulder. "Sophie—"

"Don't Sophie me." She shrugged him off, rolled up onto her knees. "We're sitting ducks here. Rodrigo has probably already sent one of his other men to come finish us off."

"Xavier is the only one left and he's injured. Rodrigo will need him to load up the getaway car and drive."

"Unless he and Kristine have already run off." She sat back on her heels, swaying ever so slight. "And only if Rodrigo decides to leave in the storm. If he comes to his senses, he'll stay put in the house."

Nelson touched her shoulder again, more to steady her than stop her. Arguments abounded on his tongue, but he kept them to himself. She was right.

There was no good answer. He couldn't leave her here, but taking her with him to hunt down Morales could kill her.

She locked eyes with him over her shoulder. "Please, Nels. This is my last shot to take Rodrigo down."

Reaching out, he carefully helped her to her feet. "Go slow," he said. "Keep pressure on your side. I can carry you if you want."

She let out a strange laugh. From pain? From him offering to be her knight in less-than-shining armor?

He got her to her feet and she reached into her pocket and handed him his phone. "Call your boss."

He punched in his passcode but there was no signal. "Storm's knocked out cell towers."

She laughed again. A crazy, low-pitched laugh that made the hairs on the back of his neck stand up. "Of course it did. Let's go."

They started toward the door, him hobbling on his busted ankle, her hobbling due to her side. She slipped on the bloody tiles and he tightened his hold, nearly losing his own balance. Now it was his turn to laugh. "We're not doing so good here."

"We're fine," she mockingly lied. "Two tough agents like us? We can handle anything."

"Don't tempt fate," he said as they started forward once more.

A boom of thunder rocked the building. Lightning zigzagged outside the window and Nelson heard the sound of a tree splitting. A huge branch busted through the window, sending glass everywhere.

They ducked.

A heartbeat later, the lights went out.

———————

Sophie blinked, trying to adjust to the sudden overwhelming darkness. "Oops."

"You had to tempt fate, didn't you," Nelson said.

Boy, were they in a pickle. If they survived this, Sophie was going to do something nice for herself. Treat herself to a spa day. Eat chocolate every night before bed. Take a desk job.

Really, there were so many nice things she could do.

Beside her, Nelson took a step forward, his hand around her waist—high enough to avoid her injury, but low enough to stabilize her—and guided her to do the same.

"Do you have a flashlight?" she asked.

"Yeah, on my phone, but I feel the wind coming through the

broken window. The door is three feet south of that. Trust me. I'll get you there."

The howling wind didn't drown out the sounds of the anaconda thrashing around behind them. "Do snakes see well in the dark?"

"How the hell do I know?"

Her cheek throbbed and her stomach threatened to heave up the previous evening's dinner. Thankfully, she could no longer feel the burning pain in her side. It had gone numb. Like her hands.

Probably not a good sign, but she could breathe easier without that pain and move faster. "Let's get out of here."

They stepped forward, glass crunching under their feet, rain blowing in. Sure enough, Nelson's internal GPS was right and they arrived at the door a moment later without the benefit of light.

"It's locked from the outside," Sophie said. "I heard Morales lock it when he left."

"Fuck."

"Can you pick it?"

"I have a better idea."

He released her and moved her gently aside. A second later, he reared back and kicked the door open.

"I like your style," she said, over the howling wind.

Debris blew in at them and Sophie shielded her eyes. The tree had blown down in front of the exit.

Nelson raised his voice. "We either climb over it or we find the back exit."

"I'm not going back inside with that...that thing loose in there. His jaws are massive. He could snap the stick at any moment."

"You've got your knife."

He was making fun of her, but in a way to take her mind off their predicament. "You're welcome to it if you want to take on a giant, man-eating snake in the dark."

"We've already come this far. Waste of time to go back."

"Exactly what I was thinking."

"Come this way," he called, edging along the building's wall. His body shifted to step over a large branch. "Up and over, Agent Diaz."

Once outside, they had to quit talking and Sophie had to duck her head. The wind blew like a vacuum against her face, sucking her breath away and plastering her hair to her skin. It seemed to take an hour just to get to the corner of the building. They finally made it and started toward the house.

What seemed like another hour passed as they trudged headfirst into the wind. Nelson finally shifted her behind him, like she had done with Lexie, making her hold onto his belt as he plowed through the gusting wind and rain.

Soon, she couldn't feel her entire left side at all. Her feet dragged, slogged down in the mud. She closed her eyes, focusing on putting one foot in front of the other, blindly gripping Nelson's shirt.

Yep, definitely putting in for a day job.

If she had a job left after this.

First, I have to make it out alive.

There were no lights on at the house. The falling tree must have taken out a power line.

If Rodrigo was still inside, what were they going to do? Neither she nor Nelson was in any condition to fight. What would they do with Lexie?

Lost in her thoughts, she was surprised when Nelson pulled up short, grabbed her around the waist again, and gently hauled her out of the elements.

They were in the kitchen at the back of the house, the white appliances seeming to glow in the dark. Gasping for air, Sophie leaned against the door and sluiced water off her face. "What's your plan?" she murmured.

Nelson stood close, catching his breath as well. "Find Morales and kill him."

"Not in front in Lexie."

"I may not have a choice."

"I have a better plan. Let me find him and arrest him."

"We have no gun, no cuffs, and no backup."

"We have each other."

"Right." He didn't sound all that confident about her plan. "How about you stay here and guard this door in case he tries to escape. I'll see if I can flush him out."

"This is my operation so it's my call. My bust."

"You're not exactly in the best condition to take him on."

She had lost steam a long time ago, but determination gave her a boost of adrenaline. "I have a gun hidden in the tiny office he let me use for the accounting stuff. Can you retrieve it?"

He hesitated. Overhead they heard footsteps, the thud of a heavy bag.

Still here.

"Where in the office is it?"

"Taped underneath the desk on the left side."

"Stay here." He kissed her forehead. "Back in a minute."

"Promise you won't kill him, Nels. I'm serious. He's mine."

"I told you from the start, I'm not here to steal your case."

As he slipped off into the darkness toward the little office down the hall, Sophie counted to ten, then silently headed for the staircase. While Nelson was busy retrieving her gun, she was going to take down the son-of-a-bitch who'd left her to die with a snake.

CHAPTER THIRTY-TWO

A gun would be nice but Nelson didn't think he'd need it and he was pretty sure Sophie didn't want it. She was in bad shape and probably couldn't make it up the stairs to track down Morales anyway.

His gut told him this trip was a goose chase. After all they'd been through, she had manipulated him out of the way so she could go after Morales alone.

He was a man who didn't admit to having his feelings hurt, but damn it. His feelings *did* hurt.

Staying in the shadows, he heard her soft, slow footsteps on the stairs. So faint, they were difficult to hear over the raging storm, but yep, she was going after Morales alone. Which in her condition was stupid.

Still, it wouldn't hurt to be armed, and as slow as she was moving, he had time to grab the gun and catch her.

His eyes had adjusted to the darkness and he moved as swiftly as his injured ankle would allow. His fingers ran across two strips of duct tape and he quickly unstrapped the weapon from its hiding place. Then he half hopped-half ran as fast as he could out of the office.

And pulled up short at the sound of a gun being cocked.

Morales's pale face emerged from a shadow near the kitchen doorway. "I should have slit your throat."

Anger surging through his limbs, Nelson flipped the safety off Sophie's gun and raised it to point at the man.

"A game of chicken, is it?" Morales gave a derisive grunt. "You think I won't shoot to kill?"

"I think if you actually managed to kill me, it would be by accident." He was ready to pull the trigger, end this here and now. Sophie's words echoed in his head. *Promise me you won't kill him.* "But either way…"

Nelson heard Sophie yell, "Nels, stop!" right before he lowered the gun a few inches and shot Morales…

…in the knee.

Morales buckled, grabbing his leg and swearing as he winced in pain. He hopped on one leg, trying to keep his gun trained on Nelson. Nelson stepped forward and kicked the gun out of his hand.

The weapon went off, the bullet whizzing past Nelson's ear and hitting the wall behind him.

"No!" Sophie hobbled down the stairs off to his right as Nelson closed the last bit of distance to Morales and kicked the guy in the balls. Morales curled up like a baby, making a choking sound.

"What did you do?" Sophie said, shoving Nelson away from the cartel leader. "I told you not to shoot him."

"You told me not to *kill* him." Nelson picked up Morales's gun and handed it to her. "And I didn't, although I wanted to. Make your bust, Agent Diaz. He's all yours."

Sophie took the gun and stared at him as he went back into the office. He grabbed the duct tape strips hanging under the desk and went back to her.

"Best I can do to tie him up since we left your cuffs in the apartment, and by the Holy Mother, I'm not going back out in this friggin' storm tonight."

She pointed at the tape. "We'll need more than that. There's a roll of it in the bottom left drawer of my desk. Should be a flashlight in there too."

"Maria-Sophia?" a tiny voice called from the top of the stairs.

"Go back to your room," Sophie called to the girl. "I'll be up to explain everything in a moment."

In the office, Nelson found the tape and flashlight. When he emerged, Sophie had slid down the wall, her hand holding the gun wobbling.

"I read him his rights," she mumbled, "but you're going to have to tie him up."

Shock.

He made quick work of tying up Morales, then went to the kitchen and rummaged around in the fridge until he found what he wanted. Snagging a bottle of Lexie's juice and a straw, he ran back to Sophie.

He made her sip the liquid. "You've lost a lot of blood. I need to have a look at the wound."

She didn't argue. "I'm sleepy."

"No sleeping. Not yet. We have to talk to Lexie." The juice would help her blood sugar level but not for long. She needed to be in a hospital with an IV and a doctor to care for her injuries.

He took out his phone and checked for a signal. Still nothing.

Morales had a landline, but those were probably out too. Wouldn't hurt to try, although he doubted he could get anyone there to help even if he could make a call.

He'd seen a lot of injuries in the field. Mostly bullet wounds and bomb casualties while in the army. A medic he wasn't, but he had basic medical training and knew without a doubt that if he didn't stop Sophie's blood loss, she'd be dead before the storm was over and help could arrive.

If there were internal injuries, she'd be dead even sooner.

Behind him, Morales moved and mumbled something. Nelson couldn't understand the words since he'd taped the man's mouth shut, but he understood the venom in them.

Taking the gun from Sophie's grip, he swung around and knocked Morales in the temple.

The man's eyes rolled up in his head and he fell silent.

"Oops," Nelson said.

Sophie laughed softly on an exhale. "What are we going to tell Lexie?"

He needed to move her to the bathroom or kitchen. Some place with running water and supplies. But with the hurricane, they needed to go to a safe, interior room. "The truth."

Scooping her up gently, he headed for the office. It took a few too many precious moments to drag Morales into the kitchen and lock him in the pantry and to check the landline, but Nelson did it anyway. There was no dial tone.

Upstairs, he grabbed Lexie and loaded the service dog's backpack with gauze and bandages and bottles of alcohol and peroxide. He gave little in the way of explanation, telling the girl that her brother wasn't feeling well and had gone to lie down, and that Sophie needed their help.

Lexie was up for the job, more to take her mind off of the storm and what she'd overheard earlier in the evening, Nelson guessed, than anything.

An hour later, he'd cleaned Sophie's wounds and packed her knife injury with gauze. He couldn't be certain there wasn't internal damage, but the bleeding had slowed. Using some odds and ends from the kitchen, he created a makeshift IV and ran his own version of saline into Sophie's arm.

"Will she be okay?" Lexie asked for the dozenth time.

The wind was still gusting and the rain continued to pour, but Nelson could tell the worst was over. They'd heard several tree limbs hit the roof and somewhere from the other end of the mansion, glass had shattered. Morales really should have put up his hurricane shutters.

"I think so," Nelson said.

The girl broke off a piece from the candy bar Nelson had given her and held it out. "Is my brother going to be okay?"

The dog eyed the chocolate. He took the piece from her. "He'll live."

"Are you going to tell me what's really going on?"

God, he sucked at lying. Criminals and cartel leaders? No

problem there. But kids? "You should wait and talk to Sophia."

"She tells me the truth about most things, but not my brother."

"She cares for you a great deal, Lexie. Remember that, okay?"

Another chunk of chocolate hovered in the air at him. "I'm almost twelve, you know. I'm not a baby anymore. I want to know what's going on. Rodrigo is not nice to other people, is he?"

Like Nelson's niece, Lexie was mature for her age. The consequence of having a disability. "No, he's not."

"He gets angry sometimes. Did he get angry at Maria-Sophia?"

"Yes, he got angry at both of us."

The girl patted her dog. "I wish my mom was here. She would know what to do. Maria-Sophia doesn't have a mom either. She needs us."

Nelson watched Sophie's shallow breathing. If he'd hauled her out of the compound when he should have, this wouldn't have happened. "I'm not so sure about that," he said.

He had the feeling he needed her much more than she needed him.

CHAPTER THIRTY-THREE

Twenty-four hours later
San Diego General

"If not for the quick actions of your partner, Ms. Diaz, you wouldn't be here with us," the doctor said. Her white lab coat was starched and pressed and nearly blinded Sophie every time she looked at the woman.

My partner. It was on the tip of her lips to tell Dr. O'Hare that she didn't have a partner. That even though Nelson had saved her life, he hadn't been by to see her since their return to the States. Hadn't bothered to call or text either.

Sophie's hospital gown was pushed aside so the doctor could examine her wound. As Dr. O'Hare ran a gloved hand over the skin, her dark bug-eyes examining every inch, she nodded as if satisfied. "There's no infection and it appears to be healing nicely. His stitches are a little uneven, so you'll have an interesting scar, but you're alive." She straightened and snapped off her gloves. "You owe him a lot."

She owed him all right.

There was a guard outside her hospital room door, and since Morales was in jail waiting for his arraignment and Agent Blue was dead, she was in no physical danger.

Plus, her boss hadn't been by to congratulate her on her bust.

Which all added up to one thing: Nelson had spilled the

beans and the Keystone Cop outside was ready to take her into custody once the doctor released her.

Still, she hated hospitals. "When can I leave?"

The doctor picked up Sophie's chart. "How are the ribs?"

Sore. She couldn't tell where the pain from her side met the pain from her bruised ribcage. Rodrigo had done a number on her, but as the doctor had said, she would live. "Fine."

"Hmm," the doctor said, still eyeing the chart. "It says here you're refusing pain meds. Is there a reason?"

Sophie covered herself and pulled up the thin sheet and blanket. The room was freezing and the linens stank of bleach. "I don't like drugs."

"I can prescribe something non-narcotic if you prefer."

"No thanks. I just want to leave."

And find out what happened to Lexie.

Dr. O'Hare finally met her gaze. "The hospital is under orders not to release you except into the care of your boss. I'm told he'll be here this afternoon."

Yep, just as she'd expected.

But she couldn't take out her fear and frustration on the doctor or nurses. They'd all been kind to her. "I see. Thank you."

After the doctor left, Sophie fiddled with a string on the blanket. The pain in her chest increased as she fought the waves of sadness and hopelessness washing over her. She hadn't felt like this since she'd lost Little Gran.

Her career was over and she was going to need a good attorney. Even if the attorney did his or her job, Sophie was looking at jail time. There was no other way around it.

She didn't have time to waste in jail. She had to keep looking for Angelique. She had to keep helping lost girls.

The door burst open and two women entered. Both were dark-haired and beautiful. They could have been sisters.

One was dressed in plain jeans, a dark blue top, and sneakers. The other was dressed in a red skirt, white shirt, and red heels.

Red Heels held out a hand. "I'm Celina. Cooper's girlfriend."

Sophie racked her tired brain. *Cooper Harris.* Nelson's boss. "Hi. I'm Sophie."

"Sara Rios," the other woman said and held up two bags. "Clothes and makeup. I cleaned out your apartment at the compound and brought all your stuff home. We thought you might want to freshen up."

Celina leaned forward with a wicked grin on her face. "Victor Dupé is coming to see you."

Sophie's insides went cold.

"From the sounds of it, he was impressed by your work on the Morales case," Sara said, setting down the clothing bag. "Maybe he's going to ask you to join his SCVC taskforce. It's a great group to work with. I've certainly enjoyed my stints with them."

Celina took the makeup bag from Sara and unzipped it, handing Sophie a brush. "No woman wants to be seen wearing a hospital gown with bedhead and no makeup, especially by a potential new boss."

Sophie wasn't used to the feminine attention, yet she was overcome with gratitude to these two near strangers. That they would do this for her meant a lot.

Even though there was no way in hell that Dupé was inviting her to join the taskforce.

She took the hairbrush and gingerly shifted into a more upright position. Her injured side cried out, but Sara took her arm and supported her as Celina adjusted the pillows behind her back.

Gingerly, she lifted the brush and dragged it through her snarled hair. "Do you know anything about Lexie?" she asked Sara. At the woman's blank look, she added, "Morales's sister?"

"No, sorry."

Celina dug out a compact mirror and handed it to her. "Listen, Cooper told me you've been undercover for nine months and you don't have a place to stay while you're on medical leave. If you need a place to crash, even if it's only a few nights, you're welcome to stay with us. We have an extra bedroom and occasionally host a taskforce member when necessary."

Medical leave? Is that what they were calling it these days? The Bureau probably didn't want it leaked to the press that she'd been smuggling illegals into the country.

The offer to put her up for a few nights was another kind gesture, however. "I don't think it will be necessary." *Especially since I'll be in jail.* "But thank you."

"No problem." Celina winked at her. "I figured you and Nelson probably had something worked out."

Sophie swallowed the sudden lump in her throat. "How is he?"

"Nelson?"

She nodded. Celina shot a confused look at Sara. "He's walking with a crutch and he has a mild concussion. Didn't he tell you?"

Sophie shook her head and tried to act like it was no big deal he hadn't been to see her. "Men. You know how they are."

Sara saw through her act, but played along, handing Sophie some eyeliner. "Being vulnerable frightens them. They have to keep up their tough act. My husband is the same way."

"Cooper too," Celina added, checking out Sophie's assortment of lipsticks. She held up a brick red and then a soft taupe for Sara to inspect.

Sara pointed at the taupe. "She doesn't need much makeup. She's a natural beauty."

"But the next time you see Nelson"—Celina held up the other tube—"go with the red." She grinned and wiggled her hips. "Va-va-voom."

The next time I see Nelson...

Sophie's heart fluttered like a teenager and she hated it. Nelson had told Dupé on her.

He'd nearly ruined her operation.

Nearly gotten himself killed.

Like she needed the death of one more person she loved on her conscious.

Love.

Yep, the flittering and fluttering inside her chest increased at the thought. She loved him. Here. Now.

For real.

But he'd betrayed her. He'd told the FBI about the lost girls and now she was going to jail.

"...else you need?"

Celina's voice snapped her back to the present.

"Um, no." Sophie examined herself in the compact mirror one last time, knowing there wasn't enough camouflage in the world to hide her bruises, but she didn't care. She looked better than she had two minutes ago, and this wasn't the end of the world.

Even if her heart said it was.

Snapping the mirror shut, she returned it to the makeup bag. If she was going down, at least her mug shot wouldn't be awful. "Thank you for this. I appreciate it."

Celina was apparently a hugger and did so, giving her a light squeeze so as not to bother her injuries. She held her shoulders for a moment as she looked Sophie in the eye. "I've been undercover inside a cartel. I know how hard it is to live in that world, and that it's harder yet to come out of that world after so long and transition back to work and real life."

She took a piece of paper from her skirt pocket. "Here's my number. If you ever want to talk, call me. We don't have to talk about the operation or anything work related. It's just good to have a friend and go out once in awhile. Do normal things, you know? Shop for shoes, grab a yogurt. I'm here."

Another lump formed in Sophie's throat. She hadn't had a friend—a true confidant—since Little Gran. Although she didn't know Celina, she felt the possibility of being friends with her hovering in the air. All she had to do was say yes. Smile. Act normal.

If only I wasn't going to jail.

Unable to form words and feeling tears sting her eyes, Sophie simply nodded and smiled, taking the paper and holding it tight.

As Celina moved off, Sara squeezed Sophie's wrist. "I'm sorry about Agent Blue. I'm not CIA anymore, and I never knew him personally, but what he did to you is wrong. I don't say this lightly, but the Agency, and possibly the world, is better off without him."

Sophie agreed. At least Rodrigo had done one thing right.

"Before you guys leave, there is one thing I could use help with," she said.

Celina brightened and Sara nodded. "Anything."

Sophie pointed at the bag on the floor. "Help me get dressed? Like you said, I don't want to meet Director Dupé in a hospital gown, and with the stiches and bandages, I don't think I can get dressed on my own."

Celina snatched up the bag. "You got it sister."

Sara helped leverage Sophie off the bed, and all together, the three of them made it into the tiny bathroom.

As predicted, getting out of her gown and into real clothes was a challenge, but she never felt embarrassed—both women were careful to keep their eyes averted as they helped her—and they were all laughing when they emerged several minutes later to find Director Dupé waiting for them.

"Sir," Sophie said, nearly jumping out of her skin when she saw Nelson standing behind him.

His gaze was hot and ate her up as his eyes glided all over her body from head to toe.

Both Celina and Sara greeted the two men, then said their goodbyes to Sophie before scurrying out.

Dupé waited patiently for the door to close before giving her a once over. "It's good to see you up and moving about, Agent Diaz."

"Thank you, sir."

"Please, return to your bed if it's easier for you."

He was an imposing man, not from his stature but from the power he wielded.

"I'm comfortable standing, but perhaps Agent Cruz would like to sit down."

She pointed to the recliner in the corner. Nelson raised a brow. His crutch was missing, even though his ankle was in a cast.

"I'm good," he said.

Dupé glanced between Nelson and Sophie. "The first stage of Operation Gangs Without Borders has been deemed a success. The Attorney General is satisfied with the evidence you provided, Agent Diaz, on the Morales cartel. Rodrigo Morales and several of his men are in custody. The Mexican *Federales* and the FBI are working together to prosecute him to the full extent of the law on both sides of the border. Agent Harris and his taskforce"—Dupé pointed at Nelson—"also discovered Morales was supplying illegal bath salts to several dealers in San Diego through a drop point in Oceanside."

He gave her a nod. "Not only did you shut down the Morales cartel, you wrapped up Project Bliss for the SCVC Taskforce."

"Did the CIA catch Kronos?"

"He's in the wind, but they're happy to have their missile blueprints back." Dupé eyed the recliner and must have decided he would use it if no one else was going to. He settled himself and rocked for a few seconds. "The CIA is, of course, upset that you blew their chance to snag Kronos. However, because of Agent Blue's actions and a few words from me, they're keeping their complaints to themselves. Although they could make your life a living hell in retribution, they won't. I've…made sure of it."

Sophie knew exactly what the CIA could do to her, and it wasn't good. That Dupé would protect her lifted a huge weight off her shoulders. "Thank you, sir."

He folded his hands in his lap. "It has come to my attention that, like Agent Blue, you played by your own rules in Tijuana."

The weight of an elephant crashed back down on her. She glanced at Nelson, but returned her gaze to meet Dupé's head-on. "I take full responsibility for my actions."

"As I would expect. You'll have to meet with the AG but I've made arrangements to lessen the fallout. Once I was aware of the situation, I told the Attorney General that you were acting on my orders to infiltrate the human smuggling ring in an attempt to investigate the resurgence of Chica Bonita. You were unaware of Blue's affiliation with the CIA and thought he was directly involved so you used your cover to play a role and figure out who all the players were. Stick to that story and you'll receive a slap on the wrist, nothing more. When you return from medical leave, I'll have to put you on desk duty for a probationary period. Then we'll talk."

"I'm not...fired?" Sophie asked.

"You're one of my best deep-cover agents, and I'd hate to lose you over an error in judgment. If it happens again... Well, we'll cross that dangerous bridge when we get to it."

"Wait." Nelson, who had been leaning against the wall, straightened up. "*You're* her boss?"

Dupé gave Sophie a questioning look. "You didn't tell him?"

Nelson shot her an accusatory look. "No, she didn't."

The cat was out of the proverbial bag. She stared at Dupé's tie and ignored Nelson. "My orders were to report to you and only you, sir, and not to share chain of command with anyone."

In the silence, she forced herself to meet Nelson's glare. "The operation was Director Dupé's idea and he's the one who sent me in undercover, but because of the sensitive nature of the operation and the extent of Ciro Morales's former contacts inside the U.S., we decided to keep my assignment a dark op until we were ready to issue warrants. That way there was no chance the details could leak out on either end."

"The warrants were ready to be issued when I arrived at the

compound," Nelson said between gritted teeth. "You could have told me."

Dupé once again glanced between them, seemingly assessing their partnership. "I assumed under the circumstances, Agent Diaz, that you saw fit to share the information with Agent Cruz since he belongs to one of my elite taskforces."

Sophie's side was killing her. She longed to lie down and cover her head with the blanket even if it did reek of bleach. "I did not, sir."

Nelson's lips looked like he'd sucked on a lemon. He leaned once more against the wall and stared at the floor.

He thought she hadn't trusted him with the fact they shared the same boss, but the truth was, she'd simply been following orders. No one inside the FBI, besides Dupé, had initially known where she was or what she was doing. He'd trusted her to work alone and bring down a monster, no matter what it took or how long. She'd done her job well.

Maybe too well.

Dupé waved an impatient hand. "What's done is done and it wasn't crucial to the outcome of the operation. No harm, no foul."

But there *was* harm. Sophie could see it in Nelson's tight stance. The tick in his jaw. "I still believe I owe Agent Cruz an apology for not informing him. I didn't think the information would help our situation, otherwise I would have."

Dupé looked satisfied. Nelson still looked pissed. "Agent Blue knew you were an undercover Fed. How did he find out?"

"I told him," Sophie said. "Part of my orders were to find him and inform him the CIA wanted him to pull out. He refused. I was waiting on orders on how to deal with him."

Shock registered on Nelson's face. "As in kill him if necessary?"

She gave a brief nod. "He had become the operation—it had taken him over—but I felt he could be rehabilitated if I got him out." She'd hoped anyway. She'd initially been so sure she could save Blue. It was easy for people like him to become so entrenched in their false lives, they couldn't ever go back. She'd feared the same thing might happen to her. "I tried to talk sense to him, tried to get him to leave on his own. When he refused, I warned him of the potential consequences. I thought he would back off, especially when I agreed to get the ledgers for him."

"But he didn't." Nelson shook his head. "If anything, he escalated, putting out the hit on you."

At least now, the whole ugly truth was out. Sophie turned to Dupé. "When can I get out of here, sir? I'm not a fan of hospitals."

She couldn't be sure but it looked as if a faint smile passed over her boss's lips. He rose from the chair and straightened his suit jacket. "I'll inform the doctor you're ready to leave, and if you're up for it, we'll reconvene in my office first thing tomorrow morning for a full debriefing with the AG."

A full debriefing. Hours of sitting in a chair giving her testimony while Nelson glared at her and her body ached all over.

"I'll be there." While she wasn't sure she still wanted it, her job was saved. She had time to figure out what she was going to do. Time to figure out the information in the ledgers that might lead her to Angelique. "The ledgers, sir. Were they recovered?"

"All of them, thanks to Agent Cruz. He confiscated them before the Agency got wind of what happened. Once the FBI is finished gleaning info, we'll of course share with the CIA and Homeland, but it could be awhile. Those ledgers are a goldmine."

"Thank you, Agent Cruz," Sophie said. "For grabbing the ledgers, and for…well, everything."

Nelson nodded without looking at her and spoke to Dupé. "I'll walk you out, sir."

Dupé headed for the door, Nelson hobbling along behind him.

Watching him leave without so much as a backwards glance

at her, her heart hurt as much as her side. She should be happy but she wasn't.

Sitting on the edge of the bed, she mentally kicked herself. She'd been so caught up worrying about Nelson and waiting for the ax to fall from Dupé, she'd totally forgotten to ask about Lexie.

She was still sitting on the bed when the nurse came in twenty minutes later with her discharge papers and a couple of prescriptions. In a pain-induced fog, Sophie nodded and accepted the paperwork, grabbed her bag and let the nurse wheel her to the exit downstairs.

"Is anyone waiting for you?" the woman asked.

Night had fallen, the stars shining brightly. The hurricane had been downgraded and was heading out to sea. Warm air touched Sophie's face and she forced herself up from the wheelchair. "Nope, but that's okay."

The nurse pulled out a cell phone. "I can call a cab for you."

Sophie felt for the scrap of paper in her pocket. She'd searched the clothing bag for her cell phone but it hadn't been there. "Could you maybe call this number for me?"

As the nurse dialed, a Ford Mustang roared up to the entrance. Nelson hopped out and leaned his arm against the hood. "Need a lift?"

Sophie's heart did that flutter thing inside her chest. She touched the nurse's arm. "Never mind."

The nurse eyed Nelson and grinned, handing Sophie back her scrap of paper. "That's better than a taxi any day," she said, wheeling the chair back inside.

On the sidewalk, Sophie stood still and took Nelson in. He hadn't shaved yet, and under the parking lot lights, his eyes were black, guarded.

Better to clear the air before she stepped foot in his car. "You told Dupé about the lost girls."

There was no one out on the sidewalk. No one paying attention to them. "I never said a word, Soph. Blue left a journal of all the undercover agents he'd made deals with. Probably how he kept track of everyone else's illegal activities in case he needed leverage or ever needed to cover his own ass. Agent Rios said it's a diary with all the illegal shit he did while undercover and who he did it with."

"What an ass."

"Agreed. But I was right. Not only was he providing you with papers for those girls, he was providing Morales with papers for the snakes and had himself a nice little stash of uncut diamonds to fund his retirement waiting in L.A."

The realization that Nelson hadn't exposed her illegal activities made her take a step backward. "I'm sorry. I thought…"

"Yeah, well, you thought wrong. I told you I wouldn't rat you out, and I held up my end of the bargain."

Her hand instinctively went to her bandaged side. "You saved my life."

"You saved mine."

"You thought I was going to miss."

"Your error margin was a few millimeters. You could have blown my brains out aiming for that damn snake."

"But I didn't."

He limped over, took her bag and guided her toward the car. "Get in. We're going to be late."

"For what?"

He opened the car door and helped her inside. "Dinner."

"Oh, I'm not up for eating out. All I want to do is go home and crawl into bed."

"You don't have a home."

"There's that."

He gently lifted her legs and tucked her feet into the foot well. "Got it covered. But we have to make a pit stop first."

The day's exertion overcame her. As Nelson drove away from the hospital, she leaned her head back and closed her eyes.

The motor cutting out woke her. She opened her eyes, saw a

house with a wide front porch and a flowery vine climbing a trellis. The porch light was on. "Where are we?"

"I thought you might want to check on Lexie."

He helped her out of the car. "It's temporary," he said, putting an arm around her waist. "Until her aunt from Texas gets here."

"That's wonderful."

They started toward the porch, Nelson hobbling but helping her keep her torso as motionless as possible. She leaned into him, helping him balance his gait. "Coop and your friend in child services worked together to get Lexie transported to this safe house. The aunt will be here first thing in the morning."

"How much does she know?"

"Pretty much everything." At Sophie's heavy sigh, he added, "She's doing okay, Sophie. She's scared and freaked out, but mostly, she just wants to see you."

"Me? But I'm the one who arrested her brother."

"That's the part I left out. I took the credit for arresting him when I told her what happened. I didn't think you'd mind."

"Mind?" She stopped him for a moment. "You didn't have to do that."

"Yeah, I did. She loves you. She deserves to keep your memory intact."

Sophie went up on her toes and kissed him, nearly knocking him off his booted cast. "You're pretty awesome, Nelson Cruz."

He grinned, righting himself. "Wait until you see what I made for dinner. Then you'll really think I'm awesome."

"You made dinner?"

"I'm no Little Gran, but I do know how to cook a steak. And Thursday, we're heading up to L.A. to have Thanksgiving with my sister and her kid. You'll like Carly. She's a special little girl like Lexie."

"I like the sound of that." Her heart was full. She tightened her grip around his waist. "And I love steak."

"Any time you want a grade-A piece of meat, *cariña*, I'm at your service."

She was pretty sure they weren't talking steak anymore. "I love you," she blurted out.

He leaned down and nipped her bottom lip. "I love you, too, Soph."

At that moment, the screen door at the house opened. "Maria-Sophia? Is that you?"

Limping the rest of the way across the lawn, Sophie and Nelson went to see Lexie.

———

The day after Thanksgiving

"You ready for this?" Nelson said, pulling into the driveway of a small house in Carlsbad.

Sophie nodded and bit the inside of her cheek. "I loved meeting Brenda and Carly, having a real Thanksgiving dinner with them." They were planning on doing Christmas with Nelson's extended family if their work schedules allowed. "I haven't had many family holidays like that."

Night had fallen and the driveway was crowded with cars. Nelson parked and shut off the engine. "But…?"

Through the living room windows, Sophie saw men and women, drinks in hand, talking and laughing. On their way home from Brenda's, Cooper Harris had called and invited them to this party. "Meeting the SCVC Taskforce is kind of…daunting."

"They'll love you." He exited the car and came around to her side, opening her door. "Come on."

Her side was much better and her stitches had started to itch. Nelson still wore a soft cast and a heavy-duty black boot that velcroed around it.

283

On the road to Brenda's, they'd talked about the future. Sophie wanted to start a nonprofit organization and name it Angel's Wings. The organization would have two main divisions, just like a pair of wings. One division would be devoted to tracking down the girls who'd been forced through Chica Bonita like Angelique. It would take time, but the recovered ledgers would help with that. Those girls who could be found would be rescued, their buyers prosecuted. Then Sophie and her group would find new homes for the girls and give them a fresh start in life.

The second division of Angel's Wings would be dedicated to helping the lost girls south of the border legally enter America. Nelson had contacted some of his immigration peers, and although it was a holiday weekend, word had already spread through the immigrant community and the federal one. Sophie had two potential donors to get her up and running financially. Monday, she was meeting with a lawyer Victor Dupé had recommended and filling out the paperwork for nonprofit status.

"How many taskforce members are there?" Sophie asked as they skirted around the cars to get to the side door.

"Only a handful. We lost Celina a while back. She decided to be a crime scene photographer. And we lost our NSA consultant a few months ago to the private sector, where she works with her husband for a security specialist. But they'll all be here, along with Thomas, Ronni, Bobby, and the temporary help Coop called in while I was in Tijuana. Mitch Holton and Sara Rios."

"I met Celina and Sara in the hospital. They're pretty cool."

Nelson rang the doorbell and squeezed Sophie's hand. She primped her hair and sucked in her stomach. Nelson's sister was an excellent cook and Sophie was sure she'd gained five pounds overnight.

The door swung open and Celina greeted them with a smile. A small brown Chihuahua ran out between her legs, wagging its tail and sniffing them. Sophie patted the dog and then received a hug from Celina who dragged her inside.

Music played, two men played a dart game near the fireplace, and everyone called hellos and how-are-yous to them. A young boy grabbed the dog and went down the hallway. Nelson exchanged manly handshakes with several of the guys, introducing her to Thomas Mann, Bianca's husband, Cal Reece, and Bobby Dyer.

On their way to the kitchen to find Cooper, she met Bianca and Ronni. Bianca was telling the other woman that scientists had found a "second earth" known as Gliese 581c, but recent findings showed it was uninhabitable.

"That's too bad," Ronni said. "I'd like to send Thomas there. By the way, do me a favor and don't ever let Thomas babysit for you."

Bianca touched her lower stomach where a slight bulge was detectable. "God, no. The kid would come home spouting inappropriate movie lines."

In the kitchen, Cooper Harris, who was big and broad like Nelson, was setting a platter of grilled burgers on the counter. "You're just in time. Nice to finally meet you, Agent Diaz."

She gave him a smile. "Thanks for sending Nelson to protect me. And for all the help reuniting Lexie with Cortana Morales. It means a lot to me to know the girl is safe and with family."

He gave her a nod and handed her and Nelson each a cold beer from the fridge. "A friend of Nelson's is a friend of mine. We stick together, right Cruz?"

He and Nelson clanked their beers and Nelson winked at Sophie over the top of the bottle. He swallowed and said, "Did you know Dupé was her boss too?"

Cooper shot her a surprised look. "Interesting. He must have a lot of confidence in you to send you in so deep without backup."

"I'm kind of a loner. Do my best work that way. Director Dupé knows that."

"The Attorney General pulled the deal with Rodrigo

Morales off the table. They decided with your intel, Blue's diary, and the Morales ledgers, they had more than enough to shut down the cartel's contacts, suppliers, and distributors. The diamonds Morales shipped into America haven't been recovered yet, but the AG doesn't care about those at the moment. Morales is going to prison for a long time, and the CIA is getting their ass handed to them over Blue."

"Good," Nelson said. "A renegade agent like Blue is a dangerous thing."

She'd been a renegade agent, too, the question of where to draw the line still haunting her. Being an FBI agent had been her way of life for so long, she'd never considered anything else. Now it no longer motivated her to get up in the morning.

She had another full week to think about it before returning to the L.A. office, but she'd already made up her mind. She wasn't going back.

"I should thank you," Cooper said to her, "for connecting the dots on Project Bliss. We've shut down the warehouses and arrested most of the distributors."

There was a time when she would have loved to take credit for wrapping up someone else's operation. Not anymore. "Nelson's the one who figured it out, not me. I knew nothing about Project Bliss. I just took him to Rodrigo's warehouse. He's the one who put the pieces together."

Nelson took her hand and squeezed. "Partners in crime. We make a good team, even if you are a one-woman-army."

Thomas poked his head in. "She's here, Coop."

Cooper tensed. "Anyone with her?"

"Another gal," Thomas said.

He relaxed and smiled. "Agent Diaz, will you go let Agent Rios in?"

"Um." Sophie looked at Nelson and he shrugged. "Sure."

Setting her beer on the table, she went to the door, the doorbell ringing overhead. She sensed Nelson falling into step behind her and the others watching her as she passed by them.

The door was a wooden one with three small glass inserts too high for Sophie to see out of. She opened it and saw Sara Rios standing under the porch light on the top step. Moving out of the way, Sophie motioned her in. "Hi. Come on in."

Sara smiled wide as she stepped across the threshold, lightly touching Sophie's arm. "How are you feeling?"

"A lot better," Sophie said, and then she caught sight of the woman standing at the edge of the drive. Sara had been blocking her from Sophie's view.

The woman was slight of frame, taller than Sophie remembered, and her hair was bleached. But her eyes...

Were they green? Under the porch light, she couldn't be sure.

And yet, her heart went manic inside her chest. For a second, she wondered if she were having a random vision. "Angelique?" she whispered.

The woman held up a hand and gave her a tiny wave. On her arm was a friendship bracelet. "Hi Soph."

Tears rushed into her eyes. Her knees shook. "Is it really you?"

Angel bobbed her head. "May I come in?"

Sophie held out her arms. In the next second, Angel closed the distance between them and fell into her embrace.

They cried and hugged and cried some more.

"I'm so sorry," Sophie said. Angel was all grown up and she had to keep touching her to make sure she was real. "I never should have left you."

"I'm sorry too, for shutting you out," Angelique told her. "I needed you so much, but all I could do was hate you for being perfect."

"Perfect?" Sophie chuckled. "I was a complete failure when it came to holding our family together."

"You were a kid, barely older than me."

"Guess where I found her?" Sara Rios asked.

Sophie held Angel's arm. She was afraid if she turned her loose, Angel would disappear. "I have no idea."

"She knew your friend Rosalie in Tijuana. I met Angelique at the bingo hall while Agent Harris and I were trying to uncover the smuggling ring. I had no idea she was your sister. Yolanda didn't know either. Angel was sending girls to Rosalie, who then sent them on to Yolanda at Chica Bonita. When Agent Cruz told me about the girl you were looking for in the ledgers, I started sniffing around." She winked. "Guess my recovery agent skills aren't limited to criminals."

"But I'm not in any trouble," Angel assured Sophie. "Neither are Rosalie or Yolanda or the others. We shut down the underground operation…unfortunately."

It wouldn't be down for long and when Sophie's organization got up and running, the operation would be legal and better than before. She squeezed Angel's arm. "I'm still going to help girls down there, and if you're sticking around, I'd love to have you help out."

Angel nodded. "Oh, I'm sticking around."

She'd always assumed Rosalie found the girls who qualified for their illegal activity, but here it had been her own sister. *Right under my nose.* "How did you escape Chica Bonita all those years ago? The men in the van?"

Angel gave her an odd look. "How did you know about the men in the van?"

Sophie didn't feel like divulging her visions in front of everyone. "Insider information."

"Well, it's a long story, but I did escape before I reached my buyer up north. I eventually made it back to Tijuana and decided to try to help other girls. It's been a crazy road, and not all of it nice, but I survived and I'm helping others survive too. To find a better life."

Nelson stepped forward and offered Angel his hand. "Nelson Cruz. Nice to meet you."

Cooper was next, also offering an outstretched hand. "Welcome to the family."

"Did you do this?" Sophie asked the SCVC Taskforce leader. "Send Sara to find my sister?"

He shook his head and pointed at Nelson. "This guy here."

Nelson ducked his head, a grin on his face.

God, she loved him.

Introductions continued as the taskforce members, old and new, crowded in. Sophie's eyes overfilled with tears as she watched them all accept her sister as easily as they had accepted her.

Wine glasses were refilled and fresh beers passed around as they toasted to family reunions. Nelson kept an arm around Sophie's waist on one side while she kept her arm around Angel's.

There was so much to catch up on, Sophie didn't know where to start. So many new steps to take in the coming days. What she did know, as the group dispersed into the living room and kitchen again, and laughter once more rang out, was that she'd finally found a place she belonged with a group of people who made her feel wanted and appreciated.

She thanked Sara profusely while Celina got Angel a plate of food. Next thing she knew, Nelson was pulling her into a corner and nibbling at her ear. "Later, I have plans for you."

They were going back to his condo. "Oh, yeah? Like what?"

"Let's just say, I'd like a repeat of Tijuana."

She giggled. "What about my sister? I have to find a place for her to stay."

"She can sleep on the couch downstairs. You two can get reacquainted for a few hours, and then you can come upstairs and get reacquainted with me."

Smacking him on the butt, she kissed him lightly, her heart happier than it had ever been. She had a family again, and good friends who would watch out for her *and* her sister. "Sounds like I better shine up my handcuffs."

He made a silly growling noise in the back of his throat. "Fifty shades of Sophie. My favorite."

"I love you, Nels."

He brushed her lips with his. "I love you, too, Soph. What do you say we get out of here and I take you and Angelique home?"

"I'd like that," she said. "No, I'd *love* that. I've been away from home much too long."

Smiling, he took her hand, and together they went to get her sister.

NOTE FROM THE AUTHOR

Dear Reader,

Nothing pulls on my heartstrings more than kids and dogs.

The World Health Organization estimates there are 1.4 million kids worldwide who, like Lexie in Deadly Intent, are blind. Historically in the U.S. blind children and youth did not receive guide dogs until they reached the age of 18.

During my research, however, I stumbled upon the MIRA Foundation. MIRA USA was founded to provide guide dogs free of charge to blind children and youth between the ages of 11-17. MIRA has been successfully pairing guide dogs with children and youth since 1991, and they remain the only organization in the world dedicated to training guide dogs for this age group.

At $60,000 per placement, these dogs present a significant expense. MIRA USA pays all of the costs associated with receiving a dog as well as all of the follow-up training that takes place after the student returns home.

Also in my research, I came across 4 Paws For Ability. Their mission is to enrich the lives of children with disabilities by the training and placement of quality, task-trained service dogs to provide increased independence for the children and assistance to their families. They place dogs with youth and veterans and assist with animal rescue when possible. A win-win if I ever saw one.

I can't say enough about these two amazing groups. A portion of the proceeds from the sales of this story will be donated to MIRA and 4Paws4Ability. I hope you'll help spread the word about these great organizations and the work they do to help kids and adults alike!

Happy reading!

~ Misty

misty@readmistyevans.com

In case you missed the first book in the
SCVC Taskforce Series…

DEADLY PURSUIT
by Misty Evans

Cooper Harris wanted to hit something. Hard.

FBI Special Agent Celina Davenport—sexy siren of his daydreams as well as evil temptress of his night dreams—was sucking face with the biggest drug cartel leader in California and there wasn't a damn thing he could do about it.

Her soft voice coming through the mic as she taunted Londano to have sex with her on the beach gave him an instant headache of giant proportions. But it was the silence that followed, broken only by the sound of them kissing, that made him want to slam the wall of the surveillance van with his bare fist.

Sucker punched. That's what it felt like.

It's her job, idiot. She knows how to handle herself.

Didn't make him any happier. Which showed what a total sexist he really was. Sure, he felt protective about all the guys on his squad, but he never second-guessed them or their skills. He never went apeshit if they kissed a mark or led her on in order to get the information to take someone down.

Celina was female and a little one at that. Short, underweight, except for a few well-placed curves, and she had a soft, almost Southern Belle persona that totally belied her fiery Cuban roots. Push her buttons and you'd see that fire, but it took an ungodly amount of button-pushing for it to surface. He knew. Out of everyone on the SCVC taskforce, he'd managed to tweak every hot button she had at least once. Most of them he'd not only pushed, but punched into the stratosphere.

He loved it when the real Celina came out. Not the professional FBI agent she'd polished to perfection, but the holy shit amazing woman underneath. The one whose emotions rose up and took over, blasting him with her clever wit and overwhelming logic even as she flushed with anger and made gestures with her hands he'd never seen before.

Yeah. *That* was the Celina he'd fallen for.

But he couldn't ever let her know that. How she tied him up in knots. How absolutely gone he was every time he was around her. He was her boss. Head of the taskforce.

He was also fourteen years, six months and four days older.

She was a baby. A rookie. A Feebie, for Christ's sake. DEA agents did not play well with FBI agents.

And he was The Beast after all. His reputation would hardly hold up under the pressure if he robbed the cradle *and* got the female rookie Fed on his team hurt in the line of duty.

So he didn't cut loose and punch the wall of the surveillance van, didn't give into the surge of acid in his stomach. Instead, he scratched Thunder's tiny square head and batted away the image of Special Agent Celina Davenport kissing Emilio Londano.

FBI agent Dominic Quarters' gaze was heavy on Cooper's neck. Fucker had the hots for Celina, too. Cooper shot him an accusatory glance. Fucker could eat shit. "What the hell is your girl doing to our op, Quarters? This wasn't the takedown we had planned."

"Pull your shorts out, Harris." The shorter man eased back in his plastic chair and shrugged. The San Diego Mafia had been formed in the early 1970s by Jose Prisco. Thirty years later, his twin nephews, Emilio and Enrique Paloma-Londano took over the business. While most cartels gained international reputations for brutality and murder, the San Diego traffickers posed as legitimate businessmen. Their unique criminal enterprise involved itself in counterfeiting, kidnapping, and drug trade, but Emilio and Enrique passed off as law-abiding citizens, investing in their country's future and earning the respect of their neighbors and the general public. The Feds wanted them gone. The DEA wanted them gone. Even the CIA thought it was a good idea. Too bad it wasn't one of the spies he'd worked with before instead of Quarters sitting next to him. "She saw an opportunity and ran with it."

An opportunity? That's what this asshole called it? "She's going to get herself killed."

Quarters did the shrug thing again and Cooper's hand balled into a fist. Punching Quarters would be way more satisfying than punching the van's side panel.

The van slowed, following a discreet distance behind Londano's car and bodyguards' vehicle. "Perp is pulling off highway and parking approximately one-quarter klick from here," announced Thomas, a West Point grad who'd held a high profile position with the Department of Defense before defecting to the DEA. The T-man was Cooper's right hand man on this takedown.

Two keystrokes of Thomas's fingers and a night-vision view of the boardwalk appeared on the screen in front of Cooper.

The surveillance van wasn't the only vehicle in the area. A few diehard surf heads always parked near the beach overnight, only moving when the cops harassed them. There were plenty of cops in the area tonight, but none would be visible until after the sting took place, thanks to Cooper's friendly relationship with the police units from L.A. to San Diego. They all wanted Londano out of business and they knew Cooper's taskforce was about to do it.

"Perp is exiting car."

Like he couldn't see that. On screen, Londano and Celina headed to the beach. Thunder, in Cooper's lap, whined. Cooper was petting the dog too hard. "Sorry, hot rod," he murmured, never taking his eyes off the screen. He wanted to watch Celina. But years of intense training and experience told him to keep his attention on Londano. "Radio the other units in the area that this is going down here and now."

Thomas made a sound of acknowledgment and began notifying their backup.

Celina kicked off her high heels and strolled into the rolling Pacific Ocean. The moon and stars lit the beach with a surreal light that even the night-vision view couldn't compete with. Cooper could only shake his head at her stupid courage and undeniable sensuality. She glowed like a beacon.

A beacon that only reminded him he was trapped in a hell of his own making.

ABOUT THE AUTHOR

USA TODAY Bestselling Author Misty Evans has published thirty novels and writes romantic suspense, urban fantasy, and paranormal romance. As a writing coach, she helps other authors bring their books—and their dreams of being published—to life.

Misty likes her coffee black, her conspiracy stories juicy, and her wicked characters dressed in couture. When not reading or writing, she enjoys music, movies, and hanging out with her husband, twin sons, and two spoiled dogs. Learn more and sign up for her newsletter at www.readmistyevans.com.

Printed in Great Britain
by Amazon